THE FROZEN WASTELAND

TALES OF THE FEISTY DRUID™ BOOK 3

CANDY CRUM

MICHAEL ANDERLE

DISRUPTIVE IMAGINATION

Thomas Ogden
John Findlay

If we missed anyone, please let us know!

Editor
Lynne Stiegler

THE FROZEN WASTELAND

Amelia sat at her desk, only just finishing writing a letter for Julianne. It was quite the surprise visit from her friend, but given all that was happening, she couldn't deny just how welcome it was.

She closed and sealed the letter, handing it to the trusted guard in her office—one of the only ones she had left in Arcadia.

"See that Julianne gets this. She's staying at the Queen's and expecting me. *No one else* is to get this," Amelia said.

The guard bowed slightly. "Absolutely, Chancellor. I'll get it there as quickly as possible."

Since Talia and Scarlett had begun taking the city, more and more people were slipping over to their side. With careful planning and Scarlett's influence over a few of the more powerful minds, they had been very successful in their plans.

But Amelia hoped that wouldn't last for long.

Perhaps Julianne could offer council on the matter. The Master Mystic had requested a meeting—but Amelia couldn't risk going anywhere except the Capitol building or her home. However, that wasn't going to stop her from meeting her friend right away.

Amelia was impressed with the speed in which the guard had delivered her letter. Julianne was in her office in no time. She just hoped her friend had taken her advice and shielded herself a little. If Scarlett realized she was in the city, things could go very wrong, very fast.

Hearing voices outside of her office, she smiled and ran to the door, flinging it open.

"Julianne!" Amelia shouted excitedly. Her dear friend smiled and stepped forward, each of them sharing a hug. "Please, come in. Your friends are welcome, too."

"This is Garett," Julianne said.

"Thank you, but I'll stay out here for now," the man said.

Amelia shrugged and pulled Julianne inside, closing the door behind them.

"I'm so sorry for the short notice, Amelia," Julianne said.

Waving a hand in the air, Amelia said, "Oh, it's fine. You have *no* idea how happy I am to see you. So much has happened and even more has changed. We've rebuilt the factory and had to set up a whole new trade industry to fund the restoration of the city."

Julianne smiled. "The work seems to agree with you."

Amelia grinned, doing her best to hide the doom she felt by what was happening in the city. She wanted to enjoy seeing her friend, even if only for a moment. "It's a lot of work, but it was worth it. Seeing it all come together like it did and knowing how we impacted the people in the city was incredible."

There was a pause before Julianne said, "I couldn't help but notice that you used a lot of past tense there. *Was* incredible?"

Amelia swallowed hard, her eyes finding her desk. Finally, she looked back to Julianne and nodded. "There is so much happening. I want to tell you, but I also just wish we could have a normal visit."

Julianne smiled, but it looked forced. Not fake exactly, but it was obvious she felt for her friend. "It sounds like we have a lot to discuss. I'm just passing through, Amelia, but I needed to speak with you. I have things that need my immediate attention as well."

Amelia's brows furrowed as she studied her friend, concerned that she might be in danger. "You first. You went out of your way to come here. It must be important."

"There was… an incident up at the temple."

Amelia sat in one of the two visitor's chairs across from her desk and gestured for Julianne to do the same. "That must have been one hell of an *incident* for you to have come here in person."

Julianne nodded. "A group calling themselves the New Dawn appeared a few days ago. I don't know who's leading them, but they're crazed, convinced that mystics are the only ones fit to rule. They want that rule to be absolute."

Amelia swallowed hard. *The only ones fit to rule.* Talia had been the one in control this whole time, but was it possible that Scarlett was calling the shots?

"Shit." Amelia shook her head. "That sounds familiar. Unfortunately, a bit more familiar than you can imagine."

"How so?" Julianne asked.

Taking a deep breath, Amelia said, "To keep a *very* long story short, I accidentally hired Adrien's bastard daughter to be the Dean of Students. More than that, she has what I could only describe as a dark mystic in her employ. I don't know if she's one of your New Dawn people, but Scarlett is definitely up to no good."

Julianne's eyes widened a bit in obvious shock before they turned white. Amelia could feel the Master Mystic brushing her mind, and she did nothing to stop her. Her eyes suddenly returned to normal before she shook her head.

"This Scarlett person is unfamiliar to me, but that doesn't mean anything. I know nothing of the New Dawn yet. It's possible she is self-taught, or perhaps she left the Temple before I met her," Julianne replied.

"How much of a threat do they pose?" Amelia asked then.

Julianne shifted in her chair. "They've managed to find some way of shielding that can't be penetrated, so I can't be sure. It seems they hail from the other side of the Madlands, which is where I'm headed now." She sighed and shook her head as she looked at her friend. "I wish I could stay to help you. I feel compelled to, but I have a responsibility to my people, and they atta—"

"No, no, no," Amelia said, reaching over to give Julianne's hand a light squeeze. "Don't do that. You don't have to make excuses to me. You always belonged in the Heights, and I belong here. We worked together to free the city, but we have our responsibilities to our homes. I know you'd stay if you could. *I* would go with *you* if I could, but my city is in danger, and I can't leave. I truly understand. Seems we have our own paths to take."

Both women smiled, but they were forced—both of them trying fruitlessly to comfort one another.

Amelia sighed. "Still, I can't help but ask. Are you sure that's a good idea? Going across the Madlands, I mean. If something happened to you out there—"

"The temple would have all the resources it needs to carry on without me," Julianne interrupted. "I've planned for the worst, though I certainly hope it doesn't come to that."

"I see." Amelia gazed over steepled fingers. "If there's anything I can do to help, I will. Our resources are thin, and I'm stuck here, but I'll commit what I can."

Julianne smiled. "No, there's no need. I only came to warn you of their presence, but it seems like you may have already been aware of it. Of the six that came to us, only three remain. I assume those three are the ones that attacked us on the mountain."

Amelia gasped. "Attacked?"

"Yes. We lost someone, not from our party but known to our rearick. I couldn't leave without telling you. Actually, could you spare a messenger? I need to let my people know what happened."

Swallowing hard, Amelia nodded. "Of course. I only have very few trusted guards, Marcus among them, though I've had him buried in responsibility training the new Guard recruits. I'll brief those who need to know and perhaps put some feelers out for more information if I can. You're sure there's nothing else I can do to help?"

Resolutely, Julianne shook her head. She could see Amelia was stretched thin already.

Amelia nodded. "Very well. Please, let me know if that changes. I'll send a trusted courier to your room at the inn tomorrow morning to take your message. I wish you all a safe journey and a fast return. Stay safe, Julianne. Irth needs you."

Amelia showed Julianne to the door. They hugged briefly, and Julianne stepped outside, Amelia locking the door behind her after a few moments.

CHAPTER ONE

The skies were wide open, only a small speckling of clouds creating any shadows over the mountain. The sun reflected off the thick snow, blinding Arryn when she looked in the wrong direction.

With every breath she took, thick white mist streamed from her mouth, but she didn't let it distract her. She bent over as far as she could, slowly moving behind a large rock. Her target was several yards away.

A beautiful white rabbit. He was quite large for being at that altitude with so little food, but she knew he would be quite the challenge to catch.

It had been several days since she'd arrived in the Frozen North; transported and abandoned on the highest peak of the tallest mountain. At first, she'd been almost too weak to move, and using magic to create a fire hadn't done much to keep her from freezing to death.

Just as Talia had told her, it had sapped her strength. But as Talia had also predicted, Arryn refused to give up. Several times a day she had thrust her hands deep into the snow, feeling for the energy in the water under and around her and pulling it into herself. It was a trick Cathillian had shown her, and for once, his advice wasn't completely useless or juvenile. It had taken several days, but she was finally feeling more like herself.

Arryn wanted to get back to Arcadia more than anything else. She needed to finish what she had started, and she needed to make sure the citizens were safe. She wasn't sure what Talia was capable of or what she truly wanted, but she sure as hell didn't want to go back home and find the entire city desolate. All life lost; only Talia left for her to return to.

Now that she was feeling a bit more normal, Arryn decided it was time to prove the bitch wrong and get her ass off that mountain. The snowy rabbit was going to help.

As Arryn shifted her weight, she saw the long white ears perk up, swiveling as they listened for whatever might be approaching. Then the rabbit turned his head, and his eyes met Arryn's.

"*Shit!*" Arryn exclaimed, shaking her head.

He jumped into action, sprinting across the snow. Arryn wasted no time as she put all the strength she had into a powerful run, chasing the rabbit across the snow while trying to avoid slipping and falling.

The rabbit was fast, and his skill at sharp turns was incredible. Try as she might, she couldn't catch him.

"Hey!" she shouted as she ran. "Give me a break! This isn't fair."

The rabbit ran straight for a massive rock. Arryn thought he would go around it on the easier terrain, but he didn't. He planted his feet against it without breaking stride and used it as a pivot point to change directions. Arryn almost had him, but was forced to drop and slide on her hip to keep from running straight into the boulder.

"*Gah!*" she yelled into the vastness around her.

The rabbit turned and stared at her as she got to her feet, as if challenging her to come for him. Her eyes narrowed and she returned the gaze, her body lowering to a crouch as she once again prepared to run.

"I *will* catch you. And when I do, you're gonna be—"

Her threat was curtailed when the rabbit took off again. She growled to herself as she lit out after him. Stiff from several days of disuse, her muscles were screaming at her, begging her to rest, but she wasn't giving up.

She knew that she would have to be strong, fast, and pay full attention to her senses if she was going to get off this mountain. The only way to get back into shape was to be extremely active.

She charged after the rabbit in the hope she would catch him, but she became careless. Her desire turned into impatience, and she quickly lost focus on her surroundings.

The rabbit made his sharpest turn yet, spinning in the snow and running directly back through her legs at the last second. As she turned, her feet slid in the snow, and she landed hard on her side. Though her breath didn't leave her, it hurt like hell.

Rolling onto her back, Arryn groaned as she cursed the rabbit and her own impatience. She grunted as the fat, fluffy, snow-white rabbit jumped onto her stomach, his little nose twitching up and down as he stared into her eyes.

She reached up with both hands and scratched the sides of his face. "I'm gonna get you next time. You just wait and see. You cheated, anyway."

The rabbit leaned his head into her touch, and she scratched between his ears before taking them between her fingers and rubbing down to their tips.

"You're lucky you're cute. Do you have any idea how hungry I am?" she asked, a smile on her face.

The rabbit bit her hand, lightly enough that it didn't draw blood, but hard enough for her to know he took offense at her comment.

She laughed. "Sorry. It was just a joke. Jeeze, you're so sensitive!"

She was just about to set him aside so she could stand when the rabbit's ears perked up, warning her that they weren't the only ones in the area. A deep, guttural sound filled the air around them. It wasn't a growl, but a warning, sounding very deep in the animal's chest as it slowly stepped toward them.

Arryn laid on her back, the rabbit frozen on her stomach as they both stared at the large, hungry snow leopard.

"Run," Arryn whispered to the rabbit.

She felt a slight movement on her stomach, but not enough to suggest he'd listened. A louder rumble from the beautiful cat warned her that time was running out. This time, she didn't give the rabbit a chance.

"Run!" she shouted, throwing him far away from her and quickly rolling onto her stomach.

The leopard pounced, but Arryn was fast enough to get out of the way. The slick snow she'd been laying on took the leopard down just as it had her. In only seconds the leopard was back on her feet, roaring loudly and charging for Arryn and her furry companion.

Hearing the rapid crunch of snow behind her, Arryn risked a look over her shoulder to see the animal coming directly for her, moving far faster than she could possibly run. The rabbit was in front of Arryn, running in a zigzag pattern but making good time.

"*Ooooh*, run, Puff-Butt, run!" Arryn exclaimed as they began scrambling down the north face of the mountain.

A loud growl sounded as a large shadow fell over her. Without looking back, Arryn dove forward, catching the rabbit in her arms and twisting, landing on her side and rolling out of the way. The leopard landed hard, sliding and rolling over, which gave Arryn enough time to get back to her feet.

Arryn was still very weak. Not only did she have very little time to try to use her nature magic to subdue the animal, but as weak as she was, she wasn't even sure she could. If it didn't work, she would be directly in front of the big cat's jaws.

Using physical magic wouldn't be much better, but it appeared she didn't have a choice. It was the guaranteed option in this instance, unlike attempting to use nature magic.

She tossed the rabbit away from her, out of the direct path of the leopard, before turning and throwing her hands out. A small gust of wind pushed the leopard back, and she encased it in ice.

But the leopard jumped forward again, breaking free of the thin ice Arryn had created in hopes of scaring it while expending minimal energy. Apparently, the leopard had no plans to back down under any circumstances. It was just as hungry as she was, and it wasn't like there were a lot of food sources in the mountains.

Still, Arryn wasn't about to let her friend be eaten after he'd helped her train and keep her reflexes strong and quick, and she sure as hell wasn't going to die.

When she swiped her hand upward, the snow from the ground lifted in a small wave and wrapped around the leopard. Her other hand jerked forward, her magic freezing the snow. The leopard fought, but the ice froze rapidly, and Arryn heard a sharp *snap* just before the cat's head slumped.

The animal fought the ice with great strength and the force had combined with her lack of magical skill to cause the leopard's death. She'd only planned to encase the cat in ice long enough for the rabbit to get away, allowing it to melt once she herself had traveled far enough that her magic no longer held. But now, she was presented with a new opportunity.

Food.

It had been two days since she'd eaten, and as strong as she'd become on her own with no sustenance and only the snow around her for hydration, she knew the leopard would gift her with both food and warmth.

Arryn quickly made her way over to the animal, melting the

ice and gently lowering her to the ground. Placing her hand on the cat's jaw, she closed her eyes.

"Though I did not mean to end your life, I promise you that your death will not have been in vain. Thank you for your sacrifice. It will not be forgotten." She started to move away, but then placed her hands over the animal again. "Besides, you were the asshole who tried to eat me first. So, you know… Fair is fair."

Having wasted the majority of her strength chasing the rabbit to keep her skills sharp and using magic on top of that, she wasn't sure how she was going to drag an animal that large back to her camp.

The chubby rabbit slowly and cautiously wandered back to her. He came to her side and looked up at her with his little nose wiggling.

Arryn smiled. "I caught you. Told you I'd catch you!"

The rabbit turned and used his back feet to rapidly kick snow at Arryn as she laughed at her little friend.

CATHILLIAN, Samuel, and Celine stood just outside the area where the sparring groups were practicing that morning as they discussed their situation. Echo had just returned, having scoured the entire southern third of the valley, but she had come up empty.

The golden eagle had searched everywhere from the Dark Forest to the border of the Madlands just outside the Arcadian Valley, and all the way down to Craigston. Fruitless.

Arryn was nowhere to be found.

They had some theories, but mainly they would just have to start looking again. Cathillian, however, had other plans.

"It's been too long since I've sent Echo to the Dark Forest. If I don't do so very soon, my mother will come here. Arryn and I joke about it quite often, but neither of you seem to realize just how serious a problem that would be. She would *not* be happy." Cathillian ran his fingers through his hair, securing it into a ponytail.

"Ye look beautiful, lad," Samuel joked as he pointed to Cathillian's long blonde hair, now tidily pulled back. "Make sure he treats ye nice."

Cathillian shook his head. "Can we stay on task, please? This is kind of important. And of course, he treats me nicely. He treats me like a princess, which is more than I can say for you."

Despite the grim conversation, Celine couldn't help but laugh. The two were always giving each other a hard time.

"Maybe you should send Echo back to the Dark Forest," Celine said. "But what message would you send? That's the real question."

Cathillian shrugged. "I've thought about that over and over again. I don't have a clue what I should do. If I don't send word, I can pretty much guarantee my mother will be here within the next two days. If I lie and say nothing is going on, I'm going to feel terrible, and the truth is, we might need her. If I tell her the truth, I don't know what will happen."

"We might get an army of pointy-eared fellas like yerself," Samuel said. "We can use all the help we can get. We need ta find our girl."

"We've been lucky up until now," Cathillian said. "The only thing that's kept us from getting our asses handed to us is the fact that Amelia is still temporarily in control. The city is on the verge of breaking. If anything else were to happen, Amelia could quite possibly lose whatever hold she has, and Talia would take over. If that happened, the Guard would have no choice but to come for us."

"Then why are we still here? Shouldn't we be on the move?" Celine asked.

"As much as I'd love to say yes," Cathillian began, "I'll have to say no. Not in the traditional sense, anyway. If I leave, I'm going back to the Dark Forest. I'm not going to stop until I can bring back an army. Problem with that is, there's now a potential war brewing in the Dark Forest as well—if what Jenna told me was true. My mom has been lying to me just as much as I've been lying to her. If they send any warriors, they risk their own walls being vulnerable. The truth is, we might not get any help at all."

Everyone sat in silence, watching the guardsmen practice the skills they had learned. Samuel and the rest had grown to trust them, and they hadn't been affected yet by Scarlett's influence.

After a few moments, Cathillian spoke. "I'm going back to the Dark Forest—I don't think there's any way around it. Like I just said, Amelia's hold on the city is fragile. We need to be ready if it slips entirely. I'm gonna take a day or two to get my things together, but then I'm heading out. I need to tell my mother and grandfather what's happened. They need to be informed, and they have every right to know that Arryn is missing."

"I'm goin' with ye, lad." Samuel patted his hammer.

Celine nodded. "Me, too."

Cathillian shook his head. "The Dark Forest is a dangerous place—well, not so much for *me* I guess, but it's dangerous as it is beautiful. There are lycanthropes, and it appears the dark druids have made themselves a threat there now, too. You should stay here where you know the streets like the back of your hand. You've spent years moving through them, dodging the Guard. This is your element. You'll be safer here."

She laughed, but the sound was cold and rather intimidating coming from a woman so small. "Like hell I will! This place is far more dangerous than some wild animals in a forest. I understand I don't know anything about the Dark Forest. Hell, I've never even been camping. But what I *do* know is that I lost my niece once. The day she came back to me I vowed I would never lose her again, and yet here we stand—without her."

"I understand that—" Cathillian began, but Celine interrupted him by taking a step forward and poking a hard finger into his chest.

"Bullshit. I'm *going* with you. I'm *going* to meet your mother, the woman who took my niece into her home and raised her to be stronger than I ever could've imagined. Either you take me willingly, or I'm going to kick your ass and force you to take me anyway."

Cathillian's eyes widened as he stared at the much smaller woman. "Damn. Okay. Look, you can come. It's only out of respect for you and Arryn, but I'll let this happen because I'm worried about my decision. If I lost you, too, Arryn would never forgive me."

Celine smiled. "Out of respect for me? That's the only reason?"

Cathillian nodded for a moment, his arms crossed over his chest. "That, and you scare the *shit* out of me, not unlike your niece... or your sister, now that I think about it. The women in your family are pretty fucking frightening, you know that? Actually, you'll fit in great in the Dark Forest with my mother. She's also terrifying."

The happy and satisfied expression on Celine's face told Cathillian she was pleased with the outcome. "Good. I can't wait to meet her."

Arryn used her feet to kick snow in all directions as she excavated toward the bare ground below. Over the past couple days, she'd slowly been clearing a large area and putting the displaced snow to good use. She'd been lucky that a true snowstorm hadn't hit yet, but from the looks of the clouds in the distance and the smell in the air, she could tell it wasn't going to be long.

Every day it snowed a little at different times, and she'd had to clear the area over and over again. Had it not been for her weakness, the task wouldn't have been much of a problem at all. In fact, the shelter would've been complete long before now.

So far, she'd cleared a circle that was ten feet in diameter, and the walls surrounding it were more than a foot thick and three feet high. While she didn't plan to stay in the mountains long, it was obvious she would need shelter until she departed.

She couldn't waste any more time and energy moving up and down the mountain searching for a cave when she had no idea if one even existed, and she definitely didn't have the strength to waste on using her magic to search through the ground for openings.

Instead, she stacked the snow high in the hope that it would block the wind. Once she had some of her energy back, she planned to stack it just a bit higher, turn it into solid ice, and build across so it had a roof as well.

While living inside an ice cube certainly wouldn't be warm, it would be a hell of a lot better than constantly being hit in the face by cold wind and snow.

Once the ground had been cleared of snow—again—Arryn sat down inside her shelter, using the walls to block the wind from blowing against the sweat on her face. She used the edge of her cloak to wipe it away, making sure her face was well hidden so the cold wouldn't freeze it before it could dry.

Arryn felt something brush against her ankle, and she pulled her cloak back just enough to see her little snow rabbit friend nestling next to her.

"Well, hello there, Sir Fuzzy Bottom." She reached out and scratched his head in his favorite spot between his ears. "You know, I really need to settle on a name for you. I'm terrible with traditional ones. I like smartass names better. But you know what they say… you get attached once you name something. I assume that mostly goes for serious names, though. I don't know how long I'll be here, so I don't want to get any more attached to you than I already am."

She sighed as she stared at the dreary sky. "I'm exhausted," she told him. "If I don't find a way to regain enough energy, I'll be stuck up here indefinitely. For every step forward I take, it seems like I go back two. But my little igloo should help with that. Time to rest up and gain my strength."

The rabbit sat on her lap, staring at her with his little nose bobbing up and down. She smiled at him and pulled him closer, enjoying the warmth he radiated.

"If I had about twenty more of you, I wouldn't even need to build a fire."

Arryn suddenly remembered the snow leopard pelt hanging over her fire, which she had repeatedly scraped, treated, and dried, curing it so it could be used as bedding. She gently placed the rabbit on the ground next to her before standing and making her way around to the eastern side of the peak.

It wasn't far away, and the tall rocks blocked the wind better than the area she had built in, but the terrain on the other side was far too rocky to make camp on. It would be very hard to make any part of the mountain completely habitable. What one area had, another didn't, and vice versa.

Thankfully, she'd been able to build a fire and cure both the pelt and some of the meat to make jerky she could use over time without it going bad.

When she'd grabbed the pelt, she could feel that it was once again dry. After looking it over for a few moments, she was happy to see that it did not need to be scraped another time; the hide had turned soft and durable. It would be perfect to lay beneath her, making a nice barrier between her and the ground below.

She went back to her camp and laid the pelt on the ground inside her partial igloo. Once she had sat down on it, the rabbit once again returned to sit in her lap.

"Well, Mr. Fluffinstuffs, it's not perfect, but it's pretty good. A few days ago, I made a big threat to one hell of a psycho bitch. I know you wouldn't know anything about that, but being stuck up here after having made an incredibly big threat is basically the equivalent of making the best argument you ever made in your life, storming out of the room, and having to go back in because you forgot your pack. Totally kills your groove."

She looked down to see the little rabbit's eyes locked on hers as she spoke, which made her smile as she scratched the sides of his face. "I guess the equivalent for you would be threatening to fight another bunny for the rights to a cute little girl bunny, only to find out that she didn't like you anyway. Actually, that's nowhere near close, but since I don't know anything about your day-to-day life, I have no idea how to relate my situation to yours."

Arryn wasn't entirely sure, but it looked like the rabbit shook his head at her. She laughed, unable to say that she could blame him.

CHAPTER TWO

In the days since the attack, Maddie hadn't run into Arryn anywhere in the city. She hadn't taught her courses, and she hadn't attended the physical magic class, not that she was surprised.

The rumor mill was in full swing, and from what Maddie could tell, things had gotten far worse. It wasn't casual chatter any longer; the people had become certain of Arryn's guilt. Students, parents, and teachers alike had begun to think Arryn had killed the students.

Not seeing Arryn at the Academy wasn't nearly as strange to her as not seeing her anywhere in the city after the battle with the remnant. She'd fought bravely, but no one saw where she went. There wasn't a body. It was as if she'd vanished into thin air, and Maddie wasn't entirely sure she hadn't—but not by choice. Someone was working awfully hard to frame the newcomer.

No matter how everyone felt about Arryn's guilt, they all seemed to agree she'd behaved heroically on the wall. So, where had she gone?

Why was *no one* asking where she was?

None of the faculty.

None of her fellow students.

No one.

Maddie had attempted to ask a few people herself, but was surprised to find they didn't care at all. For a city as cautious as Arcadia had become, not caring where Arryn had gone seemed strange, since she was a suspected murderer.

Arryn had been accused of killing several students since she'd arrived in the city. The majority of them had been Boulevard students, which didn't make sense to Maddie since Arryn's parents had been killed while trying to save those from the Boulevard.

Maddie needed some answers.

Having spent several days feeling like she was the only one holding a torch while walking through fog, she decided it was time to talk to Amelia. She could only hope Amelia would have some real answers for her, rather than having fallen into the same pit as the rest of the city.

Maddie had waited until after sundown, when the city had quieted down and the Guard was on patrol, before she went to see Amelia. While she couldn't explain the root of her feelings, she was concerned about the possibility that someone would see her, prompting her not only to wait until after dark, but to use less traveled streets to avoid being noticed.

Since Maddie had grown up as a noble, sneaking around the streets wasn't something she had much practice with. But luckily for her, she was a quick study, and she had learned a lot from her time with the Bitch of the Boulevard.

As she approached Amelia's house, she realized that remaining unseen would be an impossibility. Upon closer examination, she saw that there was a guard stationed in the Chancellor's backyard, though he seemed to be trying to conceal himself, too.

As she approached the house, she wondered why he would

take a position there instead of in front of the house. She was thinking hard, and she didn't pay attention to her footing.

There was a broken stone in her path, which crunched under her foot and alerted the guard. Her entire body stiffened as she watched him quickly jump into action, pointing his magitech rifle outward, although not directly at her.

He stayed against the side of Amelia's house as he made his way over to her, careful not to step out of the shadows, and Maddie watched as he carefully stuck his head past the corner far enough to look down each side of the street before pulling back.

"Who are you, and what do you want?" the guard asked when he reached her. His voice was hushed, as if he didn't want anyone to hear him talking.

Maddie copied his quiet tone, not only wanting to keep him calm, but not wanting anyone with prying ears to hear her speak. "I need to speak with Amelia."

He raised the magitech rifle slightly, though it was still angled enough that it wasn't pointed directly at her. "What do you want with the Chancellor?"

Maddie looked up and down the street, knowing that if even a single person heard them, they would investigate and see her standing there. She placed both hands in the air before slowly putting them in her pockets, hoping to signal that she had no plans to use magic against him.

"It's very important. I'm a friend of hers. Please tell her Maddie is here to see her, but hurry. You were hiding in the shadows, so I'm assuming you do not want to be seen. Well, neither do I."

The guard hesitated for a moment before finally lowering his rifle. "Wait right here."

He was gone for several moments, disappearing into the backyard again, and then he returned. With a wave of his hand, he motioned for Maddie to follow him around back of the house.

Amelia was standing in the back door, waiting for them. Her

body seemed rigid as she stood in the frame, leaning against it with her arms folded across her chest.

"Don't come any closer," Amelia warned. "I'm going to ask you a question and look into your mind while you answer. Understand?"

Maddie wasn't entirely certain if the woman had lost her wits and become incredibly paranoid, or if her suspicions had been correct and this was the Chancellor's way of taking precautions. Instead of asking her own questions, Maddie nodded.

"If you were anyone else, I wouldn't even give you the courtesy, but here it is. Arryn has been accused of killing several students. She's also been accused of killing two people while subduing a third in front of the Capitol building. She was seen firing on the Capitol building using her magic. And she seems to be missing now. What do you think about all that? What should I do about all that?"

The questions were strange, sure, but Maddie was certain Amelia knew what she was doing. She was nothing if not thorough and cautious.

"I came here because she's been missing for a few days and I have no idea where she is. I think the entire city has turned on her like starving dogs in a chicken coop, and I don't understand why. I understand those charges, but I seem to be one of the very few who think logic isn't really taking a part here."

Amelia nodded. "What exactly do you mean logic isn't playing a part?"

"I don't know her. I was in her class for a couple of days, and I spoke to her once. That's it. But what I do know is that she woke up every morning and trained our Guard. From what I hear, and not from her, she trained them harder than they've ever been trained before by our own men. Why would she do that if she knew those same skills could be immediately turned against her to take her down? Why would she try to teach her students to heal, knowing any damage she did to them could be healed by themselves or by another student?"

Maddie paused for a moment, but Amelia stood there, weighing her words. Maddie continued. "There's more, but those are the basics. None of this makes sense. It's like everyone is convinced of her guilt and has mysteriously forgotten all the good she has done. Sure, some of the noble girls like to chat and gossip. But it's happened with everyone, including full-grown men. Something's not right. That's why I'm here."

A few moments passed before Amelia's body relaxed and she stood up straight again, a smile spreading across her lips. "Maddie, I'm *so* glad it's really you. Please come in."

Maddie walked across the back porch and stepped inside, taking one last look at the guard outside. He gave her a nod before returning to his post in the yard. She closed the door and went into the kitchen.

"It's nice to see you, too, Amelia," Maddie said. "I didn't know what else to do. I was worried when she confronted the class about the accusations against her, and since the invasion, no one has seen or heard from her. The invasion was the last time, but no one really spoke to her. She fought for us and then disappeared."

Amelia nodded, grabbing the kettle to boil some water over a fire. "Would you like some tea before we get started?"

Maddie gave her a nervous smile before sitting down at the table. "Sure. Thank you, I'd love some."

Walking around the kitchen and working as she spoke, Amelia began. "There's a lot to the story. It's a long one, so I'm glad you decided on tea—you're probably going to need it to stay awake. You know about the accusations, but you don't know about everything leading up to them."

Amelia began to tell Maddie everything about Arryn's situation, starting with the moment she arrived. She told her about her past, her parents, the Dark Forest, coming back to Arcadia after she learned Adrien had been killed. She told her everything, all the way up to when she began teaching and came to Amelia with her fears about Talia.

She set a cup of tea in front of Maddie, along with the bowl of sugar cubes. After sitting down with her own cup, she dropped in two cubes and continued with her story.

"If I'd listened to her, we wouldn't be in this position right now. Well, it wouldn't be quite as bad, anyway. The reason we're here is because I didn't know any of this before Scarlett arrived. By the time the mystic got here, Talia had already established herself as quite the little hero of the city. Scarlett only solidified that perception by using her magic. They also have control of the remnant. This is one hell of a mess, and another mess is that Arryn is missing. I feel stuck."

Maddie took a careful sip of her tea before setting it back down. "Do we have any idea where she is?"

Amelia shook her head. "Cathillian sent Echo, his familiar, south. She searched pretty much all land south of us for any sign of Arryn, which means Talia more than likely took her north, or out of the Valley entirely. I'm not surprised—Talia was from just outside of Cella, or at least that's what I was told. She could be from another planet, for all I know. But for sake of argument, if north truly is where she's from, it doesn't surprise me that she would head in that direction."

Maddie chewed on her lip for a moment, staring at the table as she thought everything over. "But she knows you know that."

"What do you mean?"

"I don't mean to poke a hole in your theory, but why would she go north? If she's from just outside Cella, and we're going to go out on a limb here and say that maybe she really is, why would she return there? Yes, it makes sense that she would return to what's familiar. People she can trust. Terrain she knows. But she would also know we would assume that. Talia is here. Arryn isn't. That means Arryn was dumped somewhere. Or..." Maddie let her words trail off as a concerned expression across her face. "Or the worst has happened."

Amelia sighed as she sat there in silence. "It's very true. Talia definitely didn't take her south. But she would know we are aware she's from there. Okay, I'm open to suggestions."

Maddie shook her head, raising her hands into the air for a moment before lowering them. "I don't have a clue. If she's not in the south, it would make sense that she was in the north. The only thing hanging me up about it is that Talia would know we would think of it. Which means she's done something far worse. They wouldn't have taken her west, because she'd be too close to the Dark Forest. If she has control of the remnant like you say, I suppose she could have taken her to them."

Amelia nodded. "True, but I don't think so. They wouldn't have taken her east, because the remnant could've destroyed her by now, and there's no way in hell Talia would allow that. She'd want to destroy her herself. That's why she more than likely wouldn't entrust anyone to keep her either. They'd either set her free or torture her themselves."

Maddie grimaced as she considered her next words. "Common sense has narrowed down the direction, and judging by personality alone, we've determined Talia would not leave her in the care of anyone else. But—Talia is here. She was at the Academy today. That means one of two things: either Arryn is already dead, or Talia has her hidden somewhere. Alone. Not under anyone else's care."

It was Amelia's turn to grimace now. "Somewhere she can torture her. But that doesn't make sense. Talia was gone for about five days. Maybe she's already tortured Arryn to death. That's a very long time. I don't have very many guards I can trust, but none of them saw Scarlett or Talia during those five days. No one saw any movement at either of their homes, either. That means they went somewhere away from here. Outside the city. Definitely north."

Maddie took another sip of her tea before setting it down again. "Actually, there were several teachers and students missing for those five days, Jackson among them. They must have teleported outside the city."

Amelia smacked the edge of the table before pointing at Maddie with a smile on her face. "I got it. I need you to be my eyes and ears inside of the Academy. I can't go in there. I have to be absolutely perfect. With Scarlett in control of everything, I have to be very careful. I can't piss off Talia or Scarlett. If I do, the whole city will revolt against me. There would probably not be a corner in the city I could hide in. So, I need you to study everything. Follow Jackson. Do whatever you can, but don't get caught. Don't get caught, and don't let anyone know you're associated with me in any way. You were smart to come here tonight when the city was quiet."

"If things are that bad here for you, why don't you leave? No one would blame you for that. If your life is *that* in danger, you shouldn't be here. You're more valuable alive than dead. The city needs you. Arryn needs you."

Amelia gave a sad smile. "You have no idea how badly I would love to run. After all this fighting, I'm exhausted. But I can't. I took a vow when I stepped into the role of Chancellor. I made a promise to Ezekiel that I would care for his city—that I would make it a better place. I'd fulfill his dream. That I would let no one harm our people. That their children— everyone's children— would be well educated and could learn magic if they chose to do so.

"If I run, Talia will rise up. She will claim my seat, and she will have power over the Guard. The only thing stopping her from doing it now is the fact that Scarlett has a very thin hold on everyone. From what I can tell, she compelled several people, and she's using them to convince others of *her* truth about what's happening."

"She doesn't have active control over every person in the city, right?" Maddie asked.

Shaking her head, Amelia said, "From what Julianne has told me about mental magic, that would be impossible—even for the most powerful mystics. In reality, Scarlett must be exhausted. She only has control over a handful of people. In fact, if I were her, I would choose several strong-willed people who are known for rational thinking. I would choose them because they're the type of people everyone would believe. They're the ones who are calm in any situation. Dependable. If they say the sky is falling, you'd damn well better take shelter. The rest are weak-minded individuals who will believe anything they're told, especially those who like to spread gossip—and like to believe it even more. That would be the easiest path to take. It would demand far less magic."

Maddie nodded. "I don't know Arryn very well. I don't know anything about her other than what you've told me and what I've seen in class. What I do know is that she's strong. I don't know where she is or if she's alive, but something tells me someone that cruel wouldn't have killed her right away. I think Arryn is still alive, and I think she's working on a way to get herself home."

Amelia laughed as she played with the handle on her teacup. "You'd like her. She's tough, not unlike someone else we know."

"If she's anything like Hannah, then I definitely believe she's working on a way to get back to Arcadia. I also know if we put our efforts into finding her rather than saving the city, Talia and Scarlett won't be the only ones needing to save their asses." Maddie smiled. "Keep that in mind. She *will* be back, and she'll kick our butts if we haven't made any progress. I'll do what you suggested. I'll work on Jackson and the others. I'm very tiny and quiet, so I'm sure I can sneak around and get some information. In the meantime, keep yourself safe and away from any unnecessary attention. If I can't talk to you directly, how will I update you?"

Amelia shook her head. "I'm gonna have to talk to Cathillian about that. I don't know nature magic, and even if I did, the bond between familiar and master is difficult to seal. Even Arryn doesn't have a familiar. But maybe Cathillian can train a bird to deliver messages for us."

Maddie's eyes widened. "That could be fun and interesting."

Amelia nodded and replied, "I'll work on that, you work on the Academy. And for the love of the Matriarch, if anyone corners you about Arryn, act like you buy into the rumors. You can't believe you trusted her when she turned out to be a murderous psychopath. Understand?"

Maddie felt disgusted just thinking about playing such a game, but she also understood it was necessary. Not only for her own survival, but also Amelia's.

CHAPTER THREE

Talia reclined on her bed, legs crossed at the ankle, a glassful of mystics' brew in one hand as she rubbed the bridge of her nose with the other. For the last several minutes, Talia had been suffering Scarlett's hyper conversation, when all she wanted to do was drink in peace.

Things had not gone quite as she had hoped or expected, and something in her gut told her she'd made a mistake. Her instincts were screaming at her to go back to the Frozen North and find Arryn's body to confirm her death, but Scarlett had said not to.

"You can't leave right now, not when the city is still in chaos. If you do, Amelia will have control back before you can say 'Sexy Scarlett,'" the mystic had told her.

Talia's constraints were beginning to wear on her. She didn't like being told what to do, and when she knew what she needed to do, she absolutely despised being told she couldn't. Talia had to deal with the fact that her plan had failed so far.

Amelia had been slated to die.

Amelia was supposed to be dead, and Arryn had been dumped in the Frozen North to undergo a slow, agonizing death.

Talia wasn't sure either of those things would be happening anytime soon.

Arryn was a fighter. She had said as much when she dumped her on the mountain, but she had been sure her enemy would find her fate up there. It was far too cold, and the winds were far too severe. Given Arryn's blood loss and her inability to use magic in an energy-efficient way, she was doomed to die.

Wasn't she?

That was the question Talia had been asking herself for days now, and it was driving her crazy, right along with Amelia's continued existence. Everything was screwed up, as far as Talia was concerned. Amelia was alive. Arryn was more than likely alive. Their working relationship with the remnant was gone. In fact, it was more than gone. Talia had no doubt the remnant would be pissed off; certain Talia had set them up.

And she had.

Talia had known Arcadia's army wasn't well trained, but she knew they had the numbers. Numbers didn't make up for lack of skill, but the remnant would have brought twice or even three times as many to the battle if they'd known Arcadia's numbers were so high.

She'd lied when she'd told them the Guard was depleted and weak from the battle of Arcadia. She'd lied to convince them they'd only need two hundred or so to sack the city.

She'd set them up, all right.

The remnant had come with enough to take out quite a few of Arcadia's Guard and citizens, but not enough to successfully seize the city. The city had fought them off and won. That had been the plan, but she'd hoped for the beasts to kill Amelia during the battle.

She was supposed to be long gone, damn it, and Talia was supposed to be Chancellor. When she took charge of the city, she would have given the remnant whatever they might demand to keep them away in the future.

But things had gone wrong so quickly. Arryn had proven to be far more resourceful and powerful than she had imagined, and she'd taken out far too many of the remnant before they even reached the city gate. That had required Talia to do a little improvising of her own. She'd captured Arryn and fled the city before the girl could do any more damage and ruin the possibility of Amelia being taken down.

It was the only thing that had worked as planned, and she wasn't even sure of that much. Now, as she sat there with her mystics' brew, listening to Scarlett prattle on about nothing important, she worried about the inevitable.

The remnant would more than likely come for her soon, and with much larger numbers. She doubted they would take the risk of coming underprepared this time.

They may have been big, ruthless barbarians, but they understood details, and they sure as hell understood battle tactics.

"Aren't you concerned at all?" Talia asked, her voice sharp and angry. "You do realize the remnant will be back, right? I doubt they even have an interest in the city anymore. All they'd care about right now is revenge. They'll come soon enough, and you are in just as much danger as I am."

Scarlett sighed, reaching over and placing a hand on Talia's ankle. "Trust me, I've already thought of all that. Yes, our lives may be in danger, but right now there's no sign of it, and I'm not going to spend my time worrying about it. I'll deal with it if it comes. Let's not forget, Talia, that this world is a much bigger place than just this small valley. Trust me on that. This world has many places to offer, and we can go anywhere, if it comes to that."

Talia looked at her incredulously, downing the rest of her brew before slamming the glass onto the nightstand next to the bed. "Are you *serious* right now? We can just go anywhere? That's the most ridiculous thing I've ever heard. If I wanted to just go *anywhere,* I wouldn't have wasted all this time trying to secure my future here. Things are different now. At first, all I wanted was vengeance for my father, but now I want what's owed to me. The city is what's owed to me. It's mine."

"Okay, then." Scarlett folded her hands in her lap. "What's the plan?"

Talia sighed, resting her head against her headboard as she stared at the ceiling. "So far, Amelia has only worked on cleanup. There hasn't been much effort past that. She's scared to piss us off. There have been a lot of deaths, so morale in the city is obviously low. Using the remnant again is obviously out of the question, but I'm sure our group would be happy to *have more power*."

Scarlett nodded. "By *having more power*, I'm assuming you mean giving them the blood from another victim. To do that, we would have to kill someone else. The city is convinced the murders were done by Arryn's hand."

"And?" Talia asked angrily. "She's gone! No one has seen her. For all they know, she could still be lurking in the city. She proved that when she disappeared for days, only to show up out of nowhere to fight for the city. No one except us and a few in our group know what really happened to her. If we kill someone else, it *will* instill the fear that Arryn is still in the area."

Scarlett was quiet for a moment as she sat and thought Talia's words over. "Amelia isn't doing a lot right now. She's more than likely trying to keep a low profile and stay out of our way. At least, that's what I would do if I were her. If you take control and do something big to make yourself look like a better leader, it will only further the city's ever-growing disapproval of the Chancellor."

Talia smiled. "Not bad. I like it. We should talk about this later. I'm starting to feel very relaxed, and I think I need a night for me. I need some entertainment."

Scarlett winked and smiled. "Damn. Took you long enough. I thought you'd never ask."

Talia rolled her eyes. "Not you, though I'm sure I would find you very entertaining. No, I'm thinking of someone else. I'm going to get a bath started. You should go down to Sully's and look for a very tall, very broad man who answers to the name 'Eric.'"

"So, I'm not good enough for your bed, but I'm good enough to go fetch your toys for you? That's nice, Talia. And what exactly should I say to this man?"

"Tell him he's about to be shown my gratitude for the pitcher of brew he bought a while back." She smiled. "Oh, but also tell him if he doesn't like things interesting and slightly painful, don't bother. I'd hate for him to disappoint me."

BEING STUCK on the mountaintop was hell for Arryn, but it wasn't going to change until she got her energy back. Arryn had to expend some of her magic and energy every day to give herself things that would return the effort spent with interest.

For instance, she had built herself an igloo to shelter her from snow and wind, which allowed her to stay warmer at night. Being warmer permitted her a more restful sleep, which in turn gave her the energy to search for food. Food nourished her and permitted her even more restful sleep since she wasn't hungry, giving her even more energy.

Sometimes it seemed pointless, as though she had almost given up hope of ever returning to Arcadia, and sometimes she felt like she might never do so, but in reality, she was doing exactly what she needed to. Taking two steps forward and one step back was still taking another step every day.

In Arcadia, she'd taken her magic, her fighting skills, and even her teacher—her best friend—for granted. Up here, she was learning just how much she had grown already, but more importantly, how much further she needed to go. It required a great deal of patience on her part to realize her limits, but part of her welcomed it.

Arryn had finished her igloo, and last night had been the first real night's sleep she'd gotten since arriving. Part of that had been the leopard pelt she'd taken. Unfortunately, at this point she had run out of meat; she needed to find food again.

Today, she decided to hunt something that would yield even greater results. She'd seen both mountain goats and rams, even as high as she was, and knew they could be of use.

Not only could she use the hide as an extra blanket and the meat for sustenance, but she could craft weapons from the horns. She hadn't learned as much as she'd hoped in the short amount of time she attended her physical magic class, but she'd learned enough to get by.

She had found some thick, solid rock that wasn't easily broken, and she'd taken her time shaping it with the use of other rocks in her downtime. As a result, she had two six-inch-long blades that had been smoothed as much as possible by using both physical strength and magic. Once she had regained her energy, she planned to transform the rock into metal using physical magic.

The blades weren't perfect, but they would serve her. After she'd killed a ram, she could use the tips of the horns as handles, and the rest she could use for other things.

She decided that once she'd gotten down from the mountain, she would find a blacksmith who would be willing to smooth out her handiwork and perfect it. Until then, they would do her just fine.

Arryn made her way to the eastern side of the peak, where the wind blew the least. That was where she'd tanned the leopard hide for several days. It was only a small area, but it was flat, and she could easily to make a fire there when needed. Today, she had different plans.

The sun was shining that morning, and it hadn't snowed the

night before. Arryn had spent every last bit of her energy creating a fire off to the side, and kept it going all night in hopes of keeping the ground warm enough to do what she wanted to do today.

As she knelt on the bare ground, she saw green blades of grass. She'd hoped she might be able to coax some out of the earth, but her magic wasn't a strong as that of Elysia or the Chieftain. If *they'd* been marooned up there, she was positive they'd already have grown a garden of epic proportions, even with the frigid temperatures.

A loud screech cut through the air, and Arryn smiled as she looked up to see a large falcon flying toward her. Arryn held her hands out and the bird circled her, dropping something from his talons as he did.

She almost dropped the objects, but manage to catch them again.

"Yes!" she shouted. "Thank you!"

The bird screeched again before flying away. She inspected the large berries she was holding in her hands. She'd sent him to the nearest village around to find any available fruit he could fit in his talons. She regretted being so weak, because had she not been, she could've willed him to go farther. Much farther. Perhaps to the Dark Forest.

But with these, she hoped it wouldn't be a concern for much longer.

Arryn shoved several of the raspberries in her mouth, moaning as she tasted their sweetness. Her stomach rumbled, and she had to fight the urge to shove the rest of them in her mouth. She wanted to eat all of them right then, but that wasn't why she'd sent the bird to fetch them.

Taking a deep breath, Arryn laid them on the ground before digging several small holes in the cleared area. The ground was soft enough that she could do it easily, and she dropped a raspberry into each hole.

Next, she quickly placed a handful of snow on top of each before putting her hands to the ground, melting the snow before it did any damage to the berries below. The ground soaked up the warm water, drinking it in and using it for fuel for the berries.

She settled onto her knees, taking several deep breaths to pace herself. Feeling the magic in her hands, she pushed it forward, making sure not to push too hard or too fast. If she did, she would run out of energy too soon, and the result might not be what she desired.

Growing plants was something she was good at, but she'd never been as proficient as the native druids.

Arryn focused, feeling the warmth in the ground and the sun shining above, and soon she began to feel the life blooming from underneath. Within moments, several bushes had pushed up from the ground, growing and blossoming before her very eyes. The plants were small, but there were enough berries on each to sustain her for couple days and allow her to grow more if needed.

Damping down her magic, she took a deep breath and rested for a few moments before gathering all the berries and putting them into her cloak. After making her way back to her camp, she placed them on the ground, giving one to her furry little friend.

"I swear to the gods," she said, pointing to the bunny. "If you steal all of my raspberries... well, I don't know. It's hard to threaten something so damned cute. Just don't do it."

The rabbit made a little noise and bobbed his nose at her before taking the raspberry and eating it.

"Now that I have some fruit to eat," she said to him, "I'm going to go get some more meat. Mountain life is surprisingly exhausting and hungry work. Stay here, Fuzzy Lumpkins, so my falcon friend doesn't come back for you."

Arryn gave the rabbit a few quick scratches before leaving the igloo. She grabbed her makeshift blades and headed down the side of the mountain. The wind had begun to pick up, and her energy was already waning because of her magic use, so she had to stay close to her camp, as usual.

It was times like this she felt the most exasperated about her situation. She tried to remind herself that she was doing everything she could to get back home.

Arryn pulled her cloak tighter around her, trying to block the wind from her face. It was cold, and the wind chill factor made it even worse. She wouldn't have long to hunt, and she couldn't come back empty-handed; she would have a hard time healing from this endeavor without decent nourishment.

Her nose was beginning to run, and she felt the urge to cough. She realized then that she had used too much energy, and she was getting sick for the first time since before she'd come to the Dark Forest. That might have sounded like a wonderful thing to most people, but when someone never got sick, illness struck hard and fast. It would be difficult for her to recover.

Just when she was about to give up and head back for fear of moving too far from her camp, she saw a large ram not too far off. She wished that she had her bow right then—it would've made the kill so much easier. At this point, she wasn't exactly sure how to pull it off.

First, she was too weak to throw her makeshift blade hard enough to do any real damage, and she lacked the supplies needed to make a proper spear. Any wood she'd happened upon, she'd needed for her fire. Second, she couldn't use nature magic on the beast because she was already too weak, and she'd need whatever power she had left to get her kill back to camp.

She momentarily looked at the sky, saying a prayer to anyone who could hear her. She prayed that the magic she was going to use wouldn't deplete her energy so much that she couldn't get the ram back to camp, but would be enough to kill the animal painlessly.

Taking a deep breath, Arryn pulled the handle-less dagger back and threw it as hard as she could manage, using a little of her physical magic to push it harder. She hit her target exactly where she'd intended, and the magic had given her blade the added power she'd needed to achieve an instant kill.

The ram fell to the ground, and Arryn walked over and grabbed it by the horns. It didn't matter which path she chose; there were really no good choices.

Dragging the ram by sheer strength would be impossible. It was far too heavy; the energy expenditure would kill her long before she reached camp. Using magic to lighten the load would do the same. Leaving the ram here and heading back to camp would allow some other animal to carry it off for itself, while she would be left to suffer and spend several days recovering.

In the end, she decided to use both physical and magical strength, just as she had to acquire it. She pulled the animal by the horns and used telekinesis to push. By the time she made it to camp, she was ready to collapse.

As she stumbled into the igloo, landing hard on the leopard pelt, she told the bunny, "Do me a favor. If anything tries to take my ram, do whatever it takes to wake me. It might freeze before I wake up, but that's a risk I have to take."

Unconsciousness quickly took Arryn, and the weakened girl knew she had no choice but to rest. She just hoped nothing would come by and try to steal her food or kill her, or she would have to waste even more energy fighting.

CHAPTER FOUR

Cathillian stared at Amelia, who seemed to be overly intimidated by the challenge ahead.

"It's not that bad, I promise. He's tame. Granted, you won't have as much control over him as I would, but he's a smart boy. He knows how to do this. I've been working with him all morning." Cathillian smiled at the worried expression on the Chancellor's face.

"What if he doesn't like me? What if he rebels right after you leave? A single morning of training doesn't seem like very long. I know I seem like I'm freaking out, but my messages to and from Maddie *cannot* fall into Talia's hands." She looked at the large raven sitting on the back of her chair.

"Just try it," Cathillian urged. "Write something, roll it up, seal it, and attach it to his leg. Echo is a lot bigger, so she can carry larger letters. With him you'll have to keep it short and sweet. Warnings. Places you want meet. Times. Things like that. I chose a raven because those are far less conspicuous than a hawk or an eagle. They're smaller, so it'll be a lot easier to hide him."

Amelia sighed, looking from Cathillian to the bird and back. "I thought mental magic would be far more useful than nature magic. Of course, I've had a lot more experience with mental magic because of Julianne. I'm starting to think I made the wrong choice."

Cathillian laughed. "You're putting way too much thought into this. Besides, the Founder knows all three types of magic, and you said Hannah knows all three as well. Why can't you learn all three, too? Your mental magic has come in very handy, in case you don't recall. Now, quit worrying. That's not like you."

Amelia took a deep breath and nodded. "You're right. That's not like me. Well, I *do* worry, just not to the point where it's visible. So, tell me what to do. I'm still not sure about this, but I suppose there's no harm in testing it out a few times."

Cathillian nodded and smiled. "Good. Hold out your arm." Amelia did as he asked, and the raven flew across the room to land on her arm, turning its head sharply in a few directions before fixing his eyes on her. "Good job! Pet him. Talk to him. Let him get used to your voice, and let him see that you're a good person and can be trusted. It may not be a magical bond, but you can still create a bond with him."

Amelia reached out with her free hand and used the back of her index and middle fingers to rub his chest. He puffed up a little, adjusting his wings before settling back down.

"Picking a name also helps to seal a bond," Cathillian said.

Amelia nodded, staring at the bird for a few moments. "He isn't as black as some of the other ones I've seen. He's more of a dark gray. I've never seen a raven that looked like him before. Ash. I think I'll call him Ash. Do you think that's dumb?"

A smile spread across Cathillian's face. "Echo and I spent several days bonding. She was injured when I initially found her; one of her wings had been broken. I healed her and set her loose. I was only about thirteen at the time. She more or less stalked me after that, following me around the forest and circling above me. I always knew when she was there because she announced herself. Her voice carried farther than any other hawk or eagle I'd ever heard. It echoed through the skies every morning when she came to find me. After three days, she was mine, and I was hers. In other words, no, I don't think it's stupid at all."

Amelia was touched to hear the story of how Cathillian and Echo had bonded. "Well, I might not be able to form a magical bond with Ash, but at the very least we can be good friends."

"Bonded animals inherit language use from their master. They understand the language because their master understands the language. Tamed animals, not so much, but I assure you he will understand simple commands. It's the equivalent of understanding a few words of a language. He's not fluent, but he knows enough, and he will learn more as you work with him, especially if you focus your energy into it. I'll teach you more when we get back. You never know, Ash might be your true familiar one day."

Amelia smiled, her eyes sparkling a bit at the thought. "Thank you, this means a lot. It'll help me feel a bit safer while everyone is out of the city. Maddie's all I have left, and I can't put her in danger by letting Talia know we have any involvement with one another."

Cathillian said his goodbyes and made his way outside. He didn't like the thought of leaving Amelia any more than she did, but if there was a chance to get help for Arryn, he had to take it. He knew Amelia wouldn't stop working on the city, and that would be the only thing keeping Arryn from killing him once he found her. He smiled at the thought of her anger. It delighted him more than it should have.

"Is everything good to go in there?" Celine asked from the back of her white horse.

Cathillian mounted Maia, looking at the sky as Echo called out. He tightened his grip on the reins and nodded. "Everything's fine. As long as we're careful, I think it'll be okay. We just have to be smart. We need to get out of the city before the next Guard shift takes over."

Samuel nodded from the back of his own horse. "Aye, lad.

Let's go talk ta that pointy-eared family of yers and see if we can find a way ta save our girl."

TALIA STOOD IN HER OFFICE, hands clasped behind her back as she looked out the window. Scarlett had yet to come in to see her today, but this wasn't the first time. Her fun with Eric had been just that—fun. Unfortunately, it had done nothing to soothe her worried mind.

In the pit of her stomach, Talia was still feeling like something was off. It was even stronger than before, almost enough to bring her to tears. She had heard the stories about her father, Adrien, and how he'd seemed frantic, almost crazy in the end. She was beginning to wonder if perhaps that wasn't some form of real mental illness rather than simple paranoia caused by the immense and complicated plan he had put into action.

Further, she wondered if it was possible that mental illness was genetic.

As she waited for Scarlett to show, she became more and more aware that her actions spoke volumes about her mental health.

Something wasn't right. Deep down, she could feel it. Scarlett had been coming in late often, and she never offered a good reason. In fact, when Talia would ask about it, Scarlett would change the subject, and somehow, Talia bought it every time.

She's using her magic on me, Talia thought. *That bitch! That must be it! She doesn't have the strength to overpower me completely, but she still has enough to redirect me.*

Why else would her anger subside so quickly after she'd demanded answers and had received not even a smidgen of information?

Scarlett finally stepped onto the Academy grounds and Talia

watched her saunter toward the door, wondering just how the mystic had been able to get into her head so easily.

My mind must be weak, she thought. *That will have to change, and so will the company I keep.*

Stepping away from the window, Talia decided to spend the rest of the morning alone to fortify her mind, as well as to plan her next step. She needed to make a big impact, and fast. She wanted to be able to overshadow Amelia in every way. She wanted to be able to do more than the Chancellor had even thought of.

Perhaps it was time to reach out to the governor of Cella.

ELYSIA STARED AT THE GROUND, her eyes wandering over the mauled bodies of four warriors. In the middle of the night, they'd heard something outside their walls. It had been the first group that neither Elysia nor the Chieftain had accompanied, and it was certainly going to be the last.

Her men and women patrolled their borders inside the barrier, watching and listening for anything out of the ordinary. When they found it, they'd expected the worst.

The barrier had been breached more than once, and they believed the enemy would do so again if something weren't done. Instead of waiting for confirmation from Elysia or the Chieftain, Edgar, one of their higher-ranking warriors, had ordered one of their youngest back to camp to find Elysia or the Chieftain.

At that point, the group used nature magic to lift them up and over the wall instead of opening it, fearing that breaching the barrier even for a moment would leave them vulnerable. When they landed on the other side, hell itself had awaited them.

Cougars, bears, and wolves from all over the forest had gathered there, quickly surrounding the group. Some had the clouded eyes of a familiar, while the others were simply being controlled.

Apparently, the dark druids had been replacing their familiars, as well as using other animals as weapons.

By the time Elysia and the Chieftain had arrived, it had been too late. Four of them had been killed, having been down too long while the others fought. They were unable to be healed. The others had been terribly wounded, but had been saved.

The dark druids had fled, taking their animals with them when they'd heard Zobig and Chaos approaching. They'd been there to send a warning, not for battle. Not a real one, anyway.

"If not for their waning energy, I wouldn't recognize them at all," Elysia said softly.

The Chieftain wrapped his arm around her shoulders and pulled her away, forcing her head against his chest as he held her. "Just because you lead them doesn't mean you have to stare at them until we put them to rest. You've looked at them long enough. You've suffered long enough. This wasn't your fault."

Elysia shook her head against him as she clasped him tightly around the waist. Even though she was grown and had been for many years, the Chieftain dwarfed her in size, and she always felt like a little girl again in his arms. That was something she took comfort in, especially right then.

"I can't stand this anymore, Father. I have to *do* something. Our people are dying. Familiars are being sacrificed. And now our animals are disappearing in the forest. They haven't only taken the large ones, they've taken the young. Bears and their cubs. Deer and their fawns. Wolves and their pups. Cougars and their kittens. They have even taken smaller animals like foxes. Our forest is being depleted. They are always so close. What if they're living on our land, but outside our borders? We can't let this continue!"

The Chieftain gently pulled away from his daughter, his hands on either side of her face as he looked into her eyes. "And what would you do, daughter? What would you have *me* do?

Don't think we can take them head-on. We can't. We have to find out how many there are. We have to learn how strong they are."

"That's exactly right. And I intend to find out." Elysia took a step back, looking at the bodies on the ground again as she shook her head. Finally, she looked back at her father. "I'm going to take some of the *Schatten* with me since they specialize in subtlety. We're going to track them down. We'll find out how many they have, who is in charge, and anything else we might be able to determine."

"We can send someone else. I don't want you going. I can't afford to lose you. Not just because you are the only other true Elder here, but because you're my daughter. Our people need us —both of us. But more importantly, *I* need you. I can't lose my baby girl."

Elysia smiled. It always warmed her heart when her father worried about her. She knew how much he loved her, but it was never more obvious than at those moments.

"I haven't been your baby girl in almost four decades. I know you worry about me, but I have a duty. Arryn and Cat are in Arcadia. What happens when they come home? I don't want them walking into a war. I don't want them coming home to fear and bloodshed. I need to do this. We need these answers."

The Chieftain smiled. "I don't care if it's four decades or ten, you'll always be my baby girl, just like that son of yours will always be your baby boy. You and Cathillian are only children— that is the burden you both carry. Forever small and fragile in your parents' eyes."

She couldn't argue that point. Cathillian really would always be her little boy, no matter how big he got. No matter how strong he got. And that's why she had no choice.

"I'll gather my team and fill them in on everything. Tonight, we will hold the funeral. Since we can't give them a proper death ritual by the *Heilig* Tree, we will burn them on a pyre and bury their ashes at its base. Tomorrow, I leave." She looked at the bodies one last time.

The Chieftain sighed. "One would almost think I had no authority around here. Pay no attention to me; I'm just the insanely attractive but crazy old man. No need to listen to anything *I* say."

With a chuckle, Elysia said, "I know how you feel. When you're this pretty, it's hard for people to pay attention to anything that we say."

The Chieftain narrowed his eyes at his daughter for a moment, studying her. "See, it *sounds* like you're agreeing with me, but really, I think you're just being mean. Because that's what you do. You're mean."

Elysia laughed. "I love you. That's all that matters."

Just then, Nika ran up, her expression unreadable. "Elysia, Chieftain. You should come with me quickly."

All humor drained from Elysia's face as she looked at her fellow warrior. "What is it?"

"It's Echo. Cathillian is on his way back home, and he sent her ahead. By the scattered images I read from her, they're in danger."

CHAPTER FIVE

It had taken nearly two days to get back to the Dark Forest, and that was with little rest during the few short stops. Cathillian knew the forest was a dangerous place—for anyone other than the druids, though the lycanthrope posed a threat to anyone—especially when bringing along someone who was not the best fighter.

"I know the circumstances suck, but are you excited to be back home?" Celine asked.

Cathillian thought that over for a moment, though he didn't know why. The answer should have been a quick yes, but it wasn't. The Dark Forest was home—it always had been and always would be—but somehow Arcadia had become a second home. Not just a place he had been visiting or even a place he was living temporarily. It actually felt like home.

Cathillian had grown to feel responsible for the city, though he wasn't sure how much of that was due to his own emotions and how much was because of his attachment to Arryn. He'd never before had the desire to go to Arcadia except for simple visits to see the architecture and watch the people who were so unlike his own, but it had become so much more.

"I've missed home, and I've missed my family. I'm excited to see them, but I don't feel like it's where I belong right now. Once everything is settled in Arcadia, I think I'll feel much better. More than anything, I just want Arryn back. It doesn't matter if I'm here or in Arcadia; I'm not going to get any rest until I know she's okay."

Celine gave him a sad smile from the back of her horse. "I know you care a lot about her. That's the only reason I've grown to trust you as much as I do. It's obvious how good you've been to her. Not just you, but your family. I see a lot of my sister in her, but I suspect that when I meet your mother, I'll see a lot more of her as well."

Cathillian laughed. "Trust me, by the time you leave she'll have made an impression on you, too. That's just who she is." There was a brief pause as everyone joined in the laughter, but Cathillian quickly followed it up with, "I must add that it's much easier to just go along with whatever she says. I tell you that because she is one of the most terrifying people I've ever met. Arryn is the second most terrifying. At first, I thought it was because my mom raised her, but then I met you. Your whole damn family is that way; my mom just helped further the tendency."

Samuel laughed. "Ye should meet a few rearick women. In case ye haven't noticed, there ain't a lot we rearick men're afraid of. We can stare down a man twice our size with an axe or growl at the biggest and strongest remnant, but put us in a room with even a single one of our angry women and we'll be shakin' in our boots."

"As pissed off as all you seem to be, I can only—" Cathillian's smile faded as he heard a loud growl echo through the forest.

"What was that?" Celine asked as she looked around, her eyes wide.

Cathillian opened his senses to search the area, and he felt it. The presence of nature magic, but it wasn't that of any druid he was friend or family to. Realization struck his face as he sat taller, more defensively on his horse.

"I think it's Jenna, the druid who literally drained the life out of me. I'm not fucking with her this time. If I see her, I'm taking her down hard and fast." His face reflected every ounce of the rage he felt for what she had done and the threats she'd made.

"These're yer lands, lad. What'll ye have us do?" Samuel asked.

Another roar echoed through the woods, this time closer. Cathillian shook his head, his nostrils flaring as he ground his teeth. "That's a damn bear, but it's not Zobig. I think she's trying to tame it."

Without warning, Cathillian took off on his horse, urging Maia to run faster and faster. Behind him, he could hear the other horses galloping. He needed to save that bear before she completely tamed it and attempted to bond.

If she was using darker nature magic, and he assumed that she was, she would use it to dominate the bear, forcing it into submission. That didn't create lifelong familiars. It created slaves.

Cathillian saw several dark druids surrounding a black bear, Jenna among them. Just as before, it appeared that she was their leader. He didn't see Aeris anywhere around, but that didn't mean anything.

Pulling back on the reins, Cathillian slowed Maia to a stop before jumping off and rushing forward. Jenna and the rest of the group were so focused on the bear and their attempt to overwhelm it that they were too slow to react when Cathillian approached them.

Without hesitation, Cathillian stopped hard before bringing his hands up, a root ripping from the ground and tripping Jenna. She landed hard on her ass, and Cathillian used that opportunity to bring the root down on her, pinning her to the ground.

The bear roared as he whirled, snapping and swiping his massive paw at anyone standing near him. The dark druids all jumped out of the way, knowing they'd lost control of the animal when Jenna fell.

A large war hammer passed Cathillian and hit one of the druids in the chest. His eyes widened as he saw Samuel running toward the dark druids, daggers now in hand as he sprinted to retrieve his hammer.

Cathillian took that as his cue and charged as well. He drew his sword, going first after a dark druid who was pretty close to his size. As their swords met, he realized the man was equally matched in strength as well.

As Cathillian fought, he was careful to pay attention to the bear. There was no way for him to focus his attention on the battle before him while channeling the magic needed to calm the bear. If the animal decided to attack, he couldn't protect himself.

"Let me go!" Jenna screamed. "I'll kill you for this!"

Cathillian brought his sword down on his opponent's blade, the resulting *clang* ringing in his ears. He lifted his leg and kicked the man in the chest, sending him back several feet.

"Well, that doesn't sound like a very good motivator for me to let you go. If you're trapped, you can't kill me. See? That's a much better motivator for me," Cathillian responded without looking in her direction.

The girl screamed in frustration, kicking, and writhing as she tried to break free. Cathillian didn't spare her another glance as he focused on his opponent.

The sound of light footsteps came to his ears just before he saw Celine run up. He wanted to yell at her to go back, but the dark druid he was fighting had made a successful slash, catching Cathillian across the chest, and luckily only doing minimal damage.

He dropped to the ground and rolled out of the way, quickly making sure the bear was still far enough back that he wouldn't be a threat.

He heard a loud cry from one of the dark druids behind him, the one Samuel was fighting. "Nice job, lass!"

He hadn't been able to see what Celine had done, but she was safe, and that was all that mattered. Echo called from above before readying herself to dive. Cathillian thrust his sword forward, but the man he was fighting easily blocked it before swiping his sword through the air, narrowly missing Echo as she quickly pulled up.

"Echo!" Cathillian called out as he began furiously swinging his sword, his rage at seeing Echo nearly killed giving him additional strength. "Get my mom and the Chieftain!"

Echo flew away as Cathillian landed another hard kick to the man's chest. Going head-to-head with him using swords wasn't the answer, since they were equally matched. In fact, Cathillian was almost certain this man was a far better swordsman than he was. It was only luck that Cathillian hadn't already been taken down.

If he were going to win, it would have to be with magic.

Before the man could recover, Cathillian thrust his sword into the ground and dropped, putting his hands in the grass. The dark druid recovered and began to run forward, but quickly stopped, his eyes going wide before a smile broke across his face.

Cathillian heard the heavy footsteps, but didn't realize what was happening until it was too late. He was hit hard from the side and thrown several feet as a roar sounded out around him. He groaned as he rolled onto his back, trying to sit up. The wound on his chest and what he was certain was a broken rib, or several of them, prevented him from moving as fast as he wanted to.

And he very quickly regretted it.

At that moment, he realized just how careless he'd been. Not only had he underestimated his opponent, but he'd completely lost track of the bear. And now, that bear was on top of him, the only thing separating the animal's large, powerful jaws from rending Cathillian was the fact that both of his feet were planted in its chest, his broken ribs grinding against one another.

"I'm not your enemy!" Cathillian told the bear.

It responded by lunging forward, mouth wide. He pushed harder with his legs to keep the bear from successfully biting him and twisted his head to the side. As he did, he reached up with both hands and grabbed the bear, his fingers on either side of its jaws as he *pushed* his magic at him.

"I'm not your enemy!" Cathillian said again. The response this time was a growl, a low grumble from deep within the bear's chest, but he felt the message immediately take hold. "They are. I will help you. You'll be free, but not if they win."

There was another growl deep within the bear's chest, but Cathillian slowly turned his head, risking a look at the bear directly in the face. He could see the anger in the bear's expression, but the animal slowly backed away.

A loud scream sounded from his left, and Cathillian looked over in time to see vines wrap around Celine's legs and pull her to the ground before lifting her into the trees.

Jenna had gotten free, and she still had access to her positive nature magic, though it was weak enough that she hadn't been able to use it to free herself from the root. The darkness had certainly taken hold of her, but the transition hadn't been completed.

The bear growled loudly, and Cathillian looked over at him. "The girl in the tree and the short guy are mine. Do whatever you want with the rest."

There was a low grumble, and Cathillian could almost imagine the animal smiling. He roared before charging toward the dark druid Samuel was fighting. Cathillian placed his fingers in the grass, pulling nature's energy into himself.

He felt his ribs snapping back into place, and he worried he might break his teeth from how hard he was biting down. But as fast as the pain came, it was gone, and he was back on his feet.

Cathillian's eyes searched the area, finding the person he wanted most. Jenna had her hand extended, her gray eyes ringed with a faint green as she focused on Celine. Searching the ground around him, Cathillian quickly found what he wanted, smiling as he did.

His jade eyes turned dark green as he lifted his hand. A vine came out of the ground and wrapped around a large rock. He swung his hand and the vine whipped the rock into the air, hitting Jenna directly on the side of her head. She immediately fell to the ground, unconscious, and her magic released Celine.

Cathillian's other hand shot out as he focused on tightening the vines around Celine so he could lower her safely to the ground. As he did, he could hear the screams of one of the other dark druids combined with loud growls as the bear got revenge for the pain they had caused him.

Within moments, Celine was safely back on the ground, and the sound of hoofbeats rang through the forest around them. Cathillian saw Chaos and Zobig carrying their respective masters on their backs.

They'd gotten there just as everything was ending, but Cathillian was glad he'd sent Echo. Things could've gone much worse.

Elysia jumped off Chaos' back and ran to her son while she looked around and took everything in. Zobig growled at the full-grown bear in front of him. The animal was the same breed, but only half his size.

"Easy, Zobig," the Chieftain said as he climbed down.

Cathillian stepped forward. "That bear has suffered. They had him surrounded and were trying to dominate him."

Elysia sighed heavily as she looked from her son to the bear and back, then pulled him into her arms and hugged him tightly. "Gods, I can't believe how much I missed you. I'm so glad you're safe."

"It's good to see you, grandson. I'm also glad to see you're making friends," the Chieftain said, gesturing to the dead dark druids lying on the ground. "Your travels seem to have been interesting, to say the least."

Cathillian laughed. "Yeah, to say the least. About the bear... I think we should bring him back with us and allow him to cross the barrier. He deserves a safe haven."

Cathillian saw the look of wonder on Celine's face as she looked at each of the three animals. Chaos was so large that it was nearly impossible to climb on his back without him kneeling. Zobig was almost twice the size of a normal bear, and then, of course, there was the normal bear. He imagined she'd never seen animals like them before, as horses in Arcadia were typically of a smaller breed and bears didn't come around the city.

She reached out, curiosity overwhelming her as she tried to touch the wild bear.

"That one's wild, you realize. The larger one is my grandfather's familiar," Cathillian told her. "Of course, Zobig is old and grumpy, and kind of a dick. He likes to trip people and finds himself to be pretty funny, so I guess you're screwed either way you go."

To Cathillian's surprise, the bear stepped forward and lifted his nose, touching it to her outstretched and shaking hand. She squealed in delight. "He's amazing! I love him!"

While the bear had been soothed by Cathillian's magic, he was still a wild animal and couldn't be trusted, not without more training and soothing. After what the dark druids had done to him, using their magic to overwhelm, distract, and dominate him, Cathillian was surprised he'd been able to calm him at all.

Everyone jumped as Celine dropped to her knees and wrapped her arms around the bear's neck, snuggling into his thick fur. The bear grumbled, but didn't growl. In fact, he didn't do much of anything.

"Sorry, lad," Samuel said. "But I think the girl has bigger balls than ye do."

"Hey!" Cathillian feigned offense in his expression.

Samuel laughed. "I heard you screaming like a little girl over there when he came after you. Look at him now."

Cathillian shrugged, lifting his hands out to the sides. "Well, I calmed him down for her."

"I'm glad everyone is safe and the jokes have started," Elysia said, "but there are a lot of things to address here. First, why are you back? I'm happy to see you—you have no idea just how happy I am—but why are you back? Second, where is Arryn?"

Cathillian sighed, all humor leaving him. "Unfortunately, we need to talk."

A weak groan came from the far right. Everyone looked at Jenna, who was stirring on the ground. She'd been the only one to survive.

"Yeah, there are some things I need to tell you, too."

CHAPTER SIX

Although everyone was anxious to get started, they decided to deal with Jenna and get back to the tribe before talking things out. They all agreed that Jenna should not be told anything about what was happening in Arcadia, and that she should go back in chains and stay that way.

After they arrived, they tied Jenna to a tree just outside the village and put several guards on her. Cathillian made sure to let them know she was capable of much more with dark nature magic than she had ever been with pure nature magic. Once that had been settled, they made their way back to find Nika waiting for them.

Cathillian, Samuel, and Celine took turns filling Elysia and the Chieftain in on everything that had happened in Arcadia since they'd been gone. Cathillian was relatively sure his mother was on the verge of exploding, but he was proud of her for holding it together.

"I can't believe this!" Elysia exclaimed, standing and pacing back and forth. "I can't believe them, and I can't believe you. You should've told me sooner. They don't know who they're *fucking* with. I'll take our strongest men and reduce that city to nothing but rubble. That bitch will regret ever even *speaking* to Arryn."

"Now that's what I'm talking about!" Samuel cheered.

The Chieftain grunted. "Now, daughter—and rearick—think rationally. You know Arryn. She's a fighter. I highly doubt she succumbed to whatever fate those women had planned for her. You know that we are on the brink of war here as well. We can't afford to lose any men."

"Yeah," Cathillian agreed. "Plus, the whole city isn't at fault. It's just those two women, the Dean and her mystic partner. The rest of the city is innocent. Whatever hatred they hold for Arryn is because of the mystic's abilities. It was Arryn's goal to save the city, so destroying it would destroy Arryn."

"This sounds like something that would be better suited for the *Schatten*," Nika offered.

The *Schatten* were the shadow warriors of the druid community. Their magic was strong, but their skills in fighting and subtlety were superior to all others. If something needed to be done quietly, the *Schatten* were the ones to get it done.

Elysia sighed, sitting down and doing her best to relax. "You're right, but I just can't stand the thought of her being out there. We don't know if she is alone. We don't know if she's tied up somewhere. We don't know if she's being tortured. What about using Echo to find her?"

Cathillian nodded. "Echo has already searched the south for any sign of Arryn, but obviously, she came up empty. There is a lot more ground to cover in the north than in the south, though, so we're starting there next. It's more likely Talia took her north anyway."

Elysia was pleased with the plan to send Echo on another search. "Good. We'll start today. I want Echo to fly out soon. I'm going to put together a team and find out where the dark druids are hiding, and see if I can find out what their plan is."

"I suppose that just leaves Jenna. What should we do with her?" the Chieftain asked.

"After what she did to me, I'd say killing her would be quite fun. However, we need whatever information we can get out of her, though I'm betting it won't be very much," Cathillian replied. He knew she would never betray her brother, no matter how much it benefited her to do so.

"The question is, do we keep this from her parents? I worry that if they know she's here, they'll do something stupid," Elysia said.

Nika shook her head. "Don't tell them. I know Jenna well, and her parents aren't too far behind her in the deception depart-ment. I have no doubt they feel guilt, but I personally think it's nothing compared to their love for their children. If given the chance, they would do whatever it took to save their daughter."

The Chieftain stood, his eyes momentarily wandering in the direction where Jenna was being held, though he couldn't see her from their location. "For now, this stays between us. We need to learn more before we risk anything else happening."

"And for the love of all things nature, stay out of her reach," Cathillian warned. "Her death-touch is no joke. She has a lot more magic now than she did before."

Nika laughed. "Maybe if she would've spent more time prac-ticing instead of worrying about Arryn, she would've been better at nature magic. Her obsession hindered her and eventually drove her to darkness."

"All that aside," the Chieftain said, "we now know where we need to begin. Cathillian, you should go talk to Echo. Make sure she's well rested and able to make a long trip. After all, you just got back from Arcadia, and that is quite a long flight. Nika, I would like you to speak to the ones guarding Jenna. Explain to them the sensitivity of the duty, and how important it is that they keep their mouths shut. Also, relay Cathillian's message. If her dark magic is that strong, we don't want her touching anyone."

It took a couple days to recover from her ram hunt, but it had paid off greatly. Not only was she able to stay warmer by using the skin, she had also been able to craft two daggers, having enough magic now to transform the rock into steel.

She'd also grown more raspberries, and had enough to last her for a week, as well as the meat she'd gotten from the kill. Minus fires to keep warm and cook the meat, she wouldn't have to use magic anymore.

That left her with the ability to practice something new. Something she prayed would get her out of there.

Talia was from the north, so there was no doubt in Arryn's mind that if she made her way down from this mountain Talia would have spies watching for her in all directions, ready to take her and finish the job or deliver her to Talia. It was a risk she didn't want to take.

Arryn jumped a few times, loosening up her arms as she did. She took a few deep breaths and let them out, thinking to herself how much she wouldn't miss the burn of the cold air in her lungs when she got down to sea level.

Her rabbit friend sat on the sidelines, nose twitching as always, his little eyes focused on her. "Today's the day!" Arryn told him. "I'm gonna do it. I will make this happen."

The rabbit didn't respond, only continued to sit there and watch.

"You're a terrible conversationalist."

Arryn steadied herself, her eyes turning black as she began to concentrate on her magic. She'd never tried to teleport—she'd never been formally taught—but she had seen it done and felt the magic that was involved. She had faith that she could re-create it if she worked hard enough.

Just don't go far and you'll be fine, she thought to herself. *You can do this. You can do this, and you can get back to Arcadia. You can kill that bitch and end the suffering in the city. Just focus.*

Arryn focused on the magic swelling around her, slowly allowing it to surround every inch of her. She stared at a flat area about twenty feet away, concentrating on that spot in hopes that she might land there.

Taking another deep breath, she tightened her hold on the magic, drawing it to herself. The magic slammed against her, throwing her back several feet, but teleporting her nowhere.

"Gah! *Fuck!*" she yelled as she rolled onto her back and grabbed her knee. It had slammed hard onto the snow and the hidden rock beneath, tearing a small hole in her pants as well as in the flesh that lay beneath.

She sat there for a few more moments, hissing in pain before standing again.

Looking over, she saw that the rabbit had covered his little eyes with his paws. "Oh, shut up, you overgrown cotton ball. You might not actually have the ability to laugh, but I can sense it from over here."

Arryn limped back to her original spot. Her knee was throbbing, but she refused to expend the magic required to heal it. She didn't plan to use magic for anything that wasn't necessary.

Taking a few extra deep breaths, Arryn decided to try again. As soon as she had the magic wrapped around her, she pulled it in tightly again, this time making sure there was equal pressure on all areas.

She assumed she hadn't had good contact on one side or another, allowing the magic to push her back instead of carrying her where she needed to go. Of course, she had no idea how the mechanics worked; all she had were guesses.

Once again, the magic slammed into her, but this time her vision went black before she slammed into the ground. She grunted and rolled onto her back once more, wincing in pain.

"This would be so much easier with a teacher. I've never heard of anyone being launched into a wall or down the street when they learned how to teleport."

Then again, not many people are actually strong enough to try it.

She sat up and looked at her surroundings. Not only had she moved much farther, she'd landed in the spot she'd aimed for. At that moment, she realized she hadn't actually seen the journey. Everything had been black. Her eyes darted to her furry friend, who was staring at her with great interest.

"Did you see it? Did I do it?" she asked.

He squeaked at her. She pushed just enough magic to allow her to see flashes of what the rabbit had seen. It wasn't much since there was no real bond, but she did see the moment she'd disappeared entirely.

Arryn jumped up, pain all but forgotten. "Yes!" she shouted, raising her hands to the sky in triumph. "I did it! It hurt like hell, but I did it!"

Laughing from excitement and realizing she more than likely looked like a crazy person right then, Arryn made her way back over to her original spot. She felt energized, delighted by the fact that her tries weren't expending very much magic. Or perhaps her magic was getting stronger because she had no choice but to use it to exhaustion, rest, and begin again.

To her, being stuck on this mountain was equivalent to the training she'd seen the warriors go through in the forest. Train all day until collapsing, rest, wake up and do it again. Eventually, the body got used to it and grew stronger. She'd been told magic was the same, but she'd never had the ability to test the theory before.

It was possible she now had more magic than what she had come here with.

Arryn swung her arms a little bit, once again loosening herself up. Her eyes turned black as she called the magic for a third time.

I'm coming for you, Talia. Possibly, very soon.

CELINE STARED down at the throwing knives in her hand, assessing their weight. During the earlier battle with the dark druids, she'd thrown one with surprising accuracy and hit one of them in the thigh. It hadn't been a killing throw, but it *had* struck him, allowing Samuel to overpower him and take him down.

One of the warriors had been kind enough to show her to the Versuch pit so she could practice throwing at the targets set up just outside the barriers. She lifted the knife, pulling it back over her shoulder as Samuel had taught her to do, and loosed it. The blade struck the lowest part of the target, right where the crotch would have been had it been a man.

"Damn, lass," Samuel said as he approached. "That's enough right there ta make a man kill himself fer ye."

Celine laughed. "Well, what fun would it be to just end it so soon?"

Samuel chuckled. "Remind me never ta piss ye off."

Had it been anyone else, she wouldn't have wanted them around while she was practicing, but Samuel had been the one to teach her in the first place, so she didn't mind. She selected another blade from her left hand, pulled it back over her shoulder, and threw it hard. This time, the blade landed a little higher, around bellybutton height.

"Very nice," Samuel said. "Remember ta release in respect ta the height of the person yer throwin' at. I think yer releasing just a bit too late, resultin' in a lower throw. But that's good if yer attackin' someone like me."

She laughed and nodded. "Okay, I'll try to release a little sooner."

Samuel went to her right side and gently wrapped his hand around her wrist. He stood behind her as he eyed the target. Lifting her arm, he told her, "I'm just a little shorter than ye, so

I'm not sure if this is right, but try releasin' right about here. See how that suits ye."

She swallowed hard, smiling nervously before nodding again. She found herself feeling a little more sensitive to him than usual. Ever since the night he had first shown her how to throw a knife, she'd noticed there was a bit more to him than the rough exterior all rearick exhibited. He was a good man, and a gentle man. He was also a little more than a decade older than her.

Samuel had a similar nervous smile on his own face as he backed away, his eyes quickly finding the ground. "Anyway, let's see how that works."

Celine took the final throwing knife in her right hand, lifted it over her shoulder, and threw, making sure to release where Samuel had instructed her to. The blade stuck hard into the target, striking close to where the left shoulder would be.

"I did it!" she exclaimed, a large smile spreading across her lips.

"Aye, ye did! Now, go get yer knives and do it again."

Still smiling, her eyes met his. He seemed genuinely happy, even excited for her. Before she could stop herself, it came tumbling out. "Why aren't you married, Samuel?" The moment the words left her mouth, her eyes widened. "I'm sorry. That's really personal."

Samuel waved a hand in the air. "Na, it's fine. It is personal, and I don't much care for talkin' about it most days, or even thinkin' about it, but I suppose it couldn't hurt to tell ye."

She quickly went to fetch her knives and came back. "Really, you don't have to say anything if you don't want to. I shouldn't have asked. It's just… Everyone else thinks you're just a rough rearick. You fight with the rest of them, and you're damn good at it, but you're also surprisingly gentle and supportive. I've learned a lot from you in the short amount of time we've known each other. Just seems a guy like you would have someone in his life."

He nodded, his eyes focused on the ground as he shifted his

weight to his left foot and absentmindedly kicked at a rock. "Well, I appreciate that. Unfortunately, I'm not so sure that life is in the stars for me anymore. I had a wife and a daughter. The girl was just like me, only a hell of a lot cuter." They both laughed at that.

Celine was cautious as she proceeded. "May I ask what happened?"

He sighed and nodded, giving her a slight smile as he extended his hand. "I'm not much fer heartfelt conversations, lass. Hand me those knives. Maybe I'll teach ye ta throw better and distract meself while I talk."

She smiled and handed over the throwing knives, taking a step back. Samuel tossed one in the air a few times, catching it by its sharp tip every time. Then, he focused on the target, sizing it up as he prepared himself.

"Her name was Alyssa, my little girl. My wife's name was Beth." Tossing the knife one last time, he caught it by the tip, lifted it over his shoulder, and threw. The blade struck hard and dead center in the target, right where the heart would be. "My little girl loved ta go fishin' and huntin' with 'er pop, so I took 'er every time I went out. I was even teachin' 'er how ta throw a knife, just like I'm teachin' you."

He paused for a moment and stared at the blade he now held in his right hand. Then he looked at the target and prepared to throw again as he began talking once more.

"My wife was as feisty as they came. That's why I liked 'er. She was a fighter, and liked ta learn. She let me raise my little girl the same way. Unfortunately fer us, some battles just can't be won." There was a pause as a grimace crossed his face, his features showing anger. "I was on a delivery to Arcadia. That rat bastard Adrien had increased his order, so I was gonna be gone longer this time. My wife took my daughter on a hunting trip, expectin' ta be back the same day. The remnant had other plans."

Celine's hand lifted her mouth to cover the small gasp she

couldn't help but let out. She felt terrible for having asked him, but honored that he had found it in his heart to tell her his story.

"I'm so sorry to hear that," Celine stated, "although sorry doesn't even begin to cut it."

He launched another knife, the blade hitting the target right next to the first. "No worries, lass. Nothing can bring 'em back, and no words can replace 'em. But with a heart as big as yers is, I know just how much ye mean those words. Thank ye. Honestly, that's the first time I've spoke of it since just after it happened. In the end, that was why I joined the battle for Arcadia. I was a straggler comin' in toward the end and it damn near killed me, but as far as I was concerned, my family died because Adrien was a selfish prick."

"Fighting for the city was like avenging your family. It was a way of coping for you," Celine guessed.

He smiled. "I didn't deal the killin' blow—I didn't even get ta see it—but I sure as hell heard what happened to 'im. That girl Hannah did a good enough job fer me. I'll take that, and let my family's memory rest in peace. Past that, I just carry on every day. I know my little girl wouldn't want her pop pushin' the world away and actin' like an old grump." He laughed. "Well, no more 'n usual, anyway."

"You guys *are* a grumpy bunch, aren't you? Why is that? And why do you like women who are so feisty? Where I come from, men seemed to like women a little bit more subservient."

Samuel laughed. "Subservient? I take that ta mean the fancy men in Arcadia like their women not ta have any balls so it makes theirs look twice as big, eh?" He laughed again, this time much louder. "That's borin'. Where I come from, we get bored as hell havin' a woman agree ta any and all the dumb shit we say—and as stubborn old men, it's a lot. We like knowin' our women can take care of anything and everything just as well as we can. That way, when we're gone, we know they won't take any shit. Women should be strong. Don't ever let any man tell ye otherwise, or any of those women neither."

Smiling, she told him, "I should've been born a rearick. Sounds like I'd like that a whole hell of a lot more. I would get to be grumpy whenever I liked."

"Keep hangin' out with me, lass. Ye may not've been born a rearick, but yer certainly learnin' quick. That niece of yers is quite the candidate, too. The women in yer family were built tough. Ye be anything ye wanna be."

With that, he smiled and handed her the final knife before turning and walking away.

CHAPTER SEVEN

S carlett made her way through the Academy, heading for the stairs to go up to what used to be Adrien's office. Their little group was meeting, and Talia had warned her to be on time. The Dean had been showing signs of paranoia and extreme exhaustion, which Scarlett had expected for quite some time.

Talia wasn't nearly as evil as she'd like to think she was, or at least that was Scarlett's judgment. That left her vulnerable to stress.

Scarlett reached the top floor to find someone standing in the office, obviously waiting for her. It was Rebecca, a fellow teacher, and one of Talia's favorite minions. They'd grown increasingly close as of late, which explained why she was the one chosen to wait for her.

Scarlett decided to make the best of the situation.

"Hello, Rebecca," Scarlett said, her voice slightly annoyed. "Are you waiting for me?"

Rebecca gave her an almost sarcastic smile. "I was asked to make sure you made it on time."

Scarlett smiled. "Why the hostility? If I didn't know any better, I would say you didn't like me."

The woman stepped forward. She was short, right around five feet, and her long, medium-brown hair hung several inches past her shoulders. It was stringy, almost as if it hadn't been brushed, though Scarlett knew it had been. She had deep brown, almost black, eyes and a full face—her cheeks seemed to belong on someone twice her size.

She's very plain and boring, Scarlett thought.

It was obvious Rebecca found her to be a threat for more than one reason.

With a smile that was far too confident, the woman said, "That's because I don't. Talia doesn't trust you, and that means that I don't trust you."

Idiot. Did she not realize that she wasn't supposed to reveal that kind of information about the person she was minioning for? Useless... for Talia.

Scarlett had been feeling rather exhausted from using so much magic lately, but she figured this expenditure would be more than worth it. Her eyes flashed white, and all expression left the woman's face. Subtlety would be needed here, but she would need to push her influence to get it started.

"I'm sorry you don't trust me. I just worry about Talia. You see, lately she's been acting quite paranoid. I worry about her health, don't you?" Scarlett asked.

Rebecca nodded quickly. "Of course! We all worry about her, but I worry the most, I think."

Scarlett allowed a sympathetic expression across her face. "I know you do. We all do, but I agree that you carry the most on your shoulders. If Talia should fall, it would be up to you to take on all that responsibility."

The woman's eyes widened as she shook her head. "Oh, no. I don't think I could. I'm a follower. I've never been much of a leader. I'm not like you and Talia."

Scarlett nodded. "I understand. It's a hard position to be in sometimes. Talia is very sensitive about how..." Scarlett paused for a moment, exaggerating a bit as she pretended to think over her words. "Well, it hurts her to think she might not be doing a good job. It's up to us to make sure we take care of her, right?"

Scarlett knew what she was doing, but it had to be as subtle as possible. Talia was indeed becoming paranoid, and she was starting to lose control. The mystic needed the rest of them to see it, and this bitch had made herself an easy target by challenging her.

Scarlett was going to turn her need to be wedged up Talia's ass against her. The moment Talia saw her whispering to the others and talking about her, it would send her paranoia skyrocketing. Might even cause an outburst, alerting the others that Talia might not be as fit for power as she used to be.

The woman nodded again. "Yes! We need to take care of her."

"Maybe you should talk to the others. Just whisper to them whenever you can. Make sure they know they should be there for her."

Rebecca took a step closer and nodded again. "I'll talk to them tonight, as soon as we go downstairs."

"That's so kind of you. Really. See? Not so bad! We are on the same side. I worry about her, too. We have to take care of one another, don't we?" Scarlett smiled, taking a step forward. She'd only used a little bit of magic so far, but she needed to end this properly. Talia couldn't know it was her. Scarlett felt her magic flow through her as she reached into Rebecca's mind. "And all of this was your idea. You came up with it on your own. Good job. I had nothing to do with it. In fact, we never had this conversation."

Using only a tiny bit extra magic, Scarlett convinced the woman she'd only just walked in the door.

"Hi, Scarlett," Rebecca said, her smile genuine this time. "Talia had me wait up here for you. Want to walk down with me?"

Scarlett smiled. "Thank you. That's awfully sweet of you both. I'd love to."

TALIA WAITED IMPATIENTLY in the basement, pacing back and forth across the meeting space. Everyone in the room was silent, and she liked it that way. Gave her time to think. She heard the door open and turned, her eyes never leaving the stairs. Within moments, Scarlett and Rebecca descended into the basement.

"Scarlett, so nice of you to join us. Rebecca, thank you," Talia said.

Rebecca beamed at the praise. "Thank you. Oh, sorry, I mean *you're welcome*."

The girl was pathetic, but at least she was loyal.

Jackson stood and made his way over to Talia. Yet another of her loyal fans. The boy was completely obsessed with her, something that had come in very handy. If he only knew just how little he meant to her...

"Thanks for coming, everyone." Jackson opened the meeting. "As you all know, things have wound down some after the battle. It's been about a week, and everyone is starting to get back into their routine. The scars from the attack have largely been cleaned up and fixed, and people have been returning to work and to the Academy. What we decide now will dictate where the city will go."

Talia was impressed. The boy wasn't a complete and total idiot, only a partial one. "Jackson is right. Now is the most important time. I've reached out to the governor of Cella and invited what is left of his city to come to Arcadia. The reasons were simple. First, Cella is loyal to me. They know me, and they know that I'm a good person to get behind. Second, their army is weak. They lost far more people than we did because their army was small to begin with. Now it's been cut in half, so they're all but useless at this point. Even though our own city was attacked, they would still be safer within our walls."

Jackson was apparently excited by the idea and interrupted, but Talia didn't seem to mind. "On top of them being safer here in Arcadia, they would also have housing. There are still a lot of houses empty after the Battle for Arcadia, and the Boulevard is coming along nicely, too. Even more noble homes will be available once the trash goes back where it belongs."

Everyone seemed to like that idea, the idea of the Boulevard people being shoved back into the corner they'd been kept in for years. The families from that area made it easy by *wanting* to go back. There hadn't been a whole lot of pushing necessary on the part of the nobles. They knew where they belonged, and they wanted to return. The group seemed more than pleased to hear this part of the plan was going well.

Talia once again took over the conversation. "Amelia has done nothing but hide in the Capitol building. She has been beaten, and she knows it. She knows that if there's even an attempt by her to do anything in the city, we have the necessary means to take her out completely. She's been quiet because she's hoping for a miracle."

There were a few laughs from the group. Margaret, one of the students who had joined the group, seemed to find this most amusing. "She probably thinks her little druid bitch is going to come back and save them. Pathetic."

Talia smiled. "And that's exactly why she will fail. She's hoping for something that's not going to happen. Arryn is dead on that mountain. She is not coming back. Amelia knows we have control of the city, and she can't do anything. Still, we must be careful. Our control is weak. If we make one wrong step, the spell could be undone and Amelia could swoop in and save the day."

There were several nods from her attentive audience. As she looked around after her speech, she noticed Rebecca pointing at her as she whispered to one of the other teachers. For a moment, they both looked at her before turning back to their conversation.

Try as she might, she couldn't ignore it. It was obvious they were talking about her, and their expressions weren't pleased. She couldn't help but wonder exactly what they were discussing.

This came as quite a surprise to her, because Rebecca was the one she trusted the most in the group other than Jackson. Both of them seemed quite enamored with her. She made a mental note to get to the bottom of that as soon as possible. She would not be undermined by the likes of them.

Caydon and Camdon both seemed to be very excited about Talia's proposal. Caydon raised his hand before saying, "That's why we haven't taken another student, right? Because it would mess something up?"

Camdon chimed in, "Yeah, we were curious about that, because it seems like if we had more power, we could do a lot more. Nothing could stop us."

Talia almost regretted introducing them to the old myth that drinking the blood of others would allow them to harness more of their power. It had been necessary at the time to get them to play along and do what she needed them to do, but it could backfire on her.

Talia shook her head. "No. We can't do anything like that right now. If we do, it will get out into the city. Right now, they believe Arryn is guilty of those murders. If we kill someone else, they will believe it wasn't Arryn, and Amelia will have all the power she needs to regain control. Some people might believe Arryn is back in the city, but most will believe someone else is guilty."

Talia went on and on, answering questions that bored and annoyed her to no end. Scarlett was surprisingly quiet as she sat in the back watching everyone. Talia hoped she was being helpful and getting into the minds of the others, but she honestly had no idea where Scarlett's head was any longer.

At this point, all Talia had was herself. She could only trust herself. The plan for Cella to come to Arcadia was a good one. It would create hope in Arcadia by increasing the number of skilled warriors in the Guard. It would further help her because the people from Cella loved her. She'd made a lot of friends there, and that would only increase with her efforts to help them. Soon, she would have enough control to make her final move against Amelia, and soon, the city.

melia wasn't the type to sit around and do nothing, though she had been working very hard to make it look that way. She had been practicing more and more with Ash in hopes he would bond with her a bit more, and he had.

It was nothing like the bond Cathillian had with Echo, but she and the raven got along quite nicely.

Every morning, Amelia sent Ash out. Surprisingly, after having met Maddie only once, he was able to find her without issue. Things were starting to point in the right direction for her, but she did not dare become careless. She knew her seemingly good fortune could change at the drop of a hat.

Every moment of every day her enemies calculated ways to send her further into the darkness and prevent her from doing the job she had set out to do. It was true they had her trapped, but she wasn't the type to take that easily. She would do whatever was necessary to survive and help those who needed it most.

That included working with a disgraced Master Engineer.

"Have you figured out what you want to ask me to do?" Elon looked up from the bed in his cell.

Amelia smiled. "Are you going to say no?"

He sat up all the way and leaned forward a bit, his eyes burning into hers. "Is this personal? Is it for your own personal gain, or for Arryn?"

Had he responded like that two weeks ago—before he'd met Arryn—her eyes would've widened and her jaw would've hit the floor, but at this point Elon had proven himself to have more depth than she'd originally thought. His question didn't surprise her at all.

Amelia shook her head. "No. Not for me. At this point, everything I'm doing is either for Arryn or for the city."

Elon slowly nodded his head. "As far as Arryn is concerned, helping the city is helping her, and vice versa."

Amelia took a step forward, her hands wrapping around the bars. "Yes. That's exactly how I think of it."

"Good. Then I won't decline."

She gave a sigh of relief, exhaling a breath Amelia hadn't realized she'd been holding. Even though she knew Elon was using Arryn as an opportunity for redemption, her recent string of bad luck had warned her not to get her hopes up, regardless of how certain she was of his good intentions.

"Thank you," Amelia said.

Elon waved a hand, inviting her to come inside. "The door's unlocked, but I assume you know that. Come on in and have a seat, and we'll discuss whatever it is you want."

Amelia opened the door and stepped inside, not bothering to close it. Elon could have escaped at any point, but he hadn't—he had stayed there from a sense of duty to his son Gregory. She believed he stayed now because he had an opportunity to make things right with at least one of the children he'd betrayed, even though his betrayal of Arryn and her family hadn't been intentional.

"I want to talk to you about some magitech. I have some ideas, but we no longer have a Master Engineer. You know as well as I do that no one in the city is even half as smart as you are, as much as it pains me to say it. That being said, I need something designed and built that will keep the city safe. We can't risk any more remnant attacks."

He sat there for a moment thinking over her words, his eyes never leaving hers. "Well, it sounds like we might have our work cut out for us. What did you have in mind?"

Amelia went into detail, describing something she had been thinking of since soon after the last battle with the remnant. Placing inexperienced guards between the city and the Madlands was a terrible idea. If another remnant invasion happened, they would be overrun in minutes, maybe even seconds.

There had to be something else.

She'd remembered Arryn's explosive use of lightning. It had been untrained, sure, but it had burst from the sky and rained down on the attackers, taking out many before they even reached the gate. What if they had a way to do that without risking the lives of the men and women of the Guard?

"You want to build a perimeter, so to speak," Elon mused.

Amelia nodded, an excited smile on her face. "Yes. A perimeter, but only out by the Madlands. We would have to figure out a way to hide it, but we could post warning signs every so often. Since the remnant can't read, they would have no way of knowing what the signs said."

"And if they came charging through, they'd be met by certain death." Elon took a moment to ponder the idea, then smiled and nodded. "I think I can design something by the end of the day, actually. Maybe a couple days. I can't construct it here, and you can't let me loose. However, you were wrong earlier."

Amelia looked at him, confused. "About what?"

Elon smiled. "I'm not the smartest man in the city. I had a mentor, Waylon. He was a very quick learner when the city first began, and quite the inventor. I went to him because I wanted to be that good, too. He taught me a lot, and I built from it. If you go see him, he'll be able to build whatever I design."

Amelia smiled, filled with even more hope now than she'd walked in with. Elon gave her instructions and the list of things he would need to design what she'd asked for. Luckily, all those things were inside the Capitol building already. They had been seized from his house after the revolution.

She had hoped another inventor would come forward to be the city's new engineer and she could pass those things on to that person, but it hadn't worked out that way.

When she dropped everything off to him, she saw a spark she hadn't seen in quite some time. He looked at her, momentarily grabbing her hand. "Thank you for the opportunity. I won't let her down. I won't let the city down. Not this time."

Amelia smiled, somewhat satisfied that Gregory had been avenged in a way she doubted even he could have expected. She turned and made her way back upstairs, careful that no one saw her leave the jail before heading back to her office.

SCARLETT WAS VERY careful as she left the city; it was a big risk forsaking sleep to further her plan. If all went well, she was on her way to taking control, as she'd planned from the moment she'd first stepped into Arcadia. If the worst were to happen, however, her fatigue would keep her from using the magic she would need.

On the way out of the city, she made sure she controlled what those around her saw as she usually did. They never saw her leave, since she'd entirely erased their memory of her as she passed.

As she traveled, her mind wandered to the reason for this escape. It had been because of a chance meeting, one she hadn't anticipated but had certainly been excited by because of the opportunities it presented.

A couple weeks before, there had been quite the disturbance

in the city. Scarlett could sense a large amount of magic being used, and she was more than interested in figuring out exactly who and what was causing such a disruption in a city filled with mediocre magic users.

She snuck out of the Academy and went on foot. By the time she arrived, the action was over, but the instigator was still present.

She ran across the cobblestones, stopping when she saw four dead guardsmen lying by the gate. Slowly, she walked forward, studying them before coming to a stop. She looked around and saw Cathillian, Arryn's druid friend, lying on the ground.

From his appearance, she would have assumed he was dead, but she could still sense brain activity. His mind was active even though he was unconscious.

A girl clad in black sat on top of him. As she pulled her hands away from him, her eyes drifted up to see Scarlett standing there.

Scarlett smiled. "Well, hello, friend."

Without hesitation, the girl threw her hands out. Scarlett had no idea what she had planned to do, because she was much faster. Scarlett's hands also shot out, and the girl immediately grabbed her head in pain.

Arryn's friend did not move, and she assumed he wouldn't for some time. It was the perfect opportunity.

"You mistake me for someone easily overcome, someone like that young man you sit upon now. I am not your enemy, so don't make me one. I promise, you wouldn't like the end result," Scarlett had said with a knowing smile on her face.

The girl was in so much pain she couldn't scream, let alone speak. All she could do was groan in response.

Scarlett had lowered her hands, all defensiveness draining out of her posture as she looked at the girl as if they had just met at the market. "I'm Scarlett. Nice to meet you..."

"Jenna," the girl choked out as she stumbled to her feet.

Nodding, Scarlett had said, "Jenna. It's nice to meet you. I think you and I have *so* much to discuss."

From there, the two had spoken quickly about the Dark Forest, the city, and their mutual disdain for the Arcadian druid herself, Arryn. Scarlett had wanted the conversation to be longer, but she knew someone would come across the dead guards and the near-dead druid lying on the ground before much more time elapsed.

Instead, they had made plans to meet later, and meet later they had. It had been only once, but Scarlett had a much better idea who she was dealing with. Though she was a petty child, she had more reason to hate Arryn than Talia did.

After all, Talia had created her own group, and was clearly twisting them to hate and not trust Scarlett. As far she was concerned, she was simply returning the favor. Now that the remnant were out of commission, the dark druids would provide quite a backup plan.

When Scarlett approached the southernmost edge of the Dark Forest, she was met by a man with dark gray eyes. His long, beautiful face was only made more attractive to her by a scar that reached from his forehead to his chin.

He was tall, taller than most men in Arcadia, but still shorter than Arryn's druid companion Cathillian. At least she thought he was, judging by the descriptions Talia had given her as well as how long his body had looked as it laid half-dead on the ground.

His skin was unlike anything she'd ever seen. He wasn't quite as dark as those who stood behind him, but his skin lacked the normal pigment of any race she was familiar with. He somehow looked gray, although it was a much lighter color than his irises, without looking sickly. It was a strange thing to see, but it worked for him. She found herself very interested in this man

The man raised a hand, signaling for her to stop, which she did. He approached slowly.

"Are you Scarlett?" the man asked.

She nodded. "I am. I'm here to see Jenna. Are you Aeris, her brother?"

He nodded. "I am. She told me quite a bit about you, and I would like you to discuss all that with me. If you are everything she says, then you are welcome to stay. However, if I find I can't trust you, I promise you'll not be leaving today."

Scarlett smiled. "Oh, I don't think you'll have a problem trusting me. In fact, I think you and I will be great friends."

"I'm glad to hear that because my sister has gone missing, and I could use someone with your talents to help me get her back."

CHAPTER NINE

Having Cathillian back was more than a welcome distraction, but the reason behind it had been devastating. Learning what had happened to Arryn was a crushing blow. Elysia may not have given birth to her, but she was like a daughter anyway. She was family.

More than anything, Elysia wanted to rush out and search for her, stopping at nothing and leaving no stone unturned to find her. Instead, she was bound by duty to protect far more than a single life, even if that life was important to her.

She had to protect the entire druid tribe.

Though Cathillian had objected, Elysia ordered him to stay with the Chieftain. She had taken Nika as well as several other warriors, including a couple from the *Schatten*. She knew that team was her best hope in finding out what was happening.

They had spent the entire afternoon questioning Jenna, but she dodged every question. It wasn't until they had made her angry, knowing it was her weakness, that she opened up and gave them any real information. In her rage, they knew she would lack the filter that would keep her secret, and lack it she did.

In the midst of her screaming a string of obscenities and

threats, she'd let slip a general location. She'd told them as a threat that the dark druids were not far away, and had plenty of resources.

Immediately, they had assumed that an earlier theory had been correct—the dark druids had, in fact, been living somewhere in the Dark Forest, just far enough away that the druids couldn't sense what the darkness was doing to their forest.

The information led Elysia south. As an Elder and the Chieftain's daughter, she knew quite a bit about the dark druids. She knew what they were capable of, and that their magic was a perversion of her own, but when she approached the southernmost section of the forest, she was not prepared for what she found.

Elysia and her warriors stopped short, their horses stomping and bobbing their heads as they protested advancing any farther. Even Chaos displayed signs of discontent.

Elysia's jaw fell open as she looked around her. The vast difference in land from where her own horse stood and just several feet ahead was far beyond disturbing. The deep, dark colors of the once beautiful landscape looked like the very life had been sucked from it.

Tree trunks were ashy in color, and the leaves were mostly brown. As she looked farther in, she realized many of the trees were missing their leaves entirely.

"What is this place?" Nika asked, only barely able to keep her horse from bolting the other way. "This was once the Dark Forest, but not anymore."

Elysia swallowed, doing her best to hold back the tears that wanted to form as a result of seeing all the death. "It's them. They've killed everything here. They made it their home, to use that word loosely. They've been here for a while, and it looks like they're running out of food sources. That's why they want our land. It's lusher than any other part of the forest, and they could survive for years in there."

Nika looked at Elysia. "How is that possible? How do we know this didn't take only a couple weeks?"

"We don't." Elysia shook her head. "All we have to go on is what Jenna said. She said it in anger, so I believe it. She's never been able keep her mouth shut about anything of importance, which was one more reason she made a terrible warrior. At the first sign of something wrong, she would run and tell all the innocent tribesmen, filling men, women, and children with fear instead of helping her fellow warriors solve and end the problem."

There was a pause, and Elysia heard a heavy sigh beside her. "The horses won't go any farther. Shall we continue on foot?"

Elysia was silent as she stared into the barren wasteland in front of her. Her eyes then turned to search those of the men and women she was responsible for keeping safe. Finally, she shook her head.

"I'd love to run in there and save the day, but we can't. The moment we crossed the threshold, they would know we were here, just like we know when they get too close to our barrier. We would be outnumbered, and potentially overpowered. I won't risk your lives senselessly—that would serve no purpose. We came to see if we could find where they were hiding, and we found it. Now we go back and tell the others. Next time, we'll bring an army."

***

LOOKING AT THE SKY, feeling the ever-sharper chill in the air and the increase in cold moisture burning her skin, Arryn knew her luck had run out. Because of her initial lack of energy and slow progress toward regaining it, she'd been forced to stay where she'd been dumped on top of the mountain. But now, a storm was approaching, one she would have no power to chase away or survive if she didn't find better shelter.

Her igloo was well-crafted and protected her brilliantly in the weather she had endured so far, but with temperatures dropping farther and a snowstorm approaching, she would need something far sturdier—like a cave.

Before, there would have been no way in hell she could descend any part of the mountain without risking her life, but now she was stronger than ever. That being the case, she was about to use every ounce of her newly acquired energy searching for safety.

Arryn stuffed her cloak pockets with the raspberries she had grown and the meat from the ram she'd killed, both of which were frozen solid. She made her way to the flat section where she had been growing things, where the earth was the most alive because of her magic.

Kneeling, she placed her hands on the ground where the snow was shallowest. Using nature magic as well as physical magic, she pushed forward, searching the mountain for any abnormalities or openings.

The druids had taught her how to do this, but the purpose had been to sense if anyone was cutting down trees or mining within their borders. That was how they monitored the forest and kept it safe.

Arryn had never had a reason to do it—mostly because she wasn't very good at it—and the Elders were the only ones who searched that far out. Only their power was strong enough to reach any real distance.

Since her power had grown significantly since she'd been abandoned on the peak, she was able to get a faint look at what lay below her. After several moments, she found something like a large hole in the side of the mountain. Had Elysia or the Chieftain been there, they would've been able to tell her exactly what she'd found.

If she were wrong, she would be without any form of shelter whatsoever on a section of the mountain she was unfamiliar with in the worst storm she'd ever seen. Her energy, and more than likely her magic, would be depleted by the time she got there.

If she were wrong, the odds of Talia's dark wishes for her coming true were certainly not in Arryn's favor.

She pulled her hands away, took a deep breath, and stood. She couldn't allow Talia to win, not now. If Arryn stayed here, she would freeze to death—there was no doubt in her mind. If she was wrong about the cave, the storm would kill her.

As she stood there, the first few snowflakes began to fall, and she watched the clouds rolling in.

"Well, little buddy," she said, turning and making her way back to camp, her furry rabbit friend in tow, "it looks like I'm heading down the south side of the mountain. You're more than welcome to keep me company. A snowstorm is coming, and I doubt even you would make it up here."

She was answered by the rabbit hopping forward a few feet, twisting his head a bit to the side, and twitching his nose. Smiling, she turned, and he followed close behind.

Arryn grabbed her daggers, rolled and secured the animal pelts to her back using cloth she'd cut from the very bottom of her cloak, and began her descent, moving slowly but steadily. She surveyed the area around her as she moved and realized there were a lot of places too steep to walk down at all. She would have to climb down parts of the mountain, something she'd never done.

The wind had begun to pick up and the snow had become heavier as she descended; Arryn shivered and shook as she traversed the slopes. Several times she'd had to conjure heat without creating an actual fire to keep herself warm enough to stay focused, since she couldn't risk a misstep.

Unfortunately, she was growing weak very quickly.

"You can do this. You can do this. You can do this," she kept repeating to herself. "This is only temporary. You're getting back to Arcadia. You're going to find her. You're going to kill her."

When she got to a place where she needed to climb down, Arryn picked up the rabbit that had followed her and tucked him into the hood of her cloak behind her neck. He was a fat, pudgy thing for a small animal trying to survive in such terrain, and he kept her neck very warm.

Arryn began coaxing herself again as she used a bit of magic to sense the rocks in her path, allowing her to determine how to place her feet without seeing where they needed to go.

"Easy does it. Getting weaker, but that's okay. You've been doing this all along. You get weak as hell and then you get stronger than you ever knew was possible. Then you weaken yourself again, and then you get stronger still. Get to the cave. Get some sleep. Everything will be fine."

She alternated between internal thoughts and speaking aloud to herself, taking solace in the sound of any voice at all, even if it was only her own. When she realized just how comforting it was to speak, to hear a voice, she realized that had it not been for the rabbit, and even her momentary connection with the raptor bird she'd sent for the berries, she would've been far worse off than she was.

Below, Arryn could see a large area of flat earth. The wind was terrible, the temperatures were still falling, the snow was stinging her face, and she needed to rest. She welcomed the flat area, hoping she could find a protrusion of rock large enough to block the wind.

As she jumped down, the rabbit squeaked, not really enjoying the landing. She reached a hand back and gave him some gentle scratches as she walked through the snow to a place just big enough to give her some relief from the wind.

She used the time to catch her breath and warm herself again. As she was standing there, she heard footsteps in the snow. She closed her eyes, breathing heavily as she silently prayed it was another ram. She needed all the energy she had to finish her journey. She couldn't risk using any on another leopard.

A low growl sounded out, and her heart sank. She reached into her hood and pulled the rabbit free, setting him against the wall on the ground behind her in case she needed to fight. She didn't want to risk his life if the worst were to happen.

The footsteps got closer and closer, and she realized that standing there praying for the best outcome would probably be her downfall if she kept it up. Pulling her daggers free of her cloak, she took a deep breath and jumped out from behind the small wall.

Her breath caught in her throat, her eyes widening as shock filled her. It wasn't a leopard at all, or anything else she would have expected.

It was a lycanthrope. A massive, snowy lycanthrope, with a dark muzzle.

His eyes locked on hers, red and full of fury. His lips curled back in a snarl, and his long razor-like teeth glistened with drool. He took one step forward, his body bending slightly as his arms extended to the side, his large clawed hands flexing as he unleashed a loud growl.

Arryn took a defensive stance, wondering how she should take him out. Magic would be the quickest and safest, but it would also be the most draining. Physically fighting wouldn't be much better, and it would also be the most dangerous.

Magic, it is. Well, maybe not entirely.

The lycanthrope lunged for her, and she ducked before tumbling out of the way, swiping with her knife as she did. Blood spurted onto the snow, the blade having sliced across the beast's thigh.

Rolling to her feet, she turned and threw her dagger as hard as she could before he turned back around. The knife pierced the lycanthrope between the shoulder blades, just out of his reach. He growled loudly again; this time it was almost a roar. She needed to destroy him quickly before his volume brought the snow down on top of them.

The beast was full of rage by then, made even more powerful by the strong emotion. He was so fast as he turned that he almost looked like a blur. He charged her again, but she was ready.

"Today is *not* the day I die, you son of a bitch."

She turned her palms up before quickly lifting them as though she were flipping a table. The snow burst from the ground, freezing as it did. Several long shards of ice impaled the beast, the life almost immediately going out of his eyes before he collapsed to the ground only a couple feet in front of her.

Arryn sighed heavily and took several deep breaths. "Whew!" she said in relief. "Sir Cuddlepuffs, I really thought we might be dinner."

The rabbit hopped across the snow to her, and she leaned down to pick him up and put him back in the hood of her cloak as she had before. As she stood there, relishing in the warmth of her little friend on the back of her neck, her eyes drifted to the right, where the lycanthrope had come from.

For the first time, she saw dark spots on the snow. They were several feet away and visibility wasn't the best because of the falling snow, but now that things had calmed down, she could see them.

Looking at the beast on the ground, her eyes were once again drawn to that dark muzzle. She took a step forward and leaned down, her eyes widening when she realized his snout hadn't been dark in color at all. The deep color of blood had been masked by the lack of sunshine and heavy snow.

At that moment, two things ran through her mind. The first was that something had been injured but might still be alive, and the second was that it might be dead and she might have fresh meat as opposed to the frozen meat in her pockets.

While she didn't want to expend the energy to hunt for it, she was pretty sure it was close, given the newly frozen blood on the ground. She made her choice and trekked off through the snow, following the trail of blood.

The snow was beginning to fall harder now, and she was about to turn back when she saw it. It was only a little smaller than a medium-sized dog, but it looked broader and thicker.

It was soaked with blood, and she couldn't tell what it was. It was too small to be a mountain goat or ram, though it could've been one of their offspring. It was far too large to be a rabbit.

As she got closer, she saw it move, a sound of pain gargling from its throat. Her heart sank and her jaw dropped when the sound hit her ears. Forgetting about herself, she ran forward. She dropped to her knees in the snow, the rabbit protesting as he was jostled around in the landing.

As much as her heart had broken for the wounded animal when she heard its pain, it broke even more when she saw what it was. It was an animal she'd never seen herself, but had been told about, its beauty unparalleled by any other creature. And here it lay, just a baby, the cub of an even larger and more majestic animal.

A tiger cub, no more than a few months old, its fur as white as the snow around her, but stained with blood. Its little eyes—as crystal blue in color as the ice she'd seen on the mountain—opened and looked at her as if pleading for help.

Tears rolled down her cheeks, the icy wind freezing them and burning her skin. Reaching out, she laid her hands on the cub.

Before she even began, part of her regretted the decision. She would need every ounce of energy she had to survive the storm, so this might kill her, but the guilt would have been worse.

Had it been a full-grown tiger with damage this bad she might have simply drained the rest of the life force from it, but it wasn't. It was an innocent cub, and its mama would be looking for it soon, if she wasn't already. Arryn couldn't bear the thought of leaving it dead for her to find.

So, against her better judgment, she pushed her magic forward, her eyes glowing bright green as she did so. The cub took a deep breath as her power filled him, and she felt him getting stronger. She could feel his wounds closing under her hands.

She began to feel very weak, and her eyes grew heavy. Several times she blinked, trying to focus, but the falling snow had turned into a blizzard and the wind was almost unbearable.

She pulled her hands away, realizing she no longer had the strength to create enough magic to warm herself again.

How far was the cave? How much longer would she have to walk? Could she make it?

Her chest and belly suddenly felt warm, and she looked down to see the tiger cub nestling up next to her in her lap. Arryn wrapped her arms around him, holding him close and running her fingers through his blood-soaked fur.

"Where's your mama? If we don't get you out of this cold, you won't make it either. You'll freeze to death. You're soaked."

A smile had only barely begun to creep across her face when a low growl—far deeper than that of the lycanthrope she'd killed—filled the air around her. She heard the deep rumble of its anger over the wind and snow, over the sound of her teeth chattering and the aching of her body shivering in the cold.

She felt its rage.

Slowly, *very* slowly, she turned her head to the side, her eyes widening as she saw a very large snowy tiger standing there. Her back was completely straight, her shoulders pinned back, her head lowered in line with her spine. Her ears lay flat against her head, and her beautiful face was contorted in the most hideous of snarls.

Arryn didn't know a lot about such animals, but she knew they were large and she knew they were powerful. Feeling the cub moving in her arms, she also knew she was looking into the eyes of a mother staring at a strange creature she knew nothing about that was covered in her baby's blood.

Her cub was in the arms of something she believed to be his attacker.

Carefully, Arryn placed the cub on the ground in front of her. His eyes wandered to his mother before he pranced off toward her, his little footsteps as carefree as if nothing bad had ever happened to him.

Arryn didn't want to stand, fearing that the tiger might think it was a threat if she did. Instead she began retreating on her knees, moving as slowly as possible.

Unfortunately for her, the tiger didn't care about speed. Given the amount of blood on the cub, she believed he was badly injured. She also believed Arryn was the one who'd caused it.

As the tiger stepped forward, Arryn realized with great anxiety that she had no magic left to soothe the beast. There was no way for her to reach out with her magic and calm her. She had used all she had left to heal the cub.

The wind blew a hard gust at her, and as weak as Arryn was, she tipped over a bit, her hand reaching out to catch herself in the snow.

"I didn't hurt him," Arryn said, her voice smooth, but weak.

She didn't know just how strong her affinity with animals was; if they could naturally understand her, or if she had to connect to each and every one on some small level as she had the raptor bird and the rabbit. All she could hope for was the tiger would understand something.

Without warning, the tiger lunged for her, her massive jaws snapping right in front of Arryn's face as her large front paws knocked the girl back to the ground. There was a squeal underneath her, and she knew she had just landed on her rabbit friend. He quickly freed himself, sprinting back the way they had come.

"Coward!" she called after him weakly.

The tiger growled in her face again, its jaws wrapping around her throat. Arryn tried to lift her arms, tried to move, but she was too weak, and the snow was making it far worse.

The cold was taking her down faster than she'd imagined it

could. Suddenly, she heard the familiar loud squeal again, and another low rumble escaped the tiger on top of her.

Arryn's eyes fluttered open only long enough for her to see the cub running past, chasing something. The last thing she remembered before passing out was the tiger's jaws tightening around her throat.

CHAPTER TEN

Cathillian was standing at the edge of the Kalt River when he heard a familiar screech ring through the skies, and he wasted no time running back to the village. Echo had returned from her journey north, and he wanted to know if she'd found anything.

It had been a long time since he had run quite so hard, but knowing they might have an idea where Arryn was meant more to him than any exertion.

As his feet hit the bare earth of the village, he slowed down to a jog, his lungs and legs both burning. Echo had perched on the front corner of the Chieftain's roof, and there was something small in the Chieftain's hands as he stood below the golden eagle.

"What is it?" Cathillian asked, taking several extra deep breaths as he approached his grandfather. "Did she find something?"

The Chieftain nodded, extending his hand to show Cathillian the objects. They were bandages. Cloth bandages, soaked in blood. Cathillian's brows furrowed as he swallowed hard.

Looking up to meet his grandfather's eyes, he asked, "Is it hers? Is that Arryn's blood?"

The Chieftain nodded slowly. "It's hard to say, but what lingers feels like her energy. I really think it's hers."

Cathillian looked up at Echo. "You know her scent. You wouldn't have brought this back if you didn't know for sure, but I have to ask anyway. Is this Arryn's blood?"

Echo screeched. Cathillian reached for information through the bond and Echo complied, consciously remembering what she'd seen so he could see it, too.

Cathillian nodded. "It's hers. There is a cottage up north, just past Cella. Echo could smell the blood. She found it just past the cottage. It looks like those might've been dropped on the way farther north."

Cathillian was angry. Actually, he was far beyond angry. He found himself staring at the ground, unsure of what to do.

"I know your instincts are telling you go after her," the Chieftain began, "but the North is a massive place—especially the Frozen North. Echo found evidence of where Arryn *was*, not where she *is*. I think you should allow her to rest and send her back out."

Cathillian looked at him incredulously. "You would have me stay here waiting? Sitting on my ass and doing nothing while she's who-knows-where, potentially being tortured? You'd have me sit here and drink your wine while she might be dead or dying?"

The Chieftain shook his head. "Grandson, you have never been a stupid boy. You always were hyper, relatively childish, and fairly good-humored—something I always loved about you, but you were always smart in many ways. Battle. Friendships. Life. But this? Running off without knowing your destination would be very unwise. And deep down, I think you know as well as I do that Arryn is not dead."

Sighing, Cathillian shook his head as he momentarily turned his back on his grandfather, running stressed hands through his long hair. He faced the Chieftain again, his expression fierce and serious. "What would you have me do?"

The Chieftain stepped toward him. "I would have you stay here, where you're safe. Running off, anything could happen. If things are as you believe, then it's quite possible that Arryn was kept in that cottage, at least briefly. Wouldn't it stand to reason the cottage would be filled with enemies? Do you have any idea who they are? How powerful they are? Would they even know where Arryn was taken after she was out of their care? Seems to me the smart thing would be for Talia to keep her mouth shut about where she was taking Arryn, meaning you would meet with a dead end again."

"But at least I would be doing something. I wouldn't be just sitting here. I can't stand this. I can't stand not having her with me, not knowing if she's safe. I know she's more than capable of taking care of herself. She always has been, but right now she needs help, and I want to be there for her."

"Ye can't be there fer her if yer dead, lad," Samuel called.

Cathillian saw Samuel and Celine coming toward him. Celine gave Cathillian a sad smile. "I know how badly you want to fight for her and how badly you want to save her, and it makes me happy. Makes me happy knowing she has you, and she has all these people who would stop at nothing to keep her safe. They would also stop at nothing to keep you safe. He's right. You risk yourself if you leave and have no idea where you're going."

The Chieftain then said, "Let Echo rest and then send her back out, grandson. I promise you that if Echo finds more, if we get a location, I will send a group of men with you. We will get her back, but not like this. Not recklessly."

Just then, the sound of horses met everyone's ears. Elysia was the first to show on her large Shire horse, Chaos. They stopped and dismounted, Chaos kneeling for Elysia to do so.

The Chieftain smiled and opened his arms. "Welcome back,

daughter. It seems that today is the day for news. Do you have any for us?"

Elysia stepped into his expectant arms, giving him a hug before taking a step back and nodding. "The southern section of the forest is all but destroyed. Everything looks as though it has been burnt, but it wasn't fire that destroyed it. It was magic. The trees and other plants cling to life, but only barely. The leaves are all gone, and the trunks are grey and ashy in color. Plant life is wilted. They've been there for a while."

The Chieftain sighed. "It was only a matter of time. They started out as a small community—very small. It's been years; by now they would have grown their numbers significantly. They would've run out of resources in the woodland they once lived in, so they need the Dark Forest—particularly our section of it."

Celine stepped forward, her expression surprisingly angry. "No! I'm tired of the bad guys always winning. I'm sick of them always getting what they want. They've destroyed too much."

Elysia smiled, taking her hand and giving it light squeeze. "Thank you, child, but this isn't your fight. You have a war of your own. This one isn't yours to worry about, though your fire for our struggle is touching."

Celine yanked her hand away, her brows scrunching further. "That's where you're wrong. This *is* my fight. Arcadia is my home —it always has been. That's where I stayed, hoping and praying for a day when justice for my sister, my niece, and my brother-in-law would be found. But this is Arryn's home. When we met, she told me about the magic of the Dark Forest. The trees may not have true magic of their own, but now that I've been here and seen it for myself, I know exactly what she meant by magic."

Celine took a deep breath, her hands clenched tight to her sides as she stared at Elysia, who watched her with wide eyes. Cathillian was also rather shocked by the woman's unexpected anger.

When no one said a word, Celine continued, "These trees are

taller than any I've ever seen, thicker than any I've ever seen. The leaves are greener than I even knew was possible. The fruit is sweeter, and the vegetables are more flavorful. The water is cleaner. The people here are all family, whether they're related by blood or not. Everyone takes care of everyone else. No one is highborn or lowborn. No one is better than anyone else. This might not be my home, but it is Arryn's. That makes this my fight, too."

There was a pause as Elysia studied her. Cathillian's eyes flicked back and forth between the two women, wondering what was about to happen. Though Celine hadn't said anything that Cathillian would deem disrespectful, his mother did look rather shocked, and he had no idea what she would do or say.

Finally, Elysia smiled. "Do you know how to fight?"

Celine's shoulders fell slightly, her eyes wandering to Cathillian for a moment before returning to Elysia. The young woman once again straightened her shoulders, then shook her head. "No. At least, not in the sense that you do. I *do* know how to throw a punch, I'm learning how to throw a knife, and if I do say so myself, I'm a damn fast learner. I don't care how many times you break my nose, if you have something to teach me and the patience to do it, I'll learn. I made a vow to that girl when she came back, and I'm not going to let her down because I don't know how to fight."

Elysia's smile grew. "Nika, please take the young woman to be fitted in proper leathers, then escort her to the *Versuch* pit and wait for me. I'm going to talk to my father, and then we're going to have some fun."

As Elysia walked off, taking her father's arm and pacing side-by-side with him, Celine looked at Cathillian, her eyes wide. "What the hell did I just get myself into?"

Cathillian laughed. "A world of hurt, that's what. She might not look it, but that woman hits like a war hammer."

"Is she pissed? Because she seems pissed," Celine asked.

This time it was Nika who laughed. "If she was angry, you'd already be nursing a broken nose. Come with me. It's time we dressed you like a warrior. Whatever you were before dies today, as long as you're serious."

"Emphasis on the *death* part," Cathillian added.

Celine punched Cathillian in the arm, shaking her head at him.

He grabbed his arm and rubbed. "You know, I'm really starting to think people don't like me. They're always hitting me."

Nika laughed again. "You're just *now* thinking that?"

Cathillian looked at her incredulously. "And here I thought, Nika, that you loved me and we were gonna have a ceremony and have little, pointy-eared babies together."

Nika closed her eyes and shook her head, her smile fading. "Yeah, right. We both know that's not true. In fact, I'm pretty sure we all know you want little *half*-pointy-eared babies."

There was a pause and a knowing smile on both women's faces as Cathillian stared at the ground. "*Hmph.* I don't know what you're talking about. I'm not even going to dignify that with a response." He pointedly turned his nose into the air and turned to walk away with exaggerated movements, joking as always, of course.

Celine busted out in laughter. "It's okay, *nephew*. They would be incredibly beautiful babies."

"You know," Cathillian said in a dark, amused tone, turning his head just enough that his devious smile could be seen. "When Arryn gets back, I'm gonna tell her what you said. I'm gonna tell her you were suggesting she and I be together and have babies."

Both women's faces fell then, all amusement gone as they looked at one another and then back at Cathillian.

"Mmm hmm," he said, slowly nodding his head. "That's what I thought. Just as scared of her as I am. Don't make me tell on you! We all know I'm petty enough to do it!" He said that last bit with his finger pointed in the air as he turned and walked away.

CHAPTER ELEVEN

The city of Cella had been overrun when the remnant had
attacked. Their walls had been breached and more than
half of their Guard had been killed. A lot of civilians had died as
well when they'd decided to fight alongside the Guard. Everyone
was afraid, and the governor couldn't blame them.

He felt helpless at the moment, unable to give the people what
they needed, which was security. They had won, yes, but the cost
had been very high.

When the governor had received a letter from Talia inviting
him and the rest of the city to come to Arcadia, he'd been hesitant. Why take his people south to a city which had also been
breached? What good could it possibly do?

But then his son, Nathaniel, had made the point that the Arcadian Guard's numbers far surpassed their own, even though they
lacked expertise. Taking their own guards there would allow the
Arcadian Guard to be properly trained much faster than they
could learn on their own.

"There will be safety in numbers. We didn't have many, but we
had enough to stave off an attack. Do you really think that we
could do it again?" Nathaniel had asked his father.

The governor had no answer. He only had worries. He was a good man who was concerned for his people. The idea of letting them down didn't sit well with him, and he would do whatever it took to keep them safe.

"Our men could help them rebuild the Boulevard," the governor had mused, his voice barely a whisper as he stared at his desk.

"Exactly," Nathaniel had replied. "Not only that, but if we took our resources down there, we could help rebuild their city entirely. It sounds counterproductive to work on their city while our own is partially in ruins, but the new Chancellor is a good woman. You said that yourself. Imagine what we could do here once they can spare the men."

The governor looked at his son. "I suppose I hadn't really thought of it like that."

Nathaniel smiled. "We have both the manpower and enough resources here to completely rebuild the part of the city destroyed in the explosions. If we do that, maybe work in their factory, and have our Guard train theirs, they will be up and running in no time. We can fortify their borders, make them stronger than they have ever been.

"Once they have everything they need, we can bring several hundred men back here with us. Our city is much smaller, so we could rebuild much faster with their help. We help them, and they help us. I'm no leader, but I've learned a lot. I think that is the best course of action."

The governor couldn't help but smile. With every passing day, he became prouder of his son. Strong and intelligent, he was wise for his age, and he valued Nathaniel's counsel.

And that was why the governor had decided to call a town meeting and announce the big news.

At first, the city was just as apprehensive as he had been, but then he asked Nathaniel to speak. He wanted his son to talk to them as he had spoken to his father earlier, full of inspiration and wonder.

By the end of the announcement the small city had come together, cheering their loyal and faithful governor, the man who would uproot everyone if it meant keeping them safe.

But there was nowhere in the valley that was safe. Nothing was secure.

The warning bell in the town began to chime. The governor's heart immediately sank as he looked at his son, knowing that something bad was happening. The entire city was in the meeting, minus nearly the entire Guard securing their perimeters. They were all in one place, which put them at risk.

The governor jumped from his seat, instructing his son to take over in his stead. "Keep them safe and calm. I'm going to the watchtower to find out what's going on."

His son grabbed hold of his arm, pulling him closer. "Take guards with you. I don't want anything to happen to you."

The governor smiled at his son, nodding once before pulling his arm free and running from the building. As he did, he could hear his son's voice echoing through the town hall, trying to keep them calm and reassure them that everything would be okay.

As the governor approached the watchtower, he heard fighting. Loud battle cries and the clash of metal rang in his ears. Looking down the street, he saw them. Dozens of them. No, even more than that. Twice as many as had attacked them before. The remnant filled the streets, easily taking their men to the ground.

He thought of the people in that building who trusted him. He had come up with a plan to secure their future, he and his son, and now it was going to crumble before it even began. Those lives could be lost.

He couldn't let them down. Without a single idea of what needed to happen or what he could do, the governor began walking down the street, anger racing through him.

He'd attended the Academy in Arcadia many years ago, but he hadn't been the best student. Without a doubt, he knew his son

Nathaniel would be much better at magic than he'd ever been when he was able to attend and learn.

But at that moment, he was desperate.

There weren't enough men to fight off a horde this size, but he wasn't going to let his people die if he could stop it. All he cared about was them living.

Nathaniel was smart, and a good leader. He would make an excellent governor, and he would treat the people right. At that moment, he realized he wasn't only willing to die for the people of Cella, he was willing to sacrifice himself if it meant their survival.

He began running then, letting the clang of metal and the screams of battle lead him in the right direction. As he got closer, one of the larger remnant saw him and laughed before cutting one of his guards down. He turned, his evil, red eyes focused on the governor, and charged.

The governor threw his hand forward, a large stone coming out of the street to bash the remnant in the head, crushing his skull and taking him to the ground. That caught the attention of many others.

Several other remnant turned, realizing they faced a larger threat. The governor stopped in his tracks, having just passed the body of the remnant he had killed.

He leaned forward slightly, one leg extended farther than the other, his fists clenched tightly at his sides as the stones in the street around him began to tremble.

He saw death in front of him. Not just his own, but that of his people if he didn't find the strength within himself to save them.

He should have brought guards with him as Nathaniel had suggested, but there would have been no chance of any of them surviving. They had barely survived the last attack, and that had been half the number of remnant here now. Since less than half their Guard remained now, they stood no chance of winning against a horde twice the size of the first.

The remnant staring him down cried out before charging forward. The governor's entire body flexed hard, his tightened fists rising from his sides as dozens of heavy stones were lifted from the ground.

He took a step forward, throwing his hands in front of him, and stones blew past him in a blur, crushing every remnant in their path.

The screams of the men and women dying in front of him caught the attention of the others, causing just enough of a distraction for the Cella Guards to let loose. They took down several more before the others charged the governor.

His vision blurred completely as something large landed only a couple of feet in front of him. He jumped back; the largest remnant he'd ever seen was standing before him.

Pulling back his hand, he prepared to use telekinesis to push the remnant backward to allow him the space needed to kill him, but the remnant had other plans.

"Enough!" the remnant shouted.

The governor tensed his body, unsure what to do. His adrenaline was still coursing hard, but he'd never expected one of them to speak, let alone fail to attack.

The sounds of battle behind the remnant had slowed, but hadn't stopped. The beast turned his back to the governor, shifting his battle axe in his hand before taking several strides forward.

"I said *stop!*" He swung his weapon, cutting one of his own men in half.

To say that the governor was surprised would have been an understatement. He'd never seen anything like it, and had certainly never expected anything of the kind.

The remnant lifted his battle axe in the air and arced it downward to get the blood off it. The rest, he wiped on holey pants, then he turned and took several steps toward the governor. Once again, the governor tensed, ready to fight.

The remnant gave him a dark smile. "Wanna end up like my brother over there? Put those hands down. I didn't come to fight."

The governor's breath was still coming heavily, but he slowly relaxed his body and his black eyes returned to their normal color. He'd never used that much power before; he'd had no idea he was even capable of it. But for his people, for his son, he imagined he was capable of anything.

And now, he was doing the unthinkable—talking to a remnant.

"Forgive me for saying so, but if you didn't come here to fight, why are so many men dead? And did you say that was your brother?"

The remnant laughed, the sound low and terrifying. "That was my brother by blood. We don't care 'bout shit like that, means you're lucky to be talkin' to me."

The governor nodded. "Not so sure about the lucky-to-be-speaking-to-you part, but I'd definitely say I'm pretty fucking lucky to be alive long enough to have the opportunity."

The remnant laughed again and nodded, lowering his battle axe to the ground. "I wouldn't be here if I didn't have to be," he said, looking around with a nasty smirk on his face.

The governor's eyes narrowed a bit as he thought over the beast's words. It was becoming blatantly clear that he was alive for a reason. "You need my help with something?"

The remnant nodded. "Don't bother bitchin' about the death of your people. I get what I want, or the extra hundred brothers I have outside'll be excited to come in here. They're pissed and want revenge. And if they don't get it, I have to give them *something*."

An extra hundred remnant.

He couldn't imagine what a remnant would want him to do, or what revenge he would seek, but it appeared the governor had no choice but to find out.

The governor nodded. "There is no need for threats. I am a

good man, and I am responsible for the city. You are indeed talking to the right person, so let's converse peacefully."

A few moments passed before the remnant slowly nodded his head. "Betray me like the last shit, and I promise there're things far worse than death. We're experts in all of 'em."

The governor smiled, deciding to play his game. Remnant didn't respond to mercy. They only respected power, though even that was chancy. "And if you decide to break the peace and shed even one more drop of blood in the city, the power you saw me use today will be the least of your worries. I will teleport to the rest of my citizens, and we will send all of you screaming out of here with your flesh melting from your bones."

To drive his point home further, he lifted one of his hands to his chest, slowly arcing it downward as a good-sized fireball appeared in his palm. "You caught us off-guard the first time. I assure you that this time we are ready. The warning bells sounded several minutes ago, and people are all safely in hiding."

With that, the governor closed his hand, extinguishing the fireball. He was lying out his ass, but he hoped his confidence covered that fact. The logic was sound, and he anticipated it would work.

The remnant turned to his men. "I *will* have my revenge, and I *ain't* dyin' before I get it. If any of you shits put that in danger, I'll gut ya myself."

The remnant turned back, his red eyes focusing on the governor's. He lifted his hands to the side in a questioning manner, and the governor nodded.

"What can I can help you with?" the governor asked.

"Some bitch came to the Madlands, trespassed on my territory, demanded I help her, and even killed some of my men. I don't give a damn about that, but I do care about not getting what the fuck I set out to get. I kept her alive to get what I wanted. That's about to change."

The governor nodded. "I understand so far. If you're asking

me to hand over this woman, I hope she's not one of mine. If she's making deals with the remnant, deals that resulted in the death of so many of my people, I'm not so sure I can give you what you want. I'd have my own revenge to take."

Once again, the remnant laughed, amused by the man before him. "Maybe we could take 'er together. There are two of 'em." The remnant took a step closer. "The bitch is from the bigger city. Arcadia. Talia's the name."

The governor's eyes widened, his jaw falling slightly open. He shook his head slightly, unable to believe what he just heard. "What did you say? How do you know that name?"

"So, you *do* know the bitch! She wanted my men to attack the Valley. Go after the areas she wanted us to. I have a message for her. We're comin' for her. I'll show her exactly who she fucked with."

The governor was completely confused, and he wasn't quite sure he believed the words. "This doesn't make sense. Talia grew up in this area, in a small cottage on a farm a few miles outside this city. Although she grew up farming, she also spent a lot of time here in the city. Made a lot of friends, myself included. From what I know of your people, you don't make deals with anyone. You certainly don't take orders from anyone. Why would you take them from Talia?"

He smiled. "Arcadia. She promised me Arcadia, the biggest city in the Valley."

The governor's head was swimming at that point. Everything he'd said made sense, but it also didn't. He'd known Talia for many years. It was hard to believe, to say the least.

"You mentioned someone else. Who else do you want?" the governor asked.

"A month or two ago, some witch bitch, Scarlett I think, came to see me with a few friends—they were strong enough to make it to my seat alive. Most don't. It was her idea first. Planned to take Arcadia, but had some fucked-up plan to get it. I don't understand you people. If you want something, take it." He shook his head. "Talia was part of the plan. I never would've agreed if her friends didn't have some power behind 'em. I found 'er amusing. Talia, too."

The governor nodded in understanding. "When you came to take the city, their Guard defeated you."

The remnant nodded. "The bitches told me how many men to send. But they were wrong. No one fucks me over and gets away with it."

"You came here because you assumed we would be the easier city to get into. You knew there was no chance in hell of getting into Arcadia and finding Talia yourself. You would've lost all your men again."

Smiling, the remnant said, "*I* can't get in the city, but *you* can."

The governor sighed, thinking how best to handle the situation. Finally, he said, "I don't trust you anymore than you trust me. In fact, I'd have to say that you can trust me far more than I can trust you."

"Unlike the scum in Arcadia, I'd have to say that's true."

The governor nodded. "Good, we're on the same page then. I will help you, because helping you helps me. If what you say is true, Talia not only broke my trust, she caused the deaths of hundreds of people. I will find what information that I can, but in the meantime, you *cannot* attack Cella or Arcadia. I have literally nothing to offer you except Talia and Scarlett, the other woman you mentioned. If I'm to do this, I want the safety of my people assured."

It took a few moments, but the remnant finally agreed. "For now. In the future, I make no promises."

Looking around, the governor realized that was the best he was going to get. If he said no, another hundred remnant would come into the city and take it right now. If he said yes, he stood a chance of having the time to rebuild the city and make it strong enough to withstand another invasion.

"Understood. Our truce will last no less than a year. Is this agreeable?" The governor watched as the remnant nodded his head. "You have a deal. I'll ride for Arcadia tonight. In a week's time, meet me here, *outside* the city gates. I'll tell you what I've found out. I doubt I can hand her over right then, but I have a feeling the Chancellor will be more than happy to help me once she knows a traitor is in her city."

The remnant smiled. "Let's hope so."

The governor didn't like the sound of that, not in the least. The remnant turned and walked away, taking his men with him and leaving their dead behind.

CHAPTER TWELVE

Maddie hated being in the Academy. It wasn't at all what it was supposed to be. She despised it even more now than she did before, and it was rotten as hell. She wondered if it was because she was just used to the old ways, as terrible as they'd been, and now things were supposed to be better and different.

Those who had stood up for the city and fought against Adrien were now standing at the side of his daughter, having no idea who she was.

It wasn't like Maddie or Amelia could tell everyone Talia's true identity. How would they prove it? Granted, once someone knew her secret, she looked just like her father, but that wasn't enough.

There was no way to verify Adrien was her father, but Arryn had figured it out.

Arryn knew. She might even have been able to prove it, but she was gone. It would be impossible to find her, and she might not be coming back anytime soon. Maddie was worried she might not come back at all.

She still hadn't completely ruled out the idea that Talia had tortured her to death, but she didn't want to tell Amelia that. The

Chancellor was much closer to Arryn, so it was affecting her more.

As she made her way toward her class she overheard hushed voices, one of which sounded like Jackson's. It wasn't difficult to have a quiet meeting in the Academy halls at the moment because they were mostly empty.

Some students hadn't yet come back after the battle, and the rest were already in class. She was a little late, and it seemed that Jackson and whoever he was talking to had taken advantage of what they thought would be an empty hallway.

She approached a corner and stopped, standing just out of sight while listening to their conversation.

"You heard what Talia said, though," Jackson said. "If we kill anyone else, it could mess with Scarlett's hold on everyone. They might not believe Arryn was guilty anymore."

"Yeah, but we need strength. Don't you feel weaker? It's been a while. We need blood. Talia needs us to be strong for her, and we can't do that if we're growing weaker. Besides, I've already thought about what she said. We just have to find the perfect victim. Someone who was close to Arryn at one time."

There was a pause, and when Jackson finally replied, she could hear the excitement in his voice. "That's true! We can get what we need and give Talia what she needs without risking anything bad happening. We'll just have to find someone who was connected to Arryn. All we have to say is that Arryn's motive for killing that person was because she believed they betrayed her."

The thought of anything happening to anyone else at the hands of these monsters weighed heavily on Maddie. She didn't want another murder to take place, especially if she could do something to stop it. After several moments, Maddie took a deep breath, quietly exhaling as she readied herself for what she would do next.

Amelia had given her strict instructions to keep her mouth

shut about being on Arryn's side, but if she kept quiet now, someone could get hurt.

Maddie tiptoed back several feet before walking forward again, allowing her steps to fall loudly enough to echo through the hall. She stood tall with the confidence she had always shown as she rounded the corner.

"What are you two doing out here?" she asked, almost sneering at them.

Now that she was standing in the open, she saw that it was Caydon, one of the twins, who had been talking with Jackson. She hadn't recognized his voice, but she definitely recognized his face.

Caydon laughed. "I could say the same thing for you. You're just as late as we are."

Maddie pointedly rolled her eyes, shaking her head as she took a step forward. "I'm none of your business. Have fun doing whatever it is you're doing."

It wasn't like her to be so rude, but she knew it was necessary if she were to be successful. Giving them a sarcastic smile and a rather half-assed wave, she turned to walk away.

She heard several whispers behind her before she very clearly heard Caydon say to Jackson, "I know it. Trust me. She's the one. Just watch; I'll prove it."

Maddie wasn't completely certain, but she hoped that meant she'd caught their attention. She heard footsteps approaching behind her, so she stopped and turned, making sure to appear annoyed as she did.

Just as she'd suspected, both of them stopped when she did, and their eyes—particularly Caydon's—were locked on hers. "Yes? Did you need something?"

"So, how do you feel about all this Arryn stuff?" Caydon asked.

Her brows furrowed. "That's why you stopped me? To ask me about *her*?"

The men looked at one another for a moment before turning

their gazes back to her. "Yeah. Just curious. I heard you stood up in the middle of her class and cheered her innocence. I heard the accusations upset you quite a bit."

Maddie looked at him incredulously. "And that matters, why? She's gone now. Ran out of the city."

Caydon smiled, and the very sight of it gave Maddie chills. He was an attractive young man, but his good looks were marred by his terrible attitude and quest for power. He made her sick.

Caydon made a small gesture with his hands. "Actually, it matters a lot. See, Arryn is a murderer, I mean, in case you hadn't heard. And how could you not believe it? As far as I'm concerned —as far as *we* are concerned—if you stand up for her, you're no better than she was. You're a traitor to Arcadia, too."

Maddie smiled, taking a step forward. "If that were the case, we'd have had Jackson's head on a pike long ago, wouldn't we? I mean, he has very publicly cried out for the old ways. For *Adrien's* ways. Given that Adrien quite literally tried to destroy the city, wouldn't that make Jackson a traitor for supporting the former Chancellor's unbelievably stupid ideas?"

Jackson's expression turned slightly angry; he was obviously offended at her suggestion. "I think you should watch your pretty little mouth," Jackson warned. "Arryn's not around here to protect you."

Maddie's eyes narrowed as she locked her eyes on Jackson. "Was that a threat?"

Caydon shrugged, a wry smile on his face. "Take it however you want it, little girl."

"Yeah," Jackson added. "You're in the minority now. You might want to watch your back."

Maddie lashed out without warning, her knee successfully finding Jackson's balls. Before her foot had even settled back to the ground, her eyes turned jet black. Jackson cried out and hit the floor, and Caydon's eyes widened as he looked from his friend to Maddie. When he saw her eyes, he took a step back.

"I'm not sure threats are the way for you to go, boys. In fact, I find it strange. Arryn is supposedly guilty of murder, but I'm the one who needs to watch my back when I support her? *Hmm.* One would almost think that maybe she *wasn't* guilty at all. Maybe it was *someone else.*"

Caydon opened his mouth to protest, his expression telling her it was more than likely to be a threat or insult, but she stopped him. Raising her hand, she said, "In the words of another once-accused traitor and now hero-of-the-city friend of mine, you douche nuggets don't know who you're messing with."

With an overly confident smile, Maddie turned and walked away, already plotting how to get to Amelia without being seen. Her plan had worked, and now her life was in danger. She would need to make sure this opportunity wasn't wasted—and that she didn't get herself killed exploiting it.

THE ICY AIR burned Arryn's skin, but it wasn't nearly as cold as it had been before. As she laid there, trying to will herself to open her eyes, her last few moments of consciousness fluttered back through her memory. She sat bolt upright and clutched her throat as she remembered the tiger's jaws locking around both it and her head.

Looking around frantically, she studied her surroundings, quickly realizing she wasn't where she had been when she passed out. Now, she was in a rather large cave, the walls, floor, and even ceiling of which were covered in ice, giving it a beautiful blue color.

It was as if someone had created a frozen bubble inside the bluest water.

Outside the mouth of her current resting place, she saw snow pouring from the sky so heavily she could barely see through it.

A low grumble from across the cave caught her attention, and she turned to see the mama tiger standing there staring at her.

The cat's mouth was hanging open like a dog's when it panted. She didn't know much about cats, and she wondered if maybe they were like snakes. Did tigers taste the air as they breathed? Why would she need to pant in such cold weather?

"Did you save me?" Arryn asked. The tiger plopped down in response, laying her head on her massive paws. Her eyes never left Arryn.

A chill swept the air, and Arryn suddenly remembered that she'd strapped the ram and leopard pelts to her back. She pulled both free, unrolling the first one to lay on the cold ground; she would use the other for a blanket. She only hoped the tiger wouldn't realize she'd skinned a leopard to keep warm.

Would she be mad about it?

Part of Arryn wanted to trust the tiger, knowing that if she had wanted to eat her, it would have already happened. But that didn't mean she hadn't been brought here as future food. After all, the tiger would eventually get hungry again.

Another part of Arryn focused heavily on the fact that she hadn't used any magic to subdue the tiger, nor did she have the energy to do it now. It was quite possible the tiger would attack at any moment, especially if it was for the survival of her cub.

Arryn had no idea how long she'd been unconscious, but she suddenly remembered the food she'd stashed in her cloak pockets. She silently prayed the meat hadn't thawed from her body heat and the berries hadn't been crushed.

She felt around in her pockets and quickly realized she hadn't been unconscious for long. Both the berries and the meat were still frozen, though the berries had started to soften a little. She sighed in relief, popping a raspberry into her mouth to let it thaw so she could eat it.

Even though she was protected from the elements in a cave, the temperature was too low for her to stay there for long. She had no idea why she hadn't frozen to death already. Her body had been so weak when she'd passed out that it had seemed quite unlikely she would be able to survive.

In the cave, almost everything was dry. She would need to start a fire. Slowly and very unsteadily she stood, never losing track of the mama tiger as she looked around for anything she might be able to burn. Toward the back of the cave, where it was darkest, she saw what looked like the roots of a tree.

How a tree could have grown up here was beyond her. Though, it *was* still very early spring. The top of the mountain wouldn't have grown warm yet. It was possible it got temperate enough in the summer months that plant life might grow well.

As she went over to the roots, she heard little footsteps and a loud growl. Turning on her heel, she saw the tiger cub running toward her before Mama snatched her baby up by the back of his neck and carried him back to their warm spot on the ground.

Arryn sighed in relief as she realized she wasn't being attacked, and continued toward the back of the cave to investigate the roots. Not only were they dry, but they would provide more than enough wood to create a fire. In fact, there was plenty to create *several* fires, which would keep her warm for days if she stayed here. The root system extended deep into the walls, so taking the visible roots wouldn't do enough damage to kill the tree.

As with most things she'd discovered lately, the best course of action was to use a combination of physical and nature magic. Several minutes later, she brought back several chunks of wood and placed them in the area she believed would be the best for building the fire.

She had looked at the ceiling to make sure no icicles overhung the area. The last thing she wanted was to melt them enough to drip on her fire or break off entirely and impale her or the tigers.

Luckily, most of the icicles had formed toward the front of the cave, though there were quite a few sprinkled around the inside as well, none of which would pose a problem in the area she had chosen.

Arryn looked around for anything she might use to light the fire with, but was left with only a few rocks that she wasn't sure would work and sticks she had pulled away from the roots.

After setting up the makeshift firepit, she began rubbing the sticks together to start the fire. Her hands were incredibly cold, so she wasn't exactly sure how skilled she would be right now.

She caught movement from the corner of her eye and glanced at the cats. The mother had gotten up and was now slinking around the cave watching Arryn's every movement.

As she tried to create enough friction to start the fire with the sticks, the bulk of her attention was on the several-hundred-pound animal stalking her. Unsurprisingly, Arryn's hand slipped and a sliver of the wood went through her palm.

"Gah! *Fuck me!*" Arryn cried, grabbing hold of her hand and inspecting the wound.

There was a loud growl of protest from Mama. Arryn looked at her, angry. "If you're going to eat me, just *fucking* do it already! Do you have any idea how hard it is to focus on not stabbing yourself while also making sure you don't get eaten at the same time?"

The tiger grumbled but didn't move from where she stood. Her body was still in a semi-aggressive pose.

"Yeah, I didn't think so! I used the last bit of my energy to save your son's life, and you're being a real bitch. So, either eat me, or lay the *fuck* down with your baby, because I have shit to do. Not all of us are covered in fur."

The tiger seemed to scowl at her as she slunk back across the cave and flopped down next to her cub.

Arryn huffed in irritation as she turned her attention back to her hand, grabbing hold of the sliver and yanking it free. She clenched her jaws tightly, groaning deep in her throat to keep from crying out again.

Dark red blood steadily trickled down her hand from the deep wound, but she just wiped the blood on her cloak and did her best to go back to work. After several minutes, several more mistakes, and quite a few more curse words, Arryn finally achieved the spark she needed.

Once the fire had been started, it was easy for her to use just enough magic to make it thrive, since it took far more energy to create flames than it did to sustain them. Soon, her fire blazed, and she smiled as she felt the heat warming her. The smoke rose and coated the angled roof of the cave before drifting out into the outside air.

Reaching into her pocket, she pulled out a piece of meat and laid it on a flat rock at the edge of the fire. The rock would heat up fairly quickly and thaw the meat enough to allow her to ram a stick through it and cook it over the fire. It wasn't a perfect solution and it wouldn't be as neat a job as she could've done in the forest, but she was doing the best she could with the resources she had.

As she stared at the fire, a flash of something went through her mind. She shook her head and tried to push the strangeness of it away. Only a few moments later, however, it happened again, only this time she saw an image.

She saw herself from across the room.

Her gaze immediately went to the tigers, who were lying across the room. They were both watching her. It was the oddest thing she'd ever experienced, but she did her best to brush it off.

She looked at the mother and son, then reached into her pocket and put two more chunks of meat on the rock. Those wouldn't need to be cooked, only thawed.

They were her last pieces, but she knew they would be just as hungry as she was. She had the raspberries to snack on as well.

Once the meat had thawed, she tossed the tigers' share across the cave to them. Mama inspected the meat, giving it several sniffs before allowing her cub to partake. Arryn began cooking her own piece, excited at the prospect of a full belly.

She was pulling her dinner from the fire when another flash went through her mind. This time, she watched herself pulling the stick from the flames. Once again, her eyes darted to the tigers in confusion.

She took a deep breath and blew it out, doing her best to focus. "I'm just really tired," she said to herself.

Biting into the cooked meat, she closed her eyes and sighed heavily. She couldn't wait to get back to the forest. She was going to eat fruit by the handful, as well as a bowl of nuts. And wine! She planned to get good and trashed with the Chieftain. It would be a celebration. A homecoming.

After she'd finished eating, Arryn laid down on the ram's skin and covered herself with the leopard's pelt. While waiting for the skins to warm up, she continued to dwell on all the things she planned to do once she was back in the forest, and even what she planned to do once she was back in Arcadia after the city had been saved.

As she closed her eyes and settled into the warmth of the pelts, she advised the tigers, "You missed your chance earlier. You'd better not eat me while I'm asleep. I wouldn't be happy about it. I promise you the worst indigestion of your life if you do."

She'd only just dozed off when she felt something touching her. Opening her eyes, she saw the tiger cub nuzzling her chest and belly, trying to get under her covers.

She smiled, but quickly looked at Mama to get permission before she let him in with her. Mama was gone, but then she sensed something behind her and turned her head just enough to see the large tiger lying there.

Without warning Mama laid her enormous head on Arryn's side, the warmth from her body feeling infinitely hotter than the fire only a few feet away. Arryn lifted the leopard pelt and the cub climbed underneath, turning around once before plopping down with his little head nestled against her breasts.

Lowering the skin once again, she wrapped her arm around him and pulled him tight against her, her fingers scratching the sides of his face. His bloody fur had long since been cleaned; his mama had spent quite a while doing so, she imagined.

Arryn wasn't exactly sure why the tigers had decided to lie with her, but she imagined it was for her heat, little as it was. At that moment, it didn't matter. The only things she cared about were her full belly, that she was warm, and that she had shelter.

Somehow, even with a predator twice her size at her side, she felt safer at that moment than she had the entire time she'd been on the mountain.

As she fell asleep, her last thoughts were of her snowy rabbit friend, hoping he'd find his way back to her to let her know he was safe.

CHAPTER THIRTEEN

When Maddie arrived at Amelia's office around lunchtime that afternoon, the Chancellor didn't know what to think. They had been working together to train Ash to fly between them carrying messages, and things had been going well. It was far too dangerous for them to be seen together. For Maddie to have come in person, Amelia knew something must've gone wrong.

And it had. Maddie had done exactly what Amelia had told her not to do. She'd put herself in harm's way, but it had been a rather strategic plan, and one that might turn out for the best.

After quickly discussing things, Amelia had sent Maddie back to the Academy, telling her to find a way to make it obvious what she planned to do that evening. She needed Jackson and Caydon to know she would be out for a run that evening.

It appeared that Maddie had done her job well, though Amelia had been surprised. Maddie was nothing if not resourceful, and her training and guidance had been much of the reason Hannah had been so successful at impersonating a noble.

Amelia had taken a trusted guard with her and they threaded through the streets, avoiding any other guards whose allegiances might prove questionable. They climbed onto a rooftop and waited. It wouldn't be long before Maddie ran through with the boys on her heels.

Amelia had two Hunters hiding in the shadows below, waiting for the students to pass. They had to wait until Jackson and Caydon struck, hopefully not injuring Maddie in the process. But that was why Amelia and the guard were on the rooftop; to ensure Maddie's safety while the two Hunters took action.

Once the boys made their move, the Hunters would capture them and make as much noise as possible, angrily—and loudly—asking questions.

The idea was that people would hear and begin to watch what was happening. The questions had been pre-selected, ensuring that anyone peeking out their windows or listening behind their doors heard them and thought carefully about their meaning.

They needed to create doubt in the minds of others. Two students who were incredibly close to Talia going after a young woman known to support Arryn? That certainly looked suspicious, or at least it *should*. They planned to make sure it did.

The sounds of footsteps pattering down the cobblestone road caught Amelia's attention. Amelia saw Maddie turn toward the end of the street, and she looked small from that distance. Soon after, Amelia saw two shadows behind her.

Amelia wasn't the best at mental magic, but she'd learned quite a bit from Julianne in the short time she'd trained with her. She'd been getting better at it recently with all the practice she was getting.

They're behind you, Amelia sent telepathically to Maddie. *Keep up your pace, and when you hear their footsteps, I want you to run faster and make noise. If they speed up, scream. Make a scene.*

Can do, was all Maddie replied.

Maddie had passed a few extra houses when Amelia saw her look over her shoulder. She heard her say something to her pursuers, but couldn't understand at that distance. Maddie's focus returned to her run and she began to speed up as Caydon and Jackson sprinted faster behind her, just as they'd expected.

As instructed, Maddie began frantically glancing behind her and making frightened noises. The boys picked up speed; they were almost too close for Amelia's liking.

Now! Scream for help, Amelia instructed.

"Get away!" Maddie cried. "Somebody help me!"

Caydon leaped, and Amelia had a fireball in her hand before he landed on Maddie, knocking her to the ground. Amelia stood and raised her hand, ready to throw it, but the Hunters were already on them, ready to do their job. There was a flash of steel as Caydon reached for a knife and dove once again for Maddie.

The Hunter slammed him in the face with an elbow before knocking him to the ground beside Maddie and taking the knife from his hand.

Are you okay? Amelia asked.

Yeah, I'm great! Maddie's internal voice sounded excited rather than scared. She jumped up, and Amelia saw a smile on her face.

The fire in Amelia's hand dissipated as she closed her fist. As long as things continued this way, she wouldn't need it.

"Who are you?" one of the Hunters demanded. "Why are you after her?"

Amelia could see magitech lights flickering to life as the spectacle on the street began to draw attention.

"Get the hell off me!" Caydon ordered. "Do you have any idea who I am?"

Maddie took a defiant step forward. "*I* sure as hell do! You threatened me at the Academy today. You told me to watch my back. I didn't think you were actually serious, or I would have reported you then. But then again, who would I've reported you to? It sure as hell couldn't be the Dean!"

"You leave Talia out of this!" Jackson cried.

Everything was going even better than Amelia had expected.

"Is that true? Did you threaten her earlier today?" the Hunter asked. "I'll know if you're lying. I'm an *excellent* judge of character."

"Wait just a minute," the other Hunter said. He had Jackson pinned in his arms, but the boy knew better than to fight. Caydon wasn't quite as smart. "I know who the two of you are."

"Who the hell are they?" Caydon's Hunter asked.

"This is Jackson. He's the one who got the shit beat out of him by some Boulevard students not long ago. We investigated the situation when those two students were attacked and one of them was killed."

"Yeah, by Arryn," Caydon snapped. "We've done nothing wrong. Let us go."

Caydon's Hunter yanked his wrists together, snapping magitech cuffs on them. "The only reason you didn't do anything was because we interrupted you."

Maddie took a step forward and leaned down, picking something up. "This looks exactly like the knife that killed the other students. Why do you have it?"

Jackson's Hunter laughed. "That's a good damned question. You know, I'm starting to find it kind of odd. Those Boulevard students kicked your ass, and not long after, they were attacked using a knife exactly like that one right there. Now here you are, chasing down an innocent girl—"

"She's not innocent!" Caydon interjected. "She supports the murderer Arryn. That makes her a traitor."

"Is that so?" Caydon's Hunter asked. "See, you shouldn't have said anything, because now this looks a whole hell of a lot more suspicious."

"That's what I'm thinking, too," Jackson's Hunter said. "You were caught wielding a knife exactly like the one used in the murders Arryn was accused of committing, but you were using it to attempt to murder someone else, someone who supports Arryn and believes in her innocence. Maybe we didn't look at

Arryn hard enough. I'm starting to think it's possible that two noble assholes had a grudge and needed a scapegoat."

Yes! Amelia thought to herself. The Hunters were doing great. They had to deviate from the script a bit, but they still knew how to make all the details obvious to get anyone listening thinking about the possibilities that it wasn't Arryn that had killed those students.

"Like someone new to the city who no one knew very well, for instance?" Caydon's Hunter asked. "The two of you are going nowhere. There are now *many* things we need to discuss."

The boys and their big mouths had made things far easier for Amelia than she'd imagined, though she'd hoped it would turn out the way it had.

People were starting to come out their front doors now, curious about what they'd seen from their windows and heard behind closed doors. A quick look into a mind or two told Amelia her plan had worked. Doubt about Arryn's guilt had been planted, and no one had any idea Amelia had anything to do with it. The seeds just needed time to grow.

LEAVING Cella on the remnant's errand was the hardest thing the governor had ever done, but it was necessary for survival of his people. He'd made large threats, and he'd been lucky the remnant had believed him. If the remnant leader was correct, Talia had been behind the whole thing.

He wondered if the Chancellor knew of the woman's guilt. If she didn't, he planned to tell her, and if she had suspected Talia, he'd validate her theory for her.

As the governor of Cella approached the Arcadian gate, he was met by several guards. "Hello there," one of them said, stepping forward. "What can we do for you today?"

The governor smiled, having no idea what to say or how to

react. He decided to be as vague as possible, in hopes the guard would lead the conversation for him. "I'm the governor of Cella, and this is my son Nathaniel. We received an invitation, and we have come to discuss the terms."

The guard smiled. "Governor, welcome to the city. Talia is expecting you."

That was all he needed to know. The guard seemed overly excited to deliver him to Talia. It stood to reason that this man, and possibly many others, were loyal to her. He needed to step lightly.

"Thank you, thank you. It's been a long time since I've been to Arcadia. I'm excited to see it again. If you'll allow us passage, we'll head to the Academy. Thank you for your assistance."

The guard shook his head. "Oh, no. No need for all that. I will escort you myself. It would be an honor."

The governor grew very nervous, but he did his best to play it off. He forced a laugh and waved his hand. "While it's been some time since I've been here, I know how to get there. Besides, with all that's happened lately, you men are the only thing holding the city together. Our borders rely on strength, and you are our backbone. That's what I tell *my* men. They are the most important part of the city, even more than myself. I don't want to pull you away from the gate, knowing the city could be in danger simply because of my arrival."

He'd hoped flattery would get him somewhere, but it was doing no good.

"Talia *insisted*. Really, it's fine," the guard said, his expression still happy, though the governor could tell that at this point he was straining to keep it that way. The man was growing irritated.

"Talia is the Dean of the Academy, correct?" Nathaniel asked.

The guard nodded. "Yes, sir. She is."

Nathaniel briefly glanced at his father before looking back at the guard. "Shouldn't you be taking orders from the Chancellor, not the Dean of Students?"

The other guards stepped away from their post, coming closer to the two men and their horses.

The guard who had greeted them took a step forward, making sure his magitech rifle was in sight. "Things are a bit complicated in the city at the moment, given the situation. Talia has gone to great lengths to ensure that the city is well taken care of. We take our orders from her."

He looked at the other guards for a moment before returning his attention to the governor. The other guards moved forward again. Though their posture was relaxed, the governor was well aware of the threat. If they did not allow the guard to take them to Talia, they would be taken there by force.

"This can't happen," Nathaniel said to his father.

The governor turned back to the guards. "You would offer violence if I chose to see the Chancellor? The official you swore to obey?"

The guard smiled. "If that's what you choose, yes. We prefer peace, but you will not be seeing the Chancellor. No one is to see the Chancellor."

The governor sighed and looked at his son. He had taught Nathaniel some of the basics, including fireballs, but he didn't have much training. That had been the reason he'd wanted him to attend the Academy so badly. But behind his back, Nathaniel had taken it upon himself to train with the Guard, learning things the governor himself had never even learned.

When his son looked at him and nodded once, his expression deadly serious, he knew what it meant. More than that, he trusted his son with his life.

The governor turned back to the guard standing just in front of his horse and nodded. "If that is your wish."

The governor's hands thrust out in front of him, causing a large shield to burst forth. Before the guards could react, Nathaniel was off his horse and had grabbed his spear from his back.

He ran forward and slid just enough that he could reach under the barrier, stabbing a guard in the chest with his spear before rolling back behind it for safety.

The governor jumped off his horse once the guards were focused on Nathaniel and created a fireball in his left hand while focusing on the barrier. He twisted around the barrier just far enough to allow him to throw the fireball, and it hit one of the men in the back, sending him to the ground screaming in pain. Nathaniel stabbed him in the chest, quieting him for good.

The guards lifted their magictech rifles and prepared to shoot through the shield.

"*Now!*" Nathaniel shouted, pulling a large dagger from his belt.

The governor dropped the barrier and Nathaniel threw his spear, hitting one of the guards in the stomach before ducking out of the way. The last guard fired relentlessly, but Nathaniel was fast, and the guard was too poor a shot. Had it been one of the Cella guards, Nathaniel would've been dead, and he knew it.

Tumbling to the side to avoid more shots, Nathaniel rose to his knees and threw the knife, striking the guard in the chest. They had taken all four guards down within a matter of moments, and the Cellans were safe.

"Do we still think we should bring our people here?" Nathaniel asked.

The governor sighed, looking at the bodies and then at his son. He shook his head. "If we stay in Cella, we risk the remnant breaking the deal. We'd be safe here from the remnant, but then there's Talia. Son, I don't think we're safe anywhere we go. We must simply choose the lesser of the two evils. "

Nathaniel stood. "To do that, we need to talk to Amelia and find out just how bad this is, but first we need to get rid of these bodies."

They'd began dragging one of the bodies away when another guard walked around the corner.

"Shit," Nathaniel yelled.

The governor prepared to throw a fireball as Nathaniel grabbed his spear.

"Whoa!" the guard said, raising his magitech rifle. "Calm down there. You look familiar."

The governor paused, his body tense with fear and adrenaline. "I'm the governor of Cella."

Recognition struck the guard. "The governor of Cella? What the hell are you doing here?"

The governor momentarily looked at his son, who also seemed to catch the possibility behind those words. If the guard didn't realize he was supposed to be there, that he might not be on Talia's radar.

"I was invited here by Talia, but I would like to see the Chancellor first." It was a risk, but he needed to see who this man was with.

The guard looked at the other four lying on the ground. "And these men? They refused you the opportunity to see the Chancellor?"

The governor nodded. "They demanded we see Talia and forbade us the opportunity to see the Chancellor. Is that normal practice?"

The guard lowered his magitech rifle. "No, sir, but I'm sure you're aware there are a lot of things happening. Get on your horses and follow me. There are only a few of us truly loyal to Amelia. I'm sure she'll explain everything. I'll inform the next guards their shift is beginning early. They'll take care of this mess. We'll close the gate until they do."

As promised, the guard safely delivered the governor and his son to the Capitol building and the Chancellor. He hurried them inside and quickly closed the doors behind them. A beautiful woman at the front desk waved them through, and the guard did not bother knocking. He walked straight into the Chancellor's office, bringing the governor and his son with him.

"Amelia, this is the governor of Cella. The guards at the front gate tried to stop him from seeing you. They wanted to take him to Talia."

The governor stepped forward. "I'm sorry to say this, but I felt that our lives were threatened. My son and I have had disturbing news, and we came here to speak to you directly. When we were told we were being taken to her, we feared the worst. The four guards at the gate are dead by our hands."

Amelia nodded. "While I hate to hear that, I know you did what you felt necessary. At any other point in time, I could guarantee your safety in our city, but unfortunately, now is not the time. Those men are under the control of a mystic, a mystic that's in Talia's employ. If your disturbing news concerns her, you and I have a lot to talk about."

The governor laughed, but he was unamused. "Chancellor, I'm here not because of the invitation extended by Talia herself, but because I just made a deal with the remnant. A deal stating that if I delivered her, or at least got information on her whereabouts, they wouldn't rip my city apart again. I think we have quite a lot to discuss."

CHAPTER FOURTEEN

Spending time in the Dark Forest was far more intriguing than Celine could ever have imagined. Part of her wanted to abandon Arcadia entirely and live amid the beauty of the trees and wildlife. Cathillian had been right when he said it was quite a dangerous place, but most of those dangers lay outside the druids' barrier.

Inside, the animals, even the largest of them, had mild temperaments. The druids didn't have the power to permanently tame every animal within their borders, but they had made the predatory animals aware that they were not to be attacked. It was a mutual relationship—neither bothered the other.

Celine's newest and most favorite hobby was combat training. Nika had been hesitant at first, but she quickly realized that Celine had been correct. She really *was* a fast learner. Though her body ached more than she'd ever thought possible, Celine had awoken first thing in the morning every day since she'd been here and gone straight to daily training with the other recruits.

It had been a painful experience, though she had received mild treatment in comparison to the others. Even so, she'd learned more than she'd hoped to in such a short timeframe.

Nika was the hardest trainer, other than Elysia, and that was why Celine had been paired off with her. Whatever she hoped to learn would be learned much quicker with someone as brutal and as skilled as the warrior Nika.

Cathillian wandered up just in time to see Nika sweep Celine's feet out from underneath her as she planted her hand in the older woman's chest and slammed her to the ground. She landed with a hard *oof*, but it didn't seem like any real damage had been done.

"I see things are going well," Cathillian said with a smile.

Celine managed to stick her tongue out at him as she slowly climbed to her feet, stumbling back a bit as she did. "She's rough! What can I say? I've learned more with her than what you taught me."

Cathillian laughed. "Well, forgive me. I had no idea you were quite so serious. Anyone willing to take a punch in the face from Nika is clearly a real candidate. I won't underestimate you again."

Nika stepped forward. "Actually, she's doing quite well, certainly no worse than any of the other new recruits. In fact, she's better than a few of them. That's saying a lot, considering most of these druids have been training in one form or another their whole lives. They've only recently opted into the truly brutal beatings."

Cathillian's expression turned amused. "Impressive! I'm sure that doesn't sound like a compliment, but it really is."

Nika nodded towards Cathillian while looking at Celine. "He's here asking about you, but I'm kinda curious to know about him. Have you gotten weak, Arcadian?"

Cathillian's eyes widened as he smiled. "Arcadian? Crossing a line now, aren't you?"

Nika laughed as she punched her fist into her flat palm. "I don't think so. I heard how much you like those hot showers. How much you didn't want to come back. Seems to me like you're well on your way to being their newest citizen. Of course, if I'm wrong, I'd love for you to prove it."

Celine watched in fascination as the two bickered playfully. It was obvious they were good friends, but Celine couldn't help but want to see them spar.

She hadn't really seen what Cathillian could do. In the fight they'd been involved in on the way to the Dark Forest, she had been so preoccupied that she hadn't seen a thing.

At that point in time, she hadn't focused on anything other than staying alive. Watching these two spar—knowing what Cathillian could do and having seen Nika's skill—well, that would be very exciting.

"Let's see what you got," Cathillian said. "Celine, I'm going to borrow your sparring partner for a moment, if you don't mind."

Celine's eyes widened along with her smile, her eyes glistening in anticipation. She nodded quickly. "Yes, of course! I'll just get out of the way. I can't wait to see this."

Cathillian stepped into the ring as Celine stepped out. He and Nika crossed their fists over their hearts, a devious smile playing on both their faces. "You ready for this?" Cathillian asked.

"Am I ready?" Nika laughed. "In all our fights, you've only beaten me once. Perhaps you should be a bit more concerned about your own ass."

Celine watched with excitement as they playfully insulted each other, circling and sizing one another up. Without warning, Cathillian quickly drew his dagger and threw it at Nika in one fluid movement. She stepped aside and caught it, having anticipated his attack somehow. Celine's eyes widened as she saw the dagger in Nika's hand.

"Is watchin' 'im get 'is ass kicked part of yer trainin'?" Samuel asked as he wandered over to stand next to Celine.

Celine laughed. "It is right now. There's no way he's gonna beat her. I've watched her sparring with some of the more experienced recruits. She's terrifying!"

In a flash, Nika dove at Cathillian. He managed to dodge her first punch, but not the second. She caught him right across the jaw but he recovered quickly, punching her in the stomach before kneeing her in the face and sending her back several feet.

She steadied herself, reaching up and wiping the blood from her broken nose. Her smile spread as she looked at him. "Anyone ever tell you that you hit like a girl?"

Cathillian was a large man, but all druids were relatively tall. Nika was only a couple inches shy of six feet herself. She had the height, the slender frame, the reflexes, and the training to make her incredibly fast and dangerous.

"Wow, that really looks like it hurt." Celine grimaced. "She just brushes it off like nothing happened."

"If ye keep up yer training, ye'll be able ta do that too." Samuel glanced in Celine's direction and winked. "I think ye'll be quite the warrior, with how determined ye are."

Cathillian conjured a bit of nature magic, sending a gust of wind at Nika as she charged him. She was blown back several feet, but she quickly dropped to the ground and whipped her hand around, a vine springing from the ground and pulling Cathillian's feet out from under him.

Celine shook her head. "That is so badass. I wish I could do half the shit they can."

There was a bit of silence as the pair watched the opponents face off, alternating between hand-to-hand combat and nature magic. Finally, Samuel said, "Do ye really want to?"

Celine looked at him incredulously. "Seriously? Nature magic is amazing. Not only can you defend yourself, but you can heal yourself. If your teammate falls, you can heal him, save his life. I would really like to learn it. Maybe after all is said and done, I will. Why? Don't you think so?"

Samuel momentarily looked down at his hands, staring into his palms as if something were written in them. He placed his hands on the railing of the barrier surrounding the pit before focusing on the fight.

"My people've always had a natural suspicion of magic. I was raised believin' magic was a dirty weakness. If a man can't use his own two hands, he has no business bein' involved, whether it be because he's too afraid, or he ain't physically strong enough. I've always thought that way."

Celine focused on him, still trying to watch the fight out of the corner of her eye. "By the sound of your voice, I feel like there's a 'but' coming."

Samuel smiled softly, but still avoided eye contact. "After Cathillian saved the men in my friend Ren's group, he started takin' us outside the city ta learn how ta grow trees usin' nature magic. He said he could sense an affinity fer it in a few of us. Of all the people there, I was one of 'em." He shook his head and sighed. "I still can't believe it."

Celine smiled. "If you have an affinity for it, why don't you learn to use it? Nature magic could do amazing things for you. Magic isn't dirty. Well, I see why you would feel physical magic is —seems like a lot of destruction. But nature magic… I've never been around it until now, but it's beautiful. Pure. With nature magic, a family will never go hungry. Will never get sick. If they're injured, they can be healed. I can see why the druids parted ways with the Arcadians. This is a much more peaceful way of life."

Samuel shrugged. "I never thought twice about it. I never wanted ta learn how ta do any of it, and when I found out I had the potential ta learn it, I still had no interest. Not until recently."

Celine glanced from the fighting to Samuel, but he was staring at the ground. She swallowed, not knowing what he meant by that, but curious enough to ask. "Why is that?"

He shook his head lightly. "A lot has changed. Once again, I have things I risk losin'. I still don't know if I want ta learn or not, but at the very least I'm thinkin' about it."

There was a loud grunt as Nika kicked Cathillian in the chin before dropping and sweep-kicking his feet out from under him. In a flash, she was on top of him, the dagger at his throat. "I told you that you should be concerned with your own ass."

Celine cheered for Nika before noticing that Samuel was no longer beside her. She turned to find him silently walking away.

CONSCIOUSNESS ONCE AGAIN FOUND ARRYN. Warmth enveloped her, and she found herself snuggling into it even more. When she moved her head on her pillow, she became intensely aware that her pillow had a lot of very warm fur.

She opened her eyes and realized that her head was lying on the mama tiger's front leg. The female was on her side, one leg under Arryn's head and the other wrapped around her. The cub was still curled up against her chest and abdomen, but now his backside was on her thighs.

"Damn, little guy, you grow fast, don't you?" she asked. His little ears twitched before he lifted his head to see that she was awake. He flopped around until he was on his feet and began crawling all over her and his mama. "Ouch! Those big, fat, kitty paws of yours hurt! It's like getting punched in the gut every time you step on me, you little shit."

Arryn looked up, but quickly lowered her head again just in time for a massive paw to swat the little guy back down to where he had been laying. Her eyes widened as she looked at the paw—the sheer size of it was incredible.

Unable to help herself, she grabbed the big cat's paw and examined it. If she were to lay it on her face, it would easily stretch from ear to ear and from scalp to chin.

"Bitch and Bastard!" she exclaimed as she looked at it. "These things are huge! You could take someone's head off with one of these monsters. They didn't look that big last night, but then again, I was exhausted and probably not paying close attention."

The tiger pulled her paw away before stretching back out. She extended her front legs as far as they would go before curling them around Arryn and the baby and pulling them into one hell of a hug.

Once she'd finished squishing them, she let them go and pulled her leg out from under Arryn's head before standing. The tiger straddled Arryn and leaned down to lick her cub several times before raising her head to sniff Arryn's face and lave it a couple of times as well.

Arryn was too confused to say anything or stop her. She wiped her face as she stared into the tiger's eyes. They were a beautiful ice blue, the very color of the ice that encrusted the cave, but that wasn't what had caught her attention.

When those very jaws had been locked around her throat not too long ago, she'd seen just how big the predator was. Now that she wasn't facing death, though, it seemed like she'd misjudged her size, because the tiger's head looked even larger. Her body seemed bigger as well.

Arryn felt good. Better than good—she felt great. It seemed that sleeping next to the tigers had provided warmth as well as comfort. She felt better than than she had the entire time she'd been on the mountain. For the first time in a long time, she felt like herself.

Arryn placed her hand on the side of the tiger's face, risking a scratch. She hadn't used magic on these cats, minus what she'd used to heal the cub. There was nothing stopping the beautiful beast from eating her.

She wondered just how much the animal understood of what had happened. She must've understood a great deal, given that she'd saved her life.

The tiger leaned into her touch and emitted a sound that

resembled a purr. "You guys are the most beautiful things I have ever seen," Arryn declared.

Just then, the ever-growing cub pounced on her and put everything he had into a roar. Arryn laughed, unable to help herself. It was the most precious sound she'd ever heard.

It reminded her of wolf pups trying to howl for the first time. They were always so sure it was strong and terrifying, but in reality, their noises were the sweetest things you could hear.

Arryn grabbed the cub and held him to her chest as she stood, scratching the side of his head just under his ears. She looked outside the mouth of the cave and saw the sun shining. The snow had stopped falling, though it looked like it had dropped about three feet during the afternoon and night hours.

At the moment, they were trapped. No food. No easy way out. Every time Arryn had hunted, she had exhausted herself so badly that it would be nearly impossible for her to use magic anytime soon.

She needed more practice with teleportation, but they needed food. It wasn't just her now, and she hadn't used any magic to soothe the big cat to make sure she didn't become a meal.

After setting the tiger cub down, she put her hands on her hips and looked at the mama. If her plan was to work, she would need to be able to communicate with her.

As the tiger glided up next to her, Arryn realized just how big she was. She hadn't stood directly beside her before, and it came as quite a shock. Her back came almost to Arryn's elbow, her head almost to Arryn's shoulder.

Arryn silently thanked the gods for not letting her become dinner, at least so far.

Reaching over, Arryn placed her hand on the tiger's shoulder, letting just a tiny amount of magic flow through her. "If I can get you out of here, will you be able to hunt?"

The tiger grumbled in response; Arryn understood it as "yes."

Nodding, Arryn said, "I'll keep an eye on your cub so he doesn't get lost in the snow, and you track down a goat or a ram. Sound good?"

The animal turned to face her, the expression on her face deadly serious as her lips curled over her teeth and a low growl emanated from deep within her chest. Had Arryn not had the small magical connection to her, it would've sounded threatening. Well, it was still threatening, but not quite so bad. The big cat had more or less told her she would be dinner if anything happened to her cub.

With a nervous smile, Arryn said, "Understood."

Arryn broke the connection and made her way to the mouth of the cave. Conjuring wind wouldn't take nearly as much magic as melting the snow. She needed to retain all the energy she could so she could practice teleporting. Today was the day she'd nail the landing—she just knew it.

If she was going to successfully get off the mountain, she would have to precisely hit her landing every time, or she risked killing herself.

Arryn looked at her hands, then tucked them to her chest. Her eyes turned green as she thrust her hands forward. The snowflakes themselves were light, so light that the snow hadn't packed down. It was like several feet of beautiful white dust blanketing the area.

As soon as her wind hit it, it blew it outward, but it connected with the wind outside the cave, which sent it right back to its original location and beyond, coating the front of her.

The mama flopped on the cave floor not far away, making a sound that struck her as the tiger equivalent of laughter. It reminded her of the cranky old bear, Zobig—the Chieftain's familiar. He enjoyed watching the suffering of others. She imagined if he'd been human, he'd be a crotchety old man that constantly shook his fist at kids and laughed when people fell.

Arryn shook her entire body to get the snow off. The second time, she stood slightly to the side to ready herself. She thrust her arms forward again, this time blowing the snow diagonally so that when the outer wind hit it, it slammed into the mountain instead of coming back inside.

Stepping outside the now-cleared mouth of the cave, Arryn realized the snow hadn't been as bad as it looked. It had drifted, causing a foot of extra depth in the opening. She addressed the tiger. "This isn't nearly as bad as I expected. You should be able to hunt easily enough."

The mama tiger stood, stretching and shaking herself before heading outside.

"Oh!" Arryn said excitedly, suddenly remembering the risk of the tiger hunting instead of her. "No rabbits. I have a white bunny friend out there. He's been helping me. *Please* don't bring him back for dinner. Besides, we'll need a lot more than a rabbit to share between the three of us."

The tiger grumbled before leaving. Arryn felt much warmer today, as though her body was more easily able to regulate its temperature than before. While the mama was gone, Arryn played with the cub. He was so chubby and bouncy she couldn't get enough of him.

She ran around the cave, careful not to slip on the ice, and allowed him to chase her. As she did, an image flickered through her mind again—she could see herself running, but it was from a much lower point of view than her eyes.

Arryn stopped and looked at the tiger cub. Her brows furrowed as she studied him. "Is it you?"

The cub twisted his head from side to side as he stared at her, seemingly unsure of what she was talking about. As she stepped forward and reached down to pet him, another image went through her mind, only this time she was attacking a mountain goat. It was white like most animals in the mountains, but this one had some dark fur around its neck.

It ran, but she roared before pouncing on it, her claws digging into its hindquarters and pulling it toward her. She bit into its neck and shook her head, feeling the goat's neck break as its body went limp in the snow.

Arryn took a deep breath, gasping as she jumped back. "What the hell is happening?"

Arryn took several breaths to calm herself as she sat down. The cub padded across the cave floor and jumped into her lap. He seemed heavy, even heavier than he had been that morning. Curious, Arryn lay down, pulling him all the way on top of her. His backside hit her legs even lower than it had this morning.

Grabbing his paw, she put it in her hand. It was just a bit wider than her hand, and didn't quite reach her fingertips from her palm.

"I could almost swear you've grown since this morning."

Shaking her head, Arryn pushed all thoughts of it aside as she waited for the return of his mother. Within an hour, she had returned. Arryn could hear her trudging through the snow, and she ran outside to meet her.

Arryn's eyes widened as she saw the tiger dragging a mountain goat into the cave. It had dark fur around its neck, a neck that had been broken, and there were claw marks in its hindquarters.

She swallowed hard, starting to wonder if she was bonding with the mama tiger. But then, what about the baby? He was growing very quickly, and she had seen flashes from his point of view as well. As far as she knew, no one had ever had two familiars—one could only bond with a second animal after their first familiar had passed.

Arryn had been told what it was like to have a familiar, but she had never been told in detail what the bonding process was like. Was it different for everyone? Had she used more magic on them than she thought?

She shook her head, telling herself that was it. She'd used

more magic than she'd thought to soothe the animal, somehow giving her the ability to see through her eyes.

To hope for anything else was both terrifying and thrilling.

CHAPTER FIFTEEN

Fresh meat and even more rest had gone a long way toward making Arryn feel normal. Not just normal, but strong. She could feel no difference in herself today than from the day she had been taken from Arcadia.

It felt as if she had finally regained not just some, but all her strength. Something about the tigers, the cave, restful sleep, the warmth; all of it together had brought her back to where she needed to be.

Now, it was time to get ready to go home.

Arryn had spent the previous night sleeping next to the tiger and her cub again. When she awoke, the cub looked to be a couple inches bigger still, and the mother had grown several as well. Looking at them from across the cave, there was no denying it.

The mother had been fully grown, so under normal circumstances it would have been impossible for her to have grown any more. She was now large enough that Arryn could safely ride her if the big cat would allow her to do so, and the cub was growing at a rapid pace, too.

Males were always bigger than females, so she wondered if he would be even bigger than his mother.

The animals in the Dark Forest changed in various ways when they bonded. Some of them grew more intelligent. Some of them changed colors, even taking on colors that were unnatural such as pinks or even blues, like Luna's—Nika's familiar—blue-grey coat.

They weren't vibrant, but you could definitely see them in the sunlight. There were a few that changed size. Luna had also been one of those, but it hadn't been much. Only Zobig, Chaos, and Echo had changed so greatly in size.

It now appeared that she had not one but *two* familiars, each of them growing at a rapid pace. Part of her still refused to believe it. She didn't want to jump the gun and think something had happened that hadn't. It would only depress her when it came time to leave.

Still, she couldn't keep herself from wondering if it might be true. It made sense to her that she would have bonded with the cub, since she'd used her magic on him. She was unsure what had happened with the mother.

But they belonged here in the mountains. This was their home. Would they want to leave? Would they want to travel somewhere they were unfamiliar with? Was it fair for her to ask them to? She decided the best answer was to wait it out during the rest of her stay and do her best to test it before getting her hopes up.

Arryn had waited for so long to have a familiar. Deep down, she hadn't believed it was possible. She'd never been told how the process worked. Hell, she didn't even know how Cathillian and Echo had bonded. She only knew bonds existed, and that she hadn't previously been able to seal one.

The mama was lying across the room, bathing her cub when Arryn made her way to the mouth of the cave. Her goal was to use only enough magic to teleport small distances, and today she was focusing on accuracy.

She was at full strength, so she was confident she would be able to hit her target. If all went well, she would get some rest that night and head down the mountain the following day—maybe the day after.

All she would require was sunshine and a cloudless sky. If she could view the terrain below her, she could map out exactly where she needed to land.

The question was, would she be teleporting alone?

Arryn stood just outside, both tigers watching her with curiosity. She felt the swell of her magic around her as her eyes turned black. The mama tiger stood, seemingly nervous about what was happening.

She began pacing back and forth at the back of the cave where they had rested. As soon as Arryn felt confident, she stared at a place on the ground a few feet from the large animal and allowed the magic to consume her.

Everything blacked out around her for just a moment before she reappeared inside the cave in exactly the spot she'd aimed for. She had only a moment to be excited before she was pummeled to the ground by the tiger.

The animal began sniffing her all over, concerned for her and checking for wounds. When she was satisfied Arryn was safe and sound, she began licking the side of Arryn's head, making her hair a disgusting mess.

"I'm okay! I'm really okay," Arryn assured her, doing her best to shove the tiger away but failing miserably. "What's wrong? You're acting like a crazy mom. I'm fine."

Arryn felt something: an emotion that wasn't her own. Fear. Worry. The tiger had seen her disappear, but had no idea where she'd gone. Having Arryn leave her line of sight like that scared her.

When Arryn realized what had happened, she pushed a small

amount of magic forward to make sure the tiger could understand her words. "I'm fine. It's magic. It's how I'm going to get off this mountain. I have to get back home so I can save my city."

The tiger grumbled as she sniffed Arryn some more. Arryn could feel her confusion.

Arryn thought for several moments, trying to find a way to explain it to her so she would be able to relate to it. Finally, she came up with the best example she could find. "The lycanthrope that attacked your cub… Had I not been there, he would've died. You would've wanted to kill that lycanthrope for that had I not done it already, right?"

The tiger grumbled, nodding though Arryn wasn't completely sure she understood what she was conveying by nodding or shaking her head. Regardless, she felt confirmation through the temporary connection.

"There's a woman where I'm from who's killing people. Innocent people. People who did nothing to her, just like your cub did nothing to that lycanthrope. He was its prey. This woman treats the entire city like prey. I have to practice my magic so I can get strong enough to go back and stop her."

The tiger curled her lips back over her fangs, a growl rattling in her chest. Though Arryn couldn't understand the sound, somehow it was translated for her by the magic. "You want to kill her?" had more or less been the question.

Arryn nodded. "She needs to die. I don't like violence, but I will not allow her to live after all she has done. She has tortured people to death and threatened so many more. She brought me up here to die. Had it not been for you, I would've died. It will be her life for the many!"

The tiger backed away and allowed Arryn to stand. She brushed herself off and look at the big cat.

They stared into one another's eyes for a moment. "I'm gonna have to name you if the bond is really happening, but I can't yet. I can't let myself get attached to you yet. And I won't force you from the mountains. When it comes time for me to leave, if I'm sure we're bonded, we'll go together. But if I don't know without even a shred of doubt, I'm leaving you here. I don't know if I necessarily believe we are bonded. I've never had one, though I've always had an affinity for talking to animals, but I've never felt this close to another animal before. I've never been able to communicate this easily, so this must be a bond."

Arryn took the tiger's head in her hands and leaned over, kissing the cat between the eyes as she scratched her jaws. After a moment, she pulled away and walked back toward the entrance. "Now, lay down and relax. I have some practicing to do."

TALIA PACED BACK and forth in the Academy basement, drinking mystics' brew by the mug. The brew wasn't doing much good, and she wished she'd had the foresight to get something stronger.

As she heard footsteps coming down the basement stairs, she closed her eyes and sighed, her entire body slumping. The entire reason she'd hid in the basement was so no one would bother her. She'd wanted to be alone to brood over the latest failure.

Scarlett appeared at the base of the stairs. It surprised Talia that she wasn't smiling. For the first time ever, it appeared that she was actually taking things seriously.

"What do you want? Now's not the time," Talia said, a scowl on her face.

Scarlett put her hands on her hips, sighing and shaking her head. "I came down here to check on you. I haven't seen you all day, and that isn't like you. You're usually stuck in your office watching everything like a hawk."

Talia's hands went out to her sides and she gave Scarlett the most sarcastic smile she could possibly muster. "And what exactly do I have to watch from my office? Everything is falling apart. Amelia is alive. The remnant are more than likely going to come for me sometime soon. Amelia somehow intercepted the governor of Cella, and now their people are filling the city. I have no clue what is happening with them, but their Guard will be training ours.

"It's probably only a matter of time before Amelia has them convinced of my guilt, and then the entire Arcadian Guard will turn on us. Jackson and Caydon were arrested. And now, because they were so *fucking* stupid, people are talking all over the city about the possibility that Arryn might not have been the murderer. I mean, seriously? Where the hell did they get that knife? How could they have been so stupid as to use the same one?"

Scarlett shook her head, pursing her lips as she stayed surprisingly quiet. Talia took another long drink of brew, draining the cup before walking over to the desk and refilling it.

"A noble." Talia shook her head again. "A well-known noble at that. That girl was part of the revolution, from what I've been told. She worked directly with the Boulevard bitch to con everyone at the Academy. After I asked about her this morning, I didn't have the stomach to stick around for anything else. Your hold on the city is failing."

"Indeed, it is," Scarlett said. She walked over to the desk, grabbed a glass, and poured some brew from the pitcher. "It's taken quite a lot of energy, but I managed to get some of the more significant people back under control. Those from Cella will be my next targets, but more people means more power required to implant a simple compulsion. Hopefully, they will be able to convince the weaker minds. We need to make some kind of a move soon, because I'm being stretched way too thin. I'm not all-powerful. I'm not even the most powerful, though I *am* strong. Of course, I suppose I could send for some friends of mine."

Talia's eyes darted toward Scarlett. "Friends? What do you mean, friends?"

Scarlett shrugged. "I have a few friends I might be able to send for who could help us get the city under control."

Talia turned her full body to face her, her expression something between disbelief and anger. "And you didn't tell me about this, why?"

Scarlett laughed. "You don't trust me now. You haven't trusted me in a while. Are you really going to trust an entire crew of mystics? Would you have allowed me to bring them in back when things were going well?"

Once Scarlett said that, Talia understood why that information hadn't been offered sooner. Talia nodded. "You're right. I would have killed you, probably literally. Well, things are different now. We are desperate. Well, I'm desperate. You're definitely right about one thing. I don't trust you as far as I can throw you. I trust your friends even less. But if they get me control over the city, I suppose I won't complain too much."

Scarlett nodded, taking another drink of her brew. "Very well, then. In the meantime, what do you plan to do about the jailbirds?"

"They need to die." Talia's response came quickly and without a second's thought. She had no remorse in her voice whatsoever.

"Wow. Glad you put at least a moment of thought into that," Scarlett responded sarcastically.

Talia snorted. "What choice do I have? You know as well as I do that Jackson is weak. Caydon is explosive and unpredictable. If I had to guess, I'd have to say it was Caydon's doing that got them both into this mess. Jackson wasn't one for disobeying me. Still, his past loyalty is not in question here. It's his future loyalty. The jail is in the Capitol building. If Amelia threatens him just right, we're fucked."

There was a pause as Scarlett studied Talia. Talia wondered if she was trying to get in her head or if she was simply debating the next thing she would say.

"The others seem to think you might be getting a little paranoid. It seems I'm not the only one. Perhaps you should take a step back. Give this some time and think about it. Jackson has been very good to you. If he dies in custody, the others will turn on you."

Talia had already thought about that, but she didn't care. Things were falling apart right and left, and she didn't want any loose ends. "They die. The other twin should probably go as well. Camdon's no better than that impatient imbecile brother of his."

Before Scarlett could protest, Talia waved a hand to signal she would hear no more of it.

Scarlett replied anyway, her voice coming off annoyed. "I'll get rid of Amelia myself. I think I have a plan that will do just fine. And I'll have Jackson and Caydon taken care of while I'm at it."

Talia nodded before turning her back on Scarlett without another word, silently telling the mystic the conversation was over and she expected Scarlett to carry out her orders.

She couldn't be certain, but she was relatively sure she heard angry mumbles coming from the woman as she left the room and headed back upstairs.

CHAPTER SIXTEEN

It had been a long day for Amelia. Bringing in the citizens from Cella and placing them in available homes had been quite a feat. Luckily, there were plenty of empty homes, and more were currently being built in the Boulevard.

Amelia and the governor of Cella had spent quite some time talking, working everything out. He'd been forced into a corner by the remnant, compelled to make a deal with them.

Amelia couldn't fault him—she found she respected him for it. He'd put aside his own safety to buy his people some time. She'd also admired his honesty. He'd told her what he had done, even though he didn't have to.

While he wasn't comfortable being in the same city with Talia, he also didn't feel that his people would be safe if they stayed in Cella, which lacked the necessary resources to protect against another attack if the remnant decided not to hold up their end of the deal. Amelia honored Talia's offer, and the two struck an agreement.

Both cities had fallen. Cella had no way to protect itself, and some of the buildings near the southern wall of the city—not far from the entrance—had severe structural damage from fires that had been set.

Arcadia had gone through hell with Adrien, and it had just barely been starting to show signs of healing when the remnant came for them, too. On top of that, whatever Talia had in mind had yet to be revealed. It was a simple decision.

Arcadia needed the support, and Cella needed the shelter and defensive capability.

Everything was agreed upon exactly as the governor and his son Nathaniel had hoped. His people would band together and help rebuild the Boulevard as quickly as possible, bringing all the resources they could transport along with them.

Those who weren't needed for building would work in the factory and help build extra resources—magitech lights, weapons, sinks, beds, whatever they might need.

Amelia had sent Ren with an order for amphoralds—the crystals that powered magitech—for extra weapons like the ones Elon was working on, as well as for the lights that would be needed for the Boulevard's new housing. Also, the Cella Guard, who were very experienced fighters, would train the Arcadian Guard.

Within a very short period of time, Arcadia would come to life again.

The accommodations were made with the understanding that once Arcadia was back on its feet and under no threat, no less than two hundred men would return to Cella to reinforce its walls, rebuild the homes that had been damaged, and supply whatever resources they could manage. Amelia herself could not have planned a better arrangement.

Both cities won, both cities lost. They would truly become allies, not only in this fight, but in future battles as well.

The governor had never been a fan of the previous Chancellor, and he had avoided setting foot in Arcadia when he could. But now, an alliance had been forged between the two cities,

Amelia having proven herself to him as someone worth fighting beside.

He also vowed that the Cellan Guard—as long as they did not fall victim to the mystic's tricks—were hers to command as she saw fit, provided it was for noble and just causes.

After a full day of welcoming everyone and making arrangements, Amelia was exhausted. Exhausted, but excited. She felt hopeful. Though this hadn't been her own plan, it had nevertheless fallen into her lap, and she'd made the best of it.

Wherever Arryn was, she hoped she would be happy with the steps she had taken. She also sent a silent prayer that Arryn would return safely.

"You look bored, Mattias," she said to the guard who accompanied her. Given everything that had happened, she never stayed at home alone. She always made sure to have someone inside the house with her, as well as outside.

Mattias smiled. "Not at all, Chancellor. Though, I *am* wondering when we will get our hands on the Dean."

Amelia laughed. "Hopefully soon. Arryn has been gone for quite some time now. I'd have to say it's about time for her to return."

Mattias' expression turned uncertain for a moment. "If she's still alive."

Amelia looked at him with a sad but reassuring smile on her face. "I know it seems impossible, but she's not dead. Don't ask me how I know—I just do. I've met people like her, and they are damn near impossible to kill. If she's not on her way back right now, she will be very soon."

The guard smiled and nodded, opening his mouth to say something. He was cut off by sound of his own screams. Amelia quickly joined him, both gripping their heads as pain overwhelmed them. She fell from the couch to the floor as blackness surrounded her.

AFTER WHAT FELT LIKE AN ETERNITY, Amelia's eyelids started to flutter open. She found herself straddling the guard Mattias with a dagger in her hand. His throat had been slit. Her breath began to come quickly as she looked around her. She was covered in blood, but it wasn't hers.

"What…" Amelia said, her voice barely a whisper, struggling to put pieces together. "What the hell?"

The last thing she remembered was talking to him. Everything had been just fine. He was a sweet man, and had a way of treating her nicely. It confused her to think he might have done something that warranted her attacking him. It didn't make sense.

Unfortunately for Amelia, there wouldn't be time to think it over.

Amelia's door burst open and several guards ran inside with their magitech weapons leveled at her. Their faces fell as they took in the sight in the room. Amelia knew exactly what they saw —a dead guard, her covered in blood with no wounds, and the murder weapon in her hand.

"I had nothing to do with this. All of you know me. You know I would never do something such as this." She dropped the weapon to the floor, hoping her words would reach some part of them that still understood logic.

"We want to believe that," one of the guards said. He was a younger man with golden blonde hair. "You helped to lead us to victory against Adrien. You fought to get the city back under control. But one of our own is dead, and you're sitting right on top of him covered in his blood and holding the murder weapon. What else are we supposed to think?"

"The bitch must've been helping Arryn all along," another one of them said. He was taller and had black hair. "Arrest her."

"What do we do now? She's the Chancellor," the blonde guard asked.

For the life of her, she couldn't remember their names. Of course, at that moment she didn't really care much.

The black-haired guard looked at him with disdain. "We arrest her, lock her ass up, and go get Talia. If the Chancellor is unfit for her position, control falls to the Dean. Talia will know what to do."

"I have *got* to put some better safeguards in place," Amelia said to herself, shaking her head.

The black-haired guard laughed. "You won't be doing anything. Well, except rotting in a jail cell." He motioned toward her, and two guards approached to put magitech cuffs on her. "Take her down to the cells. Make sure she doesn't have anything on her. Then we'll go tell Talia what happened."

Amelia wanted to fight. She wanted to fight, kick, bite, and scratch her way out of her situation, but she didn't do it. She knew it would be pointless. There were too many of them, and she was alone. As they walked out her back door, she saw a dead guard lying on the ground and realized just how wrong she was.

If she fought, she might be killed in the process, and that just couldn't happen. Arcadia needed her. Besides, when she was in the dungeon she wouldn't be alone. Elon was down there, and one way or another he had become a friend. Maybe not *her* friend, per se, but they had a mutual friend, and that meant that they had a mutual agreement. Elon would get her out safely.

The guards made sure to create as much noise as possible as they toted Amelia through the streets, catching the attention of onlookers as they walked. She heard footsteps following them, lighter and different than those produced by the guards' boots. Looking around, she saw Scarlett walking along the sidelines, making sure to stay in the shadows.

But Amelia saw her.

Yes, there it was.

Scarlett stepped into a bit of moonlight and Amelia could see the dark circles under her eyes and the fatigue in her face. There was no shine to her hair, and her skin looked worn.

Scarlett was having a hard time.

The mystic was using far too much power continuously, and she was exhausting herself. Right now, she was convincing the guards to be loud, a small task for someone like her. She had more than enough power to do such a thing, and it would only cost a small amount of magic.

If Scarlett kept using so much magic, her mind would become fragile—she would drive herself crazy. That was why she'd gotten rid of Amelia. This was the coup she and Talia needed. Amelia was accused of murder and had been caught in the act, so the entire city would be against her. Talia would have power then, and Scarlett would no longer need to use quite so much.

Scarlett had worn herself out to get a vacation.

The guards hustled Amelia down the steps and across the dungeon floor, walking past the many empty cells to the last one on the right. Amelia was careful not to turn her head, but she did sneak a peek; Elon was watching with wide eyes as she passed.

Good. She wanted him to know she was there. She wanted him to know exactly how bad this had gotten. The time for action was now, and she hoped he had what she needed.

There was something wrong, though. There were a couple of faces she'd expected to see down here, but she hadn't.

Jackson and Caydon.

Neither one of them were in their cells, and she couldn't help but wonder what had happened to them.

"Be a good girl," the black-haired guard said, giving her ass a slap. "Get in there and don't say a word."

They shoved her into the cell and she whirled, white-hot rage on her face at having been treated in such a fashion.

The black-haired guard laughed, his head falling back slightly as he did. When he looked at her again, his dark brown eyes glared at her. His smile never left his face. "Aw, don't be angry. I know you're sad that we can't have alone time together now. Maybe I'll come back later." He slammed the door, the magitech lock clicking into place.

Amelia gave a dark smile of her own. "Be careful now. If you *do* come back, you'll be the *only* one choking on your dick."

The man stared at her, his smile fading as he swallowed hard. Amelia hoped the look on her face told him all he needed to know—that she would make every effort to ensure that happened if he approached her again.

Without saying another word, the black-haired guard stomped away, the others following closely behind. She heard the door at the top of the stairs slam, and she listened for the exterior doors as well. It would be hard to hear from where she was, but she wanted to make sure they had truly left the building.

She heard a faint noise upstairs and used her mind to search for anyone in the area. The only people in the building at that moment were her and Elon, exactly as she'd hoped.

"Hey, roomy," Amelia said, moving to stand by the cell door.

There was a click followed by a loud creak before she heard footsteps approaching. Within a short few moments, Elon was standing in front of her cell with his arms crossed and a slight smile on his face. After a prolonged silence, he sighed and rolled his eyes, shaking his head slightly.

"Turn around," he said in an exasperated tone, though his expression told her he found this amusing.

She turned and backed against the bars, doing her best to shove her hands through.

"Did you see two young guys brought down here? Jackson and Caydon were their names. They were arrested and should be down here," Amelia asked.

She heard him step away for a moment before coming back.

"Yeah. They were here. Emphasis on *were*."

"What the hell happened to them? Were they set free?" Amelia asked.

"A woman came in here. They called her Scarlett. I'd never seen her before, but they knew her. She never opened the cells, but I heard screaming just before they hit the ground. I laid in my cell and acted like I didn't give two shits. I didn't really, but I wanted to make sure she knew it," he replied. "Anyway, the guards that just brought you in came earlier to carry their bodies out."

In no time at all, there was the familiar click of a magitech lock, and he pulled the cuffs free.

Rotating her hands to loosen her wrists, she said, "Scarlett is a mystic. She probably overwhelmed them. They were little bastards, but it's just one more thing to show how planned all this was. Damn it. Oh, and thanks. For setting me loose, I mean."

Elon sighed again. "Don't mention it. What did you do?"

She held her hands out to her sides, palms up, to show him that they were covered in blood.

"I was set up," she told him. "They finally made their play. One minute I was sitting in my living room talking to the guard who watched out for me, and the next I was on top of him with a knife in my hand. His throat was slit, and I was drenched in his blood."

Elon nodded. "Talia now has everything that she needs. You're out of the way. Arryn's out of the way. The people love her. This is definitely a big problem."

Amelia nodded. "I'm hoping you have some good news for me."

He nodded before going to work on the magitech lock on the cell door. Within seconds, she heard a click again just before he opened it. "Come with me. I have so many fun things to show you."

Amelia followed him to his cell, and he reached under his mattress to pull out the parchment she had given him. On the sheets were elaborate designs she couldn't understand in the least.

He handed them to her and smiled. "Now, before you ask, I'll just go ahead and explain. This one on top—this round device—it's an explosive charge. You were worried about the remnant coming back into the valley? This is your answer."

She looked from the designs to him. "That certainly sounds interesting. What do they do?"

On the designs, the device was shown put together as well as broken apart into its component pieces. He began pointing to the different elements. "These will be very difficult to make, but my mentor should be able to do so easily. Inside, just like any other magical device, is a magitech core. Also, inside is a pressure switch and a timer. At first, I thought an initial charge would do the job, but then I remembered that remnant come in hordes, not a single line."

He pointed to what looked like a button on the top. "When the remnant come through, they will step on it, hitting the pressure switch and triggering the first explosion. It will pulse several times thereafter, setting off a predefined number of charges. Magitech can only be shot off so many times before it needs to cool down, or it will explode.

"Designing them this way ensures they can be reused without ruining them. If the timers continue to function properly and don't allow too many shots to go off, they should last for quite a while before needing to be replaced. As long as any magitech rifle, I calculate."

Amelia was more than impressed. It was far more than she had expected. "This is incredible, though of course I shouldn't have expected any less. You really are a genius."

Elon smiled and winked. "Don't get too sappy on me yet. I actually learned this technique from Gregory. He discovered that crushing an amphorald created an explosion by releasing all the energy inside. While we aren't crushing the amphorald in these, I still took from that idea. Also, I have more."

Amelia excitedly watched as he shuffled through the sheets and handed her the next design. She saw that this one was a secondary device for an arrow. It would be a few inches long and cylindrical, attaching to the shaft of the arrow just below the arrowhead. There was a flat plate on the bottom that looked as though it shoved something inside the cylinder, which held a small amphorald.

"These can be clipped onto any arrow and it only take a second to do so. When the arrow is shot and hits its target, it puts pressure right here," he said, pointing to a tiny plate just behind where the arrowhead would be.

"This will crush the amphorald inside the tubing and create an explosion. This is where I really employed what I learned from Gregory. These devices should only be used in areas where enemies are thick. If they were to be used too close to allies, our people would be killed. In a horde of remnant or an army of any kind, these will come in very handy for her. And the tubing the amphoralds sit in will keep them secure, so they won't explode."

Amelia was about to speak, but he pointed to one last thing. "I also drew an attachment for her quiver. That way she can put these in there and attach them when needed. She'll have to practice a bit, though because these will alter her arrows' balance. She won't be able to use them at a great distance at first until she gets some experience with them, but I have faith in her."

Amelia couldn't believe her eyes. The first device alone was enough to make her feel safer when she thought about emplacing them to keep the remnant back. On top of that, she could give Cella the same design. She would be able to bring peace back to them and make them feel safer in their own homes once their deal had been completed.

"You have no idea what you've done here. You haven't just created a safety net for our city, you've done so for Cella as well.

This is good. Better than good. Now, I just need to figure out how to get them made."

"I don't know if you've thought about this or not, but you need to leave. You can't stay here anymore. Your time is up."

Amelia shook her head. "I can't leave the people. They're in danger. Not only that, but I just brought in all of Cella. Well, minus the Arcadian refugees who left after Adrien's death. I can't leave them here under Talia's control."

Elon sighed, looking at the floor for a moment as he thought. He turned his attention back to Amelia. "There has to be somewhere safe you can go, and a place for the people of Cella as well —even if they just go back to their city."

Amelia stood there, shaking her head as she ran several scenarios through her mind. "Flee the city? *Again?* You do remember that we had to do this before, right?"

He nodded, his eyes narrowing as a look of concern crossed his face. "Yes. And you must do it again. You're going to need an army, Amelia. Talia already has hers. She has the entire Arcadian Guard."

Amelia's eyes widened. "She doesn't have all of it. The Cella governor knows what's going on. He knows Talia has been controlling the remnant and attacking the cities. He promised me that his Guard was mine to command, as long as it was for a noble cause."

"Well, I think this is pretty damned noble, don't you?" Elon asked.

Amelia began absentmindedly tapping her hand on her leg as she stood there for several moments, considering her options. Finally, she said, "Do you think your old mentor would be awake this time of night?"

Elon laughed. "You know my son Gregory. You know me. Have you ever caught me asleep down here?" Amelia shook her head. "That's because it's very rare. Gregory is the same way.

When you have a brain that invents or creates things, your mind never sleeps. My mentor will definitely be awake."

Amelia nodded. "Good, then here's what we're going to do. I'm going to go upstairs and get Ash. I'll write a letter and have Ash take it to Maddie to let her know what's happening. I will instruct her to tell the governor of Cella, and have him send his Guard toward the Dark Forest. Once I send the letter, we'll sneak through the city to your mentor's house and drop these off. Give him a quick rundown of what's happening, and have him start building right away. From there, we'll steal a couple of horses and ride for the Dark Forest. I have friends there. They may not choose to get involved in the war, but they will shelter us until we can get ourselves together."

"And what about the citizens?"

Amelia sighed, shaking her head. "They're lost to me right now. I wouldn't be able to convince them to come with me, and if I tried, I would waste so much time that I would put everyone in greater danger. Mostly because I'd be dead. We'll take the Cella guard. Talia wants to rule, so if everyone plays along, they will stay safe. For now, this is the plan we have to stick to. Are you with me?"

Elon nodded. "When do we get started?"

CHAPTER SEVENTEEN

Amelia and Elon carefully and quietly snuck upstairs and headed into her office. She wrote the letter as quickly as possible, detailing what had happened with her as well as what would soon happen in the city.

She attached it to Ash's leg, telling him to fly as quickly as possible to Maddie. She cautioned him to fly away if anyone else was around, hoping he understood her. No one but Maddie was to get that letter.

Once the raven had flown out of her office window, she and Elon headed toward the receiving area of the Capitol building to make their escape. As they did, they heard a familiar voice arguing and protesting as it got closer and closer to the front doors. They quickly ran to hide in a corner behind Marie's desk, Amelia watching in anger as two guards brought Marie in.

"Oh, no. That's not fucking happening," Amelia whispered.

Elon put a hand on her back, stilling her. "That's the same jerk guard that brought you down. He will notice we aren't there and immediately send for the others. The hunt will begin right now, and we won't make it out of here."

Amelia watched Marie fighting back, questioning them as to

why she was even being arrested, then looked at Elon. "What do you propose we do?"

One of Elon's brows rose. "You can't tell me you don't want to make good on that promise you made after what he said to you." Amelia glanced at the black-haired guard before turning back to him. He continued. "How do you know he wasn't going to visit you right now? Or do the same to her?"

Amelia realized he was right. It was entirely possible the guard was coming back to make good on his promise, and it was her duty to make sure he didn't take it out on Marie in her absence.

Twisting her hand, Amelia created a small fireball in her palm. As the guards shoved Marie forward hard enough to throw her through the door leading downstairs, Amelia took her shot. The fireball flew across the room, hitting one of the guards in the shoulder and causing him to stumble back a bit.

Amelia stood and waved a hand over the desk she hid behind, lifting a couple pens and a small knife Marie used to cut parchment into the air. Before the guards could lift their magitech rifles, she whipped her hand forward and the objects sailed across the room.

The pens stabbed into the chest of one of the guards, and in a stroke of good fortune, the knife struck the black-haired guard in the throat.

Amelia walked across the room, her eyes never leaving his. By the time she reached him, he had fallen to his knees and was grabbing at the knife. "Oh, no, *sweetheart.*" Her voice was as cold as ice. "I wouldn't do that. The faster you pull it out, the faster you die."

The knife wasn't very long, only a few short inches, but it was plenty long enough to pierce his trachea. She heard him struggling to breathe, and she leaned over and placed her face only inches from his.

"I just wanted you to take a moment to appreciate this,

because I am. I promised you earlier after your *gracious* offer that it wouldn't be me choking on anything, but you. I said I'd shove your dick down your own throat after what you said to me," she then smiled and wrapped her hand around his on the hilt before whispering, "but this is just as good."

Amelia jerked her hand back, pulling his hands with it. His eyes widened as he began choking even worse on his blood. Within seconds, his body crumpled to the floor, as his life ended.

Amelia looked to her left and saw Marie sitting on the floor with wide eyes. "You okay?"

There was a pause before Marie nodded her head. "I was just scared. Luckily, they didn't do anything to me."

Amelia pointed to the man she'd just killed. "Yeah, well, that probably wouldn't have been the case for very long. That one right there was a little handsy."

Elon walked over and extended his hand, and Marie hesitantly took it. He was surprisingly gentle as he helped her from the floor, placing his hand on the small of her back and helping her walk.

"Officer Dickhead over there probably let slip what he had planned. They won't come looking for him for at least half an hour, I would say. At the very least, they would have assumed he'd run into issues with one or more of us. So, we have *some* time, but not much. We need to get across the city to Elon's mentor."

Marie gave Elon a quick, reassuring smile as she took a step forward. "Tunnels were built under the city to control flooding. They run directly under the Capitol. If we can get to one of the access points, we should be able to move anywhere we like within the city."

Amelia sighed, a slight grimace on her face. "I really hadn't thought about that, but I suppose it's our only option. I'm surprised you know about them. *I* didn't even know about them until I took over as Chancellor and saw the city records. Of course, I'm sure Adrien played a part in that."

Elon nodded. "Would you want to let people know there was a way to sneak in and out of the city and bring it crumbling down if you were an evil, narcissistic, asshole dictator at serious risk of a mutiny?"

Amelia thought for a moment before finally nodding. "Good point. I can see why he kept it quiet, though it doesn't make me any less annoyed. Probably could've saved a lot of lives. Anyway, did I mention that I hate rats and snakes? Because I imagine there are a lot of both down there."

Marie and Elon led the way, since both had studied the blueprints of the city at one point or another—no doubt for different reasons. Arcadia sat in one of the deepest areas of the Valley, putting it at risk of flooding when heavy rains fell.

The tunnels had been small when the city was first built, just as the city itself had been small, but as it grew Adrien had them expanded. He took no chances that *his* great city would be destroyed by something as simple as a flood.

Elon's Master, Waylon, had designed them with a secondary plan in mind—safety. If ever the city was attacked, the citizens could access the tunnels at multiple points to escape, and many could be saved. He'd kept that to himself, though he'd told only one other person: Elon.

One by one, they quietly made their way down the front steps of the Capitol building. They were ready for a fight, but hoped one wouldn't come. Amelia's earlier assumptions had been that no guards were in the immediate area, though she had no doubt they would soon be on their way.

They ran around the back of the Capitol building and found what looked to be doors leading into a cellar. Pulling tools out of his pocket, Elon quickly picked the lock and opened the doors to find steps down into the darkness.

"All other entry points were barred by Adrien's Hunters,

though I think there might be at least one more open because a rebel... Uh... I mean, one of your friends was able to sneak into the city. Adrien planned to only keep this entry and the one behind the Academy open in case the city was ever attacked and he needed to go below," Elon said.

"That's disgusting," Amelia exclaimed with obvious disdain in her voice and expression.

A guilty look crossed Elon's face. "That was partially my fault. Back when Arryn's parents were alive, he'd worried that a successful coup might be staged. I opened my big fat mouth and told him the purpose of the tunnels, a secret my mentor had told me that I was supposed to keep to myself in case the citizens ever needed to escape."

Marie's brows furrowed. "You really have a lot to make up for, don't you?"

Elon pulled the doors the rest of the way open and shook his head. "You have no idea."

Without another word, Elon jumped inside, quickly making his way down the stairs until he was standing ankle-deep in water. Amelia was the last one down, and she made sure to close the doors behind her.

After Elon put his hands together and pulled them apart, several little balls of light hovered in the air. He tossed them over his head to illuminate the area. "Waylon placed magitech lights down here long ago, and I even replaced them once, but they've long since burned out. We'll have to go through using magic."

"This is really gross," Marie said as they walked through the water that soon came up almost to their knees.

"This is where the wastewater goes," Elon informed them. "It hasn't rained in a long time, but it's been a cold winter. Most of this was more than likely ice, but now it's melted. Come summer, this will be much lower. Unless it rains, of course."

It seemed to take forever to wade through the water and the

tunnels, but they finally approached a vertical grate at the top of the wall, but even with the street.

It had been locked shut from the inside, but Elon had his tools ready to pick the magitech lock. They soon heard the familiar click, and he pulled the lock free before throwing it into the water.

Elon grunted as he pulled hard several times to free the grate from the position it had been in for so long. They had nearly been sealed in by Father Time, but the engineer finally managed to open it.

After pulling himself out, Elon looked around before sticking a hand back down and helping both women out. "We don't have far to go. My mentor's house is just down the street."

They ran behind him, following Elon as closely as possible as he led them through backyards and kept as close to the shadows as possible. It was strange for Amelia to be working with him after all he'd done, but right now he was also doing all he could to save the city.

In just a few minutes they came to a large backyard behind a massive two-story noble home. Even without Elon's announcement, Amelia would have known this was an engineer's house. The backyard was full of trinkets and sculptures and other interesting things she'd never seen before.

"I used to collect portraits and paintings from before the Age of Madness. I was introduced to things from that era because of him. Some of these sculptures are replicas of things he's seen in recovered books or other such pictures," Elon told them as they made their way to the back door.

Amelia grabbed Marie's hand and held it, giving her a reassuring smile before letting it go. They both stood back and waited for the once-Master Engineer to knock and announce their presence. Within moments, a man with shoulder-length snow-white hair and a long beard to match answered the door.

Though he looked incredibly old—and Amelia imagined he

was—he appeared to be quite fit and healthy. His back was straight, his shoulders broad and pulled back. He stood with a noble's confidence.

The old man beamed as he looked Elon over before greeting Amelia and Marie. "Boy, I never thought I'd see you again. I heard what you did. If you're here with the Chancellor—at my back door, no less—I suspect that the city is in danger and you've joined the winning side. Well, the good side, at the very least."

Elon nodded. "You'd be guessing correctly. Tell me, do you have a stash of amphoralds handy?"

The old man's smile grew. "Do you even have to ask? Of course, I do. Now, get your asses inside before someone sees you. We have a lot to talk about."

MADDIE CAREFULLY MADE her way through the city, being as quiet as possible and as invisible as possible, just as Amelia had instructed in her letter. The Chancellor had been arrested and thrown into the Capitol dungeon for a crime she never would have committed. She and Elon had escaped and were coming to the defense of the city.

Amelia had known it was a risk when she'd allowed Cella's Governor to bring his people in, but so had he. They'd made the arrangement knowing the worst could happen. As far as both were concerned, it was less dangerous than a remnant attack.

Now, Amelia needed Maddie to call on the governor for his aid and to secure the services of his Guard. Not only that, but to warn him that he needed to get his people out of the city before morning. Amelia had instructed Maddie to take the governor and his Guard and whatever other people he could manage to the entrance behind the Capitol building and through the tunnels. She'd read the letter twice to make sure she got it right.

M,

This is the last letter I can send for now. The worst has happened—I've been arrested for a murder I didn't commit, which was Scarlett's doing.

The city now believes I'm just as guilty as Arryn, and they'll turn to Talia. You must warn the governor of Cella. He and his son need to get his Guard and as many of his people he can round up out of the city before the sun rises.

Have them take the tunnels behind the Capitol building. It's wet down there, but it's a straight shot outside the walls according to Elon. I'd forgotten, but Parker once said he used those tunnels to sneak in and out of Arcadia. Get them to safety. Get yourself *to safety.*

I'm heading to the Dark Forest. Meet us there. I've heard it's a dangerous place, so make sure they're ready. The druids will welcome us, and I have faith Cathillian will see us to safety.

Please take care of yourself.

- A

Maddie was small, and capable of sticking to the shadows. It took quite a while, but she reached the home where the governor was staying without any fuss. She knocked on the door, looking over her shoulders and nervously shifting her weight from one foot to the other. As soon as the governor opened the door, Maddie ran inside.

The governor closed the door and Maddie held out her hand, the letter between her fingers.

"What is this?" the governor asked.

"It's from Amelia. The city has fallen. You need to get your people out of here and head to the Dark Forest."

The governor's eyes went wide. "The Dark Forest? Did I hear you correctly? I've never seen one myself, but the druids—"

Maddie waved her hands in front of her, shaking her head as she interrupted him. "Forget all that. The Dark Forest is danger-ous, but not nearly as dangerous as Arcadia is right now. Amelia and I have friends there. Well, Amelia has friends there. My druid friend has been kidnapped and taken out of the city. She was born here but raised in the Dark Forest from the age of ten, so I know they aren't entirely bad. Besides, it's the safest place we could go right now. Talia has control of the Arcadian Guard, and if she believes for an instant you aren't on her side, she will have all of you arrested—or worse. Right now, your Guard are the only hope we have."

The governor sighed, then took the letter and read it. After several moments, he looked up and nodded. "I'll get my son. We'll ride out tonight."

CHAPTER EIGHTEEN

Talia had been awakened in the middle of the night by the Guard, who informed her what had happened with Amelia. Scarlett had promised she'd take care of her, but she didn't specify how. The guard seemed to have no idea, having been convinced it truly had been Amelia that killed the guard, Mattias, but the Dean knew better…

It had been Scarlett.

Her mood had begun to improve when she'd heard that Amelia was out of the way and locked away in the dungeon. She hadn't been able to sleep for the rest of the night, but was smart enough to stay home so she didn't appear too eager. Just after dawn broke, Talia got up, took a shower, made herself presentable, and went straight to the Capitol building.

The Chancellor was no longer housed in Adrien's office. Her office was in the Capitol building in the heart of the city. As Talia made her way into the building, she saw the blood spatter on the walls and floor. Her brows creased as she wondered exactly what had happened.

Annoyance began to overtake her triumphant mood as she slowly began making her way to the building. Talia walked through the receiving area to a door that led downstairs, and she shook her head as she briskly descended the stairs toward the dungeon. The magitech lighting clicked on as she stepped into the large room.

As she looked into the first cell, she realized Elon was no longer in residence. Her nostrils flared as anger threatened to overwhelm her. She stomped through the rest of the room, looking in each cell but coming up empty. Even Jackson and Caydon were gone.

"*Fuck!*" she shouted. "Where the *fuck* is everyone?"

"Trouble in paradise?" Scarlett inquired from the entryway.

Talia turned. If looks could kill, Scarlett would have died a thousand deaths. Talia stomped over to Scarlett with her fists clenched at her sides and her face full of anger.

Without warning, Talia lashed out, slapping Scarlett right across the face. Scarlett's face turned with the blow, but her expression revealed nothing. No shock. No anger. Not even pain. Talia didn't care to dissect her reaction… or lack thereof.

"I have no patience for your stupid shit right now. She's gone. Where the *fuck* is she? The boys, too." Talia demanded.

Scarlett moved her jaw gingerly, causing a loud pop to echo through the dungeon. Her eyes blinked slowly, lingering shut for just a moment before she fully turned her face back to Talia. Though the Dean couldn't see any anger in her expression, she could certainly see the rage in her eyes.

"Jackson and Caydon are *dead*. As per your orders. As for the fucking Chancellor, how the hell would I know, *my Queen?*" Scarlett asked, her voice full of scorn.

Talia took a step closer, ignoring her smart comment. Her nose was almost close enough to touch Scarlett's. "Find out. Because if you don't—"

Scarlett's eyes flashed white, causing Talia to jump back. The Dean continued to retreat as Scarlett moved forward. "What? What will you do?"

When Talia didn't answer, Scarlett continued, "Let me tell you what's going to happen. You will *never* strike me again. If you do, you and I will be right back here in this dungeon. I will bring a dull, serrated blade, and I will give it to you. When I do, you'll smile at your gracious host. You will sit down in that corner right over there, and I will sit in that chair just to your right. I will watch as you cut away parts of yourself, piece by tiny piece.

"I won't let you scream—it would only give me a headache. But I will *gladly* watch you cry. Believe me when I say that whatever convoluted torture you could imagine in your own mind, is *nothing* compared to what I can force you to do. It would be nothing compared to what I can come up with, mostly because I have already envisioned it. Do you understand me?"

Talia swallowed hard, nodding as she did. She'd never seen Scarlett quite so angry, and it wasn't until that moment she realized just how strong and how demented the mystic was.

Scarlett smiled, her eyes still white. "Good. Because I've put up with a lot of your shit. Let's not forget… You may be able to set me on fire, but I promise you it won't be fast enough. I can overwhelm you before you even finish arcing your hands over your chest. You're only in your current position because I *allowed* you to be. Fuck with me again, and I'll make sure to rectify that problem. Now, if you're quite finished with this pissing contest, your adoring fans await."

Talia blinked a few times, doing her best to shake away the chill moving through her body. "My adoring fans await?"

Scarlett nodded. "Quite a few people saw the Chancellor arrested last night. Word spread fast. They know you're here, and they're turning to you for answers. It's time for you to seal the deal. Get out there and claim your throne. No one set up a proper line of succession after Adrien died. No governor was elected. The next most powerful person in the city is the Dean— you. They're expecting you to speak to them, since you're their new Chancellor."

Talia nodded, nervously plucking at her shirt. "Well, let's go address them."

As Talia passed her, Scarlett put her hand out, placing it on Talia's chest and stopping her in her tracks. "There's one more thing."

Talia looked down at the hand on her chest before glancing at Scarlett. She didn't look angry, and her eyes were no longer white, but she didn't look happy either. "Yes?"

"I'm leaving the city tonight. I wasn't planning to tell you, but now I don't really care," Scarlett said.

Talia had no idea what to think at the moment. Something in the back of her head told her this was the beginning of the end. All her paranoia had pointed to this very moment. Or had it?

Talia tried to convince herself that Scarlett was loyal, that she was only acting this way because Talia had wrongfully struck her. It made sense, and Talia would've reacted in the same way had the roles been reversed.

But that nagging feeling in the back of her mind—be it paranoia, intuition, or some kind of genetic mental disorder she'd inherited from her father, Adrien—told her to watch her back. The end was coming.

***

Scarlett stood silently to the side and watched as Talia made the announcement that she was taking over as Chancellor. The city was mixed in its reaction. Some screamed for joy, crying out for justice for the lost guards Amelia had been accused of murdering. Others wanted peace. They were angry, and didn't seem convinced Amelia was capable of such a thing without good reason.

Scarlett alone didn't have the power to force these people to believe what she needed them to swallow, but she soon would.

Four of her friends would be arriving, and with their help she would be able to convince the city of anything she wanted.

Once Talia's usefulness had run its course, Scarlett planned to get rid of her. Although she was now strongly considering fulfilling the promise she'd made after Talia had slapped her, she would more than likely just kill her in some normal fashion when the time is right.

Her brows furrowed as her expression turned angry. Talia and her underestimating things had screwed with some of Scarlett's plans, but she knew she'd get them back on the right path.

The most recent of which was the Cellans coming to Arcadia. Somehow, Amelia had not only escaped, but she'd taken the potential allies from Cella as well.

The governor had snuck in somehow and spoken to Amelia without their knowledge. Scarlett still hadn't figured out how, since all guards in charge of the gate had been instructed to deliver the governor to Talia immediately. That hadn't happened, and the governor and the Chancellor must've struck a deal between them, allowing him and his people to come into the city without putting Talia in a position of power over them.

That made Amelia the one they would be loyal to.

They must have escaped with her, or at least shortly after. She would have them on her side now, and they were much better fighters, though their numbers where only a tiny fraction of Arcadia's Guard.

Cella had about twice as many people in their population as Arcadia did in the Guard—at a population of about two thousand, their army was only a few hundred. That number had been cut drastically after their fight with the remnant.

Still, they would be quite an enemy to go against if they *were* Amelia's allies. At the moment, it wasn't Scarlett's concern. She had appointments to keep.

Scarlett had struck a deal with the dark Chieftain's closest ally, Aeris, who also happened to be the brother of Jenna, the girl who had so easily taken Cathillian down in front of the city gates.

It never hurt to have friends, no matter where those friends came from. Scarlett had learned that lesson long ago, which was why she had reached out to the remnant in the first place before she'd ever made her presence in Arcadia known.

The mystic was nothing if not resourceful, especially when it came to planning for her future.

Making friends with the dark druids would definitely come in handy, especially with that life-sucking thing they did. Scarlett had no idea how it worked, but she loved the entire idea of it.

From what Aeris had told her, the druids of the Dark Forest also had that ability, but they rarely used it—only for hunting or if an animal was suffering in the woods and couldn't be healed enough to live.

Boring.

Scarlett much preferred the company of the dark druids, and they'd requested that she help them retrieve Jenna. She'd convinced them to hold off, explaining that a direct attack so soon after Jenna had been taken would've been expected. They would be ready, and would rip them apart.

But now was the time. It was a great opportunity for many reasons. One, it built a stronger foundation of friendship between Scarlett and the dark druids. Two, it forced Talia to deal with things on her own.

At this point, she was so paranoid that the slightest hiccup would drive her insane. Striking Scarlett had been a terrible mistake on her part, but it had forced the mystic to show her dark side. She hadn't wanted to do that so soon, but now she realized it would fester in Talia's mind like an infection, growing out of control and making her even crazier as she worried about the possibilities.

Talia's time was coming; of that Scarlett was certain. It was just a matter of when. And how, of course. She hadn't quite decided how she wanted Talia to go yet, but she wanted it to be poetic. After all, Scarlett had shown her friendship, however false it may have been, and Talia had never once been appreciative. That was a mistake she would pay for.

Scarlett made her way into the Academy, searching for Bernice, one of the other teachers in their group who was capable of teleportation. She found her sitting alone in her classroom, reading.

"Bernice, I need you to take me to the southern edge of the Dark Forest," Scarlett said.

Bernice smiled confidently. "And does Talia know about this?"

Scarlett had hit her quota of snooty bitches for the day. Her eyes flashed white, and fear covered Bernice's face as she looked down, frantically kicking and clawing at herself.

"What's happening? They're everywhere!" the woman screamed.

Smiling, Scarlett advised, "Don't move too quickly, now. Snakes respond violently to quick movements."

The woman was visibly shaken. Her entire body trembled as her phobia came to life. "Please help me! They're everywhere, and I can't move."

Scarlett allowed her eyes to return to normal and the illusion to fade. The woman across the room sighed heavily as she frantically looked around the area, searching for any snakes that might still be lying around, but coming up empty.

"Why? Why would you do that?" Bernice asked.

Scarlett slowly took a few steps forward, each click of her heel on the floor a dark threat. "Because I asked you to do something for me, and I was met with rudeness. I'm sick of the disrespect around here. Talia would be *nothing* without me. She would've already gotten herself killed by now, most likely by that bitch Arryn. So, unless you want the image of those snakes burned into your brain for eternity, I'd suggest being a little more helpful."

Bernice nodded, quickly rising and moving across the room to stand in front of Scarlett. "Of course. Anything you need."

With a genuine smile, Scarlett said, "Good! Now, teleport me to the southern edge of the Dark Forest. You'll stay with me, then you'll teleport me back when I'm ready. When your part is all done, I'll compel you to forget all about this. Understand?"

The woman nodded, wringing her hands.

Scarlett gave a quick nod. "Good girl. Now, take my hand. Let's go."

CHAPTER NINETEEN

Today was the day. The sun was shining. The wind was barely a breeze. It was warmer than it had been for the past several days because of the snowstorm.

It was time.

Arryn walked out of the cave, her body and her mind both feeling stronger than ever. The past couple of days had been spent training hard in teleportation skills. With how strong she had gotten, she had been able to practice several times a day without completely exhausting herself.

Sleeping with the tigers had kept her from needing fires, though she usually built one a few hours before dawn when it got the coldest.

She'd gone back and forth, questioning whether the animals were her familiars or not. The cats didn't seem to have an emotional bond with her, and she didn't have one with them, except for her general love for all animals.

Her rabbit friend had come back, having snuck into the cave in the middle of the night. She'd tried to tell the tigers not to eat him, but they hadn't understood. She'd had to use magic to get through to the cats and arrange to keep her long-eared, chubby friend alive.

Had it been a bond like Cathillian's had with Echo, she could've just spoken the words or simply thought them.

Perhaps it wasn't a true bond.

Arryn made her way to the edge of the mountain, looking down to find a good path. From where she stood now, it looked like it would be easy for her to walk in a zigzag down a natural walkway that had been carved out by wind and erosion, but that would only last so long.

Eventually, she would have to climb down twenty or thirty feet, maybe more, to the next landing. That would take a lot of skill, patience, and sure footing.

"Fuck it," she said out loud to herself. "I'll just teleport down to those places. Not gonna risk it."

She checked her pockets and found jerky from the last ram the tiger had brought in, and she tied her knives to her belt. She had everything she needed.

As she stared down the path, rechecking her route, something felt wrong. She felt worried. Paranoid that something bad was about to happen. Taking several deep breaths, Arryn did her best to calm herself, but it didn't work very well.

The sound of crunching snow filled her ears. The tigers had stepped out of the cave and were approaching. She walked over to them, kneeling to pull the cub into her arms. As she reached out to him, he stood on his hind legs and put his paws in the air. A big smile spread across her face as she picked him up and held him tightly, scratching the side of his face and his favorite area under his ears.

"Well, I guess this is it. I'm heading back to Arcadia. I have a score to settle." Arryn pulled the cub's little face closer and kissed his nose, his cheeks, and between his eyes before hugging him one last time and setting him down.

When she turned to the mama, she had to stand. The tigress

was now tall enough that Arryn could look her directly in the eyes.

"You are *huge*. It doesn't feel like we've been around one another very long, but I think you're almost twice the size you were when I met you."

Arryn stepped forward and wrapped her arms around the big cat's neck, hugging her tightly. To her surprise, the tiger wrapped one of her front legs around her thighs and tipped her head sideways, leaning into a hug. She rubbed her cheek on Arryn's head and shoulder several times before letting go.

"Marking me as yours?" Arryn asked, smiling as she pulled away. "I promise, where I'm going we don't have anything like you. I've seen some panthers and leopards, but nothing like you."

Arryn stepped back, tears filling her eyes suddenly. She laughed as she rubbed them away. Before her face was dry, she felt something hit her leg. Looking down, she saw that the cub had flopped down on her feet and was wrapping his legs around her.

More tears filled her eyes then, so many that she couldn't see. "I can't take you from your home. This is all you've ever known. If we were bonded it would be different, but I don't think we are. It's inconsistent—nothing like what I've been told. You're used to the cold. I can't take you to the forest without knowing that's where you belong."

She began to sob as she leaned down, picking up the tiger cub and carrying him back over to his mother. She set him down in front of her paws. "I don't understand," she said between sobs, sniffling as she stood and looked into the ice blue eyes of the mother tiger. "You grew so big. He grew. I thought you were mine. After all this time, after all these years, I thought you were mine."

Arryn once again started to leave, momentarily looking at the sky as she took a deep breath and exhaled. She did her best to push her emotions aside.

"Maybe the bond is just taking longer. Maybe it started, but we haven't had enough time to fully seal it." She sighed, exasperated. "Then again, if you leave the mountain and we aren't bonded at all—if this was just some strange thing that happened—then I'll have ripped you away from your home for no reason."

Arryn wanted to go, she felt certain she could go, but it hurt to think about it. Just then, something hopped across her foot. She looked down and smiled at the rabbit, who was looking up at her with his adorable nose bobbing.

"Hop Hop!" She picked the rabbit up, nuzzling her face against him. "I'm glad you came to say goodbye. All my best friends. If it wasn't for all of you, I would've either gone crazy up here or died."

She kissed his little nose and set him back down on the ground. With a sigh, and more tears threatening to fall, she looked at each one of them one last time.

"I love you. All of you. Be good to each other. Baby snow cat and mama snow cat, no eating my little Hopsicle. We're all family."

Having said her goodbyes, Arryn turned, did her best to stifle the oncoming tears, and headed toward the edge of the mountain.

THE CHIEFTAIN HAD ONLY JUST LAID down to sleep when he felt the presence of dangerous magic. He sat up in bed, calling on his strength to reach out through the interconnected life in the forest, which allowed him to see what was happening.

In a flash, the Chieftain was on his feet and out his door, alerting everyone in the area to head south.

"What is it?" Elysia asked. Her own internal alarm had gone off when something approached the barrier.

"The dark druids. From the amount of magic being used, it

looks like there are several." The Chieftain turned, searching the assembled crowd of warriors for Nika. He found her and ran over. "Send Luna to find the warriors and tell them about the barrier. They may be patrolling and not in the immediate area. She's the fastest."

Nika only nodded before turning and running in the opposite direction. The Chieftain closed his eyes for a moment, and a loud roar echoed through the forest as Zobig answered his silent call. Thunderous hoofbeats sounded as Chaos answered Elysia. Each climbed onto the back of their familiar before racing for the border.

Other horses joined the fray as the warriors followed their leaders into what was sure to be a battle. Howls and growls sounded from other familiars as they raced alongside the Elders' steeds. The moon was high, but the light only shone through every so often because of the thick canopy overhead.

The Chieftain could sense magic in the trees, and he realized that the *Schatten* warriors were quickly traveling through their branches. He'd ordered some of them south from the northern-most village in the tribe to help in cases just like this one.

"Do you think they're coming for Jenna?" Elysia asked.

"They've been suspiciously quiet since she was captured. I'd have to say that's exactly what they're after. If that's the case, they probably have a sizable pack with them."

As they approached the wall, the Chieftain sensed a large amount of magic being used in one specific spot. Just as they came into seeing distance, the Chieftain watched the plants in the barrier darken, all life inside being drained as they shriveled.

"Shit!" Elysia shouted. "They must have a ton of men to accomplish that!"

She wasn't wrong. The Chieftain knew their death touch was strong. It was what had destroyed the southernmost edge of the Dark Forest, and it was also what would one day destroy the rest if they won. But a small number wouldn't have been strong enough to break through that wall so quickly.

There had to be at least thirty, maybe more.

Just as they got close enough to engage, several dark druids broke through the barrier, having cleaved their way through the weakened wall using swords and what looked like scythes. As Elysia and the Chieftain dismounted, the *Schatten* began dropping from the trees, snatching up the enemy and taking them into the canopy before dropping them again with their throats cut.

The Chieftain ran forward, and Zobig wasted no time before charging several enemies, grabbing them by their throats with his powerful jaws and slamming them into the ground.

Staff in hand, the Chieftain swung as a dark druid approached him, striking him in the head and taking him down before delivering the finishing blow. Vines began shooting from the canopy, wrapping around ankles, yanking the men and women up and slamming them against the thick trees, ending their lives immediately.

Very quickly the Chieftain realized he'd underestimated their numbers. Elysia ran up, her face frantic. "There are too many of them, and Aeris isn't here. Something's not right."

When he looked around, the Chieftain saw that his people were evenly matched against theirs. Though everything was happening quickly, the actual progression was slow. The *Schatten* were killing from above, thinning the horde as those on foot charged forward with their companions.

The Chieftain looked at Elysia. "The village! This is a distraction."

Elysia's face fell. "Cathillian and Samuel are guarding Jenna."

"I'm about to finish this. Go. Quickly. Get back to the village and save them," the Chieftain ordered.

Elysia nodded once before jumping on Chaos and taking off. The Chieftain took several steps towards the crowd, his eyes glowing bright green as he lifted his staff to the night sky, causing thunder to crack hard above the forest. Clouds began to blow in, covering all available light.

"Let us end this!" the Chieftain called as lightning struck the top of his staff.

Cathillian looked at the sky as clouds began to blow in.

"That's some loud thunder," Samuel said.

Cathillian shook his head. "That's not real thunder. That's my grandfather."

Laughter echoed around them as Cathillian glanced at the young woman still tied to a tree. "They must be coming for me. Cathillian, my dear, I'll forgive all of this if you untie me and take me to my brother. He's going to get me anyway, so you might as well live through it. Or... Maybe we could just have one night together before you die."

Cathillian grimaced as he looked down at Jenna. Even in the fading light, he could see her dark smile. She made him sick.

"Fuck you," he spat.

Jenna laughed again. "I'm trying, but you're not cooperating."

Cathillian shot her an annoyed look. "Hey, I'm the only one around here allowed to hand out witty one-liners. And I won't ever give in to you, not in any way, shape, or form. You might as well get that through your stupid head."

"Lad," Samuel said, readying his hammer, "she's baitin' ye. Don't listen to her. She's tryin' ta distract ye while someone sneaks up on us."

Cathillian had no more than listened to Samuel's statement when someone grabbed him around the throat from behind, shoving a knife through his lower back. He cried out as he thrust an elbow into his attacker's ribs, throwing her far enough away he was able to reach back and pull the knife from his kidney. He turned and jammed it into his attacker's throat, twisting it for good measure.

He focused his energy, healing the area a bit, but careful not to use more energy than what was needed for a simple close. He'd do a deeper heal later.

Samuel ran forward, swinging his hammer just over Cathillian's head into the chest of another approaching dark druid. A knife whistled through the air as it passed between the men and struck another attacker in the face. Both men turned to see Celine standing there with a smile on her face.

"Thanks for that last lesson, Sam," she said before waving her hand, her telekinesis pulling the knife free from the attacker's face and bringing it back to her.

Samuel smiled. "Glad ta see it paid off fer me, too."

There were screams coming from the village, forcing Cathillian to make the decision between leaving Jenna alone, knowing she would be taken, or staying and abandoning the other druids in the community.

Having seen the dilemma on Cathillian's face, Samuel smashed another dark druid in the chest before saying, "Go, lad! I can handle this."

"Be careful. Her brother *will* come for her. Don't let them touch you. You remember what happened to me." Cathillian spared only another moment, giving his friend a nod before running toward the screams.

More cries echoed through the forest, leading him to a mass of dark druids invading the actual village. When he got there, he realized they were all women. "Ladies! Ladies! Hey, no fighting. There's enough Cathillian to go around. All you had to do was ask."

A dagger whizzed by his head, one he hadn't seen coming but which had luckily missed.

"Hey!" he said, pointing a finger at the one who had thrown it.

"That's no way to treat a guy you like. Unless, of course, that's just how you flirt."

Just as it was in the sparring match with Nika, his hand was a blur as he drew his knife and threw, hitting the woman directly in the chest.

"Did I mention that I flirt harder?" he asked.

There were five of them, and all five charged at him at once, clearly not amused by his sense of humor. Lifting a hand into the air, Cathillian was able to grab a thin branch which creaked as it angled down far enough for him to reach. The branch quickly lifted Cathillian as he swung his body upward to stand on the end.

The women stopped, anger all over their faces.

"Now see, if you guys weren't evil psychos, you'd still be able to use your nature magic. But no. The trees don't like you now," Cathillian said, then childishly stuck his tongue out at them.

He only barely dodged another knife flying at his head before he once again reached for the sky. A vine shot down from one of the overhead limbs and wrapped around his wrist. He held on tightly and jumped from the branch he stood on, swinging downward and wrapping his legs around one of the dark druids as he passed her. He arced high into the air and released her, dropping her from a height that was enough to kill her on impact.

As he arced back down, he broke the vine at the lowest point and dropped to the ground, tumbling once and landing flat on his back. From his position on the ground he kicked one of the dark druids in the gut as hard as he could, sending her flying back several feet.

Scrambling to his feet, he unsheathed his sword to meet the last two coming for him with blades and staffs. They weren't nearly as well trained as he was in close-quarter combat, so he was able to cut them down easily. The last one had recovered from the hard kick he'd given her and was now coming at him with a staff.

It struck him as odd that they would use staffs at all, because the druids believed that the weapon helped them connect better with nature. The dark druids were more or less an abomination of nature, their magic taking life instead of giving it.

She came at him, screaming out a war cry. He easily ducked out of the way, spinning once and hitting her in the back of the leg with the broad side of his sword. When she was on the ground, he lowered the point to her throat, pushing it in just hard enough to draw blood.

"How did you get in?" Cathillian asked.

"That would be me, big boy," a sultry feminine voice said.

Cathillian looked up to see a woman with white eyes approaching. He'd never met a mystic, but he had a feeling this was the very one Arryn had told him about. The woman on the ground shifted, attempting to get away from the sword, but he didn't give her the chance. Thrusting the sword downward, Cathillian ended her fight.

"What the hell are you doing here?" Cathillian asked. "Aren't you the mystic helping Talia in Arcadia?"

The woman bowed slightly. "Scarlett. So nice to meet you, Cathillian. I've heard all about you. I just must say, you are much more delicious in person. Before you ask, I have an Arcadian with me. Stashed away. A large group invaded the southern border while I came farther north. The Arcadian teleported me inside the barrier, and I used my special abilities to convince a few of your people to open the barrier here to let my friends in. Really, it wasn't that hard."

Cathillian shook his head. "Why are you telling me this?"

She shrugged. "I felt like it? I don't know. I don't really have any reason not to. I mean, I'm getting out of here. I'm perfectly safe, so why shouldn't I? Anyway, I made a deal with Jenna after she nearly killed you outside the Arcadian gate. I can't exactly get *my* side of the deal if she's here in your custody, so her hot brother asked me to help. As soon as I'm done here, I'll be teleported out to safety, away from all you savages."

"Where's Arryn?" Cathillian no longer cared about this woman or her game. He knew she was stalling for some reason, but he didn't give a damn. At that moment, the only thing on his mind was Arryn.

Scarlett laughed. "Took you long enough to ask! And if I'm to be completely honest, I don't know."

Cathillian took a few steps forward, but Scarlett smiled and held up her hand, wagging a finger at him. With her eyes white, he knew she could take him down before he could even get close to her. And if he attempted to use magic, she would know what he planned before he did it. Now he understood why Arryn was so obsessed with shielding her mind.

He had so many regrets. So many things to apologize for.

"You *do* know. You wanted to take her. You were probably one of the people who kidnapped her," Cathillian said.

Scarlett shook her head. "Actually, I'm not lying. You are correct, I did have a hand in taking her. During the battle with the remnant, we bled her out and weakened her so she couldn't heal easily. Took us a couple days to get where we were going, but we finally dumped her. Talia wanted her to suffer alone before she died."

Cathillian growled, "She isn't dead. I can promise you that."

Once again, the mystic laughed. "Well, I certainly hope not! You see, I need her. I need her to come back to Arcadia with all the rage that has probably been building the entire time she's been fighting to get out of that deathtrap we left her in. I need her to kill Talia. If Arryn's dead I'll have to change my plans, and I'm not a big fan of doing that."

Cathillian couldn't believe what he'd heard. Though it pissed him off more than he could comprehend, he also felt hopeful. This woman had been one of her captors, and she wanted Arryn to survive.

The woman sighed heavily. "Please don't go and cry on me

now. It'll totally ruin the image I have of you. Let me just say, I plan to use that to my advantage later tonight, if you know what I mean." She winked and smiled.

Cathillian could hear heavy hooves and knew his mother and Chaos were coming.

"Oh! Our time is up. I'll be seeing you soon." Scarlett winked again. "Very soon, I'm sure. Tell your mother I said hello."

The whites of her eyes suddenly brightened and pain shot through Cathillian's head, overwhelming him and causing him to slump to the ground. Darkness surrounded him as he fell unconscious.

SAMUEL HAD FAILED. The dark druids had proved to be too much for him when a small group attacked from all sides. Celine had managed to take a few down with her newly acquired skills, and Samuel had taken almost all the rest, but one had managed to get through and free Jenna. He imagined that one had been her brother.

As the final body hit the forest floor, Samuel turned to find Celine, and his heart jumped into his throat when he saw her lying on the ground with blood pouring from her stomach and shoulder.

"*No!*" Samuel cried out as he rushed to her side. He dropped to his knees and slid his arm under her head, his free hand going to the side of her face. "Not again. Please. Don't go. Just hold on, and I'll get ye ta Cathillian or one of the others. Just hold on!"

He could feel a pulse in her neck, but it was weak. Her breathing was shallow, and he wasn't sure if she would make it long enough to reach anyone. He didn't care. He would do whatever it took to save her.

Sliding his hands under her body, he lifted her, struggling to stand. Samuel had lost quite a bit of blood himself during the fighting, and even more energy. His body was weak, even with the fear racing through him.

Samuel tried several times, dropping back to his knees every time. Tears began to fall down his bearded cheeks as he screamed for help, praying someone would hear him.

"Please hold on just a little longer. I'm gonna run and get help. I'm too weak ta carry ye," he pleaded. "I'm so sorry."

As Samuel started to climb to his feet, he heard a tiny groan. He looked down to see her eyes weakly open before shutting again.

"No." It was only a single word, but it shattered him into a thousand pieces.

He pulled her into his lap, cradling her face against his chest as he kissed her forehead. "I've got you. I got you."

He looked down, lifting her shirt enough that he could see the wound. It looked very deep. His eyes shut as more tears escaped to his cheeks, and he pressed his hand tightly against the wound in the hope that he would be able to stop the blood enough to keep her alive until someone else got there.

Please. Please. Please. I was responsible for ye. Ye've saved me arse more than once. Please live long enough so I can save yers.

Samuel felt warm, warmer than he should have, given that he was holding the dying girl in his arms. The heat in his body rose, but was highest in his hands. It didn't matter to him. All that mattered was that Cathillian needed to get his ass back here and fast.

The rearick open his eyes, preparing to search the area again for anyone who might be close enough to call out to, but he was interrupted by the woman in his arms taking a deep breath, her eyes darting open as she sat up and panted for air. They stared at one another in confusion.

As Samuel's eyes focused on hers, he saw a green glow in them, but quickly realized it was the reflection of his own eyes.

He quickly shifted his gaze downward, moving his hand away from her stomach to see that the wound had stopped bleeding.

Celine had noticed the same thing, and her hands wiped at her abdomen, cleaning it enough to see that the wound had closed, though it wasn't perfect. If she moved around too much it could easily bust back open, but he'd done it. He'd healed her.

Celine smiled and said in a whisper, "You did it. Samuel, you used magic to heal me. You saved my life."

Samuel heard voices approaching, but his mind was swimming and his eyes were suddenly heavy. "I..." That was all he managed before his eyes rolled back in his head, and he hit the ground, unconscious.

CHAPTER TWENTY

It took all day and well into the night for Arryn to reach the bottom of the mountain. As soon as her feet touched the green grass she smiled and dropped to her knees, her fingers combing through the blades.

Several times on her way down she'd had to stop to block the cold wind or use a little magic to warm herself. There were also times she had to stop because she couldn't quit crying. Leaving the tigers had been incredibly painful, more than she'd ever imagined it would be.

But no matter how much it broke her heart, she couldn't bring herself to take them from their home if she wasn't truly bonded to them. They weren't hers to keep. Besides, she knew that if the bond had been real, they would've followed her no matter what.

Painful or not, she knew she'd made the right decision.

When Talia and the others had taken Arryn to the top of the mountain, they'd stopped in several places for the others to rest between teleporting. Arryn had no idea where those places had been, so she needed to be careful where she stopped to prevent anything bad from happening.

She came to a small village with only a hundred or so people in its entire population. It was small enough that it wasn't even mentioned on the maps of Irth she'd seen.

Of course, it was also possible the tiny area had grown, as hard as that was to believe, since the maps had been created.

Keeping her head up, Arryn made her way through the street. There was only one street, so it allowed her to observe everything the village had available. It was late evening when she arrived. The sun had set, though there was just enough light remaining in the sky to illuminate her path.

She saw the sign with an anvil and hammer on it hanging over the door of one of the buildings. She pulled her knives from her belt and examined them. They had been crudely put together, and though she was sure the metal was strong, it had originally been stone, which she had transformed by magic. If she wanted them to be what she'd intended, she would need a blacksmith.

Arryn went over to the shop and knocked on the door, hoping someone was inside and would see her. She needed food—something other than ram jerky. She also needed sleep.

On the way down the mountain, she'd been forced to teleport several times. The distances were small so the magical use had been light, but it had been conjuring heat and healing herself when she'd miscalculated one of her landings and nearly broken her leg that had drained her.

She had no doubt she could make it back to Arcadia tonight, but then what? She sure wouldn't have the energy to do what she'd come to do, which was destroy Talia.

A man came to the door, which pulled Arryn from her thoughts. He wiped his hands on a towel as he stared down at her. "Yes, girl? What can I do for you?"

She gave a nervous smile, having no idea how to ask what she needed to. "I know this will sound strange to you, but I promise there is a reason. Do I look familiar to you?"

Arryn turned a little, allowing the light to strike her face. He stared at her for a moment, studying her features before finally shaking his head. "No, you don't. You do, however, look like you've been through hell."

That statement brought a knowing smile to her face. It wasn't funny to her, but she still found it amusing. "Yeah, you could say that. I spent the last couple weeks on those mountains. *Way* up at the top."

He looked at her curiously. "And why would you do a fool thing like that?"

"Because I was teleported there and dumped by a heinous bitch. That's why I asked if I looked familiar. They had to stop several times to rest between jumps." Normally, Arryn wouldn't have given out quite so much information, but she felt he was on the verge of helping her, and she needed to know for sure that he hadn't helped Talia.

As soon as she'd spoken the words, his eyes widened before he stuck his head out the door, looking in each direction. "I guess maybe you are familiar. Get your ass in here before anybody sees you."

He grabbed her arm and pulled her inside, taking one last look out the door before shutting and bolting it. Arryn's eyes went black before he'd even turned around. As his gaze fell upon her, he stopped hard, swallowing nervously.

"I take it I'm familiar to you now?" Arryn asked.

The man put his hands in the air, and she saw that they were dirty and calloused. He must've been the blacksmith. "I never saw you personally, not your face anyway. I saw them carrying you. I thought maybe you were very ill. They took you to the Widow."

It was Arryn's turn to look confused now. "The Widow? Who the hell is that?"

The man walked across the room, nervously pulling back the curtains an inch or two to peek outside. "She's been married five times, but none of her husbands have survived. She came here a long time ago. Rumor has it before she moved here, she'd had a daughter, coal black hair and beautiful, but the daddy was never around. He'd left her to take care of the child by herself. No one had ever seen him or knew who he was. Something about the whole situation drove her crazy. She ended up taking a husband when the daughter was around five or six—after she was certain he wasn't coming back—but he died in a barn fire."

When he paused, Arryn asked, "So, what happened next? What about the daughter?"

"She married again when the girl was around ten. He only lasted about six months before he was killed. Drowned in a pond in the horse pasture. The next one came a couple years later, and he caught a fever. People suspected poison, but there was no way to prove it. She married the next one a few years later; that was supposed to be a hunting accident. Then the woman came here, but there was no daughter with her. No one here had ever seen her; only heard about her from people who had traveled south."

Arryn swallowed. There is something deeply disturbing about the story—far more disturbing than she thought possible. "Then what happened? That's only four."

"It was a few years after she lived here. Several actually. That woman was always quiet and withdrawn. Everyone said she was crazy, but when I'd run into her at the market, she didn't seem crazy. She seemed broken. Beaten. She herself had long black hair and porcelain skin. Gorgeous. Of course, I wouldn't go anywhere near her. With a name like 'the Widow,' you don't exactly take chances. Well, *I* didn't, anyway. Someone else did. She'd lived here for several years before she took any interest. He was a friend of mine. They married, even though I warned him against it. Within a few months, he was dead. Hanging."

"And everyone thinks she was one who did it?" Arryn asked.

The man nodded. "Everyone except me, of course."

Arryn shook her head. "Why didn't you believe it?"

His sad smile was unamused. "Because he met her daughter."

Arryn's eyes widened. "What did he say? What was she like?"

The man walked across the room, grabbing a couple mugs and pouring some ale. Arryn imagined it would be cheap and more than likely taste like shit, but she didn't care. She couldn't wait to taste something other than snow.

"He said she had the most beautiful hair, skin, and face he'd ever seen. She'd come here from just outside of Cella to see her mother after the marriage, but he said his wife swore she never invited her. He also said she was cold and calculating. He met her more than once. He said that every time he saw her, she made some condescending remark about him never measuring up to her father. That her mother was a fool for trying to replace him."

"Talia." The word was only a whisper on her lips, but his eyes widened briefly before he nodded. Something seemed oddly familiar about the physical description and creepy behavior, but the second he'd said 'Cella," she knew.

"You know her?" he asked, cocking his head to the side.

Arryn smiled. "Who do you think put me on that mountain? I've been there for a couple weeks. I need rest and food, and I need my weapons fixed because I plan to march right into that city and rip her fucking head off. Unfortunately, I don't have the money to pay for any of it."

He handed her the mug of ale with a smile on his lips. "My name is Roger. I don't have much to offer, but I have shitty ale, food, and a bed you can sleep in while I work on your weapons. My services are yours, and you don't have to worry about paying for them."

"You don't even know me. Why would you help me?" she asked.

"I saw them bring you through the village. I saw that woman. It was only a flash, but when I saw her and where she was heading, I knew it had to be her. Talia. She killed my friend. She killed several people's friends. Fathers, sons, brothers—whoever they were to someone else. And when she brought you here, I let her walk right by because I was terrified of her. I wasn't man enough to confront her, mostly because she had a group with her. Regardless of all that, if you survived that long on the mountaintop by yourself with no resources, there's no way in hell I'm gonna stand in your way. You're more man than I ever will be."

"Thank you—" Arryn was interrupted by Roger suddenly darting over toward the window. "What is it?"

His eyes widened as he looked out the window, and his jaw dropped. He just stood there, unable to speak.

"Roger? What is it?" Arryn asked again.

"I've seen some pretty big animals come through here when it's at its coldest in the mountains. They come down to hunt sheep. But I ain't never seen anything like that."

As soon as the words left his mouth, Arryn felt warmth rushing through her as hope filled her chest. *If it's you, scratch on the door. Twice, no, three times. Scratch twice and then pause before the third. Please, please, please.*

Tears filled Arryn's eyes but didn't spill over as she watched the door, terrified to open it. She could've handled anything on the other side, but if it wasn't them, she didn't want to see whatever it was.

And if it *was* them… She didn't use magic when she spoke the words to herself. She only thought them. If one or both was her familiar, her *true* familiar, they would hear the command through the link—through the bond.

Arryn's body went rigid when there were two scratches at the door. Roger looked at her as though she were crazy when a big smile spread across her face and a tear spilled on each cheek.

"Are you okay?" he asked.

She shushed him and held up a finger, waiting for just a moment. And then it came, the third and final scratch. Arryn ran for the door, and Roger nearly tripped as he darted after her, trying to keep her from opening it, but he was too late.

As the door opened, the giant snow-white tiger leapt at her, knocking her to the ground before lying on top of her and rubbing her face all over Arryn's. Arryn wrapped her arms around the big cat, scratching her and kissing her cheek. The cub ran up and pounced on her, too.

"So... I take it we're *not* going to be their dinner?" Roger asked.

"No," Arryn said, giggling. She sat up, and the tiger stepped around and grabbed her by the cloak to lift her off the ground. When Arryn was finally back on her feet, she looked at Roger with a huge smile on her face. "They're mine—and I'm theirs!"

AMELIA, Elon, and Marie had made it to the Dark Forest without issue. They approached from the eastern side, having decided it would be the easiest route to travel. The governor of Cella and Maddie had caught up to them with his Guard and what few people he had been able to get out of the city. They would all seek asylum in the Dark Forest, free of Talia and whatever else might come their way.

A thick wall came into view; Amelia knew the druids would sense them coming soon. Holding up a hand to halt everyone, she reined in her horse and waited for the rest to follow suit.

The governor and his son rode forward to flank Amelia. "What is it?" the governor asked.

The Chancellor pointed toward the barrier. "That's the entry point to the real Dark Forest, where the druids are. I'm going to approach alone so they don't think the worst."

The governor nodded, his expression revealing nothing but concern and admiration for Amelia. She turned and began to walk her horse toward the barrier.

As she approached, she heard a voice from above. "Who are you, and what do you want?"

Amelia looked up, but she saw no one. That made her nervous, but she knew the druids weren't murderous. They wouldn't hurt her for no reason.

"My name is Amelia, and I am Chancellor of Arcadia. I have been helping Arryn and Cathillian. I was forced out of the city, and I brought all the innocent people I could manage with me. We are all refugees seeking asylum, for now."

There was a pause before the druid spoke again. "Those don't look like any innocents or refugees I've ever seen. They look like warriors."

Amelia nodded as she looked from treetop to treetop, having no idea who—or where—she was actually speaking to. "They are. It's a long story, one I would gladly tell, but I would prefer not to repeat it. I'm quite fine waiting outside the barrier while you send someone for Cathillian, his mother, or the Chieftain. Or, I'll offer myself as a prisoner. You can lift me over the barrier and bind my hands to take me to them. You have my word that no man or woman here will cause any harm to the forest or to your people."

"I won't risk the lives of our Elders. I will take your second offer. As long as they honor your promise, you will stay safe," came the reply.

Amelia nodded, sliding off her horse. She turned the mare and walked her a few feet closer to the governor so she would continue her path back to the others. After letting go of the reins, Amelia returned to her negotiating spot.

A vine dropped from the trees, expertly wrapping around her body in a way that would distribute the weight evenly so there would be no pain as she was pulled into the trees. Once she was high in their branches, the vines unraveled and she saw her host.

It was a young woman only a few years older than Arryn—maybe just a little older than Celine. Her face was flawless, her skin medium-toned, and her hair auburn. Her face had been painted, and there were green and white symbols she did not recognize running down her cheeks.

"My name is Alehah. I'll escort you to the tribe," the woman said. Her voice was stern, but also gentle.

Amelia smiled and nodded. "Understood. Thank you."

Without being asked, Amelia turned and placed her hands behind her back, allowing the woman to bind them. It was the first time Amelia had ever seen the Dark Forest, and it was every bit as stunning as Arryn and Cathillian had described.

Instead of thinking of herself as a prisoner, Amelia focused on the landscape surrounding her, allowing her mind to escape as she was taken to the Chieftain to do something that had been done once before not too long ago—when the Founder had come to him, his old friend, begging for his assistance to beat Adrien in the upcoming war. Amelia was going to make a similar request, only this time it was to shelter the lives she'd brought with her so they might be free of Adrien's daughter.

CHAPTER TWENTY-ONE

Arryn awoke several hours later—she imagined it was just around midnight—lying on a bed surrounded by the warmest creatures on the planet. She sat up and scooted to the end of the bed, which was only a mattress on the floor. Standing up, she rubbed her eyes and made her way across the house to find Roger on guard at the window. He looked out once more before turning around and seeing her.

He smiled. "Did you sleep well?"

She nodded. "I did, thank you. I'm sorry to have put you out, but I really do appreciate the help."

He shook his head, setting the mug down on the table next to the couch. "Don't worry about it. Trust me, it's for a good cause. Besides, it gave me a chance to work. I have something for you."

Arryn followed the man into the kitchen. He lifted one of her daggers from the table and handed it to her. The steel was now smooth and shiny. It had an edge on it that was sharp enough to slice someone through with little effort, and the point at the end had been sharpened as well.

The tip of the ram's horn she'd used as a handle had been properly cleaned and coated with something that gave it a glossy appearance. On top of that, it had been appropriately attached instead of the crude fastening she'd designed in the mountains.

"I got them finished while you napped," he said.

She smiled and turned her gaze on him. "Thank you. They look amazing! How did you do it so fast?"

He shrugged. "I don't know much magic, but fire I'm an expert in. That's why I took up smithing. I can make quite a bit of money in a short amount of time. Travelers come through here all the time, so I do pretty good. They head north to the land beyond the mountains. There's a town full of stormcallers there. From what I hear, they're persecuting the nobles from Arcadia who fled there after the old bastard Chancellor was killed. Sinking their ships and shit. Can't say I'm really torn up about it. Some of them came through here, and they were assholes. They deserved what they got."

"Can't say I am either after what I've been told about what happened in Arcadia before I got back there. Anyone who fled the city was an enemy of the current Chancellor, and I happen to know she's a pretty good person. Anyway, thank you for everything. This is a huge help."

He nodded, jumping a little when the tigers walked into the room. The mama tiger was as tall as Arryn. "If you need anything, don't hesitate to let me know. I wish you the best on your journey, and I hope you get to take that bitch down. For yourself, but also for the Arcadian people and for my friend. It ain't much, but if you ever need shelter, I have it here for you."

Arryn reached out and gave him a hug, thanking him one last time. She made her way outside with the tigers, eyeballing the mama. The big cat looked at her, her eyes narrowing as she grumbled.

Arryn gave a toothy, exaggerated smile. "Come on, you knew this was gonna happen. You didn't wander all the way down the mountain to find me without having at least *thought* about the fact that I might have to ride you."

The tiger grumbled again as she knelt on the ground. Arryn reached for the cub, and he stretched out his front paws again, waiting for her to pick him up. After straddling the tiger, she set the cub between her legs, making sure to hold him tight.

"Take it easy at first. We *all* need to adjust. Then we need to move as fast as we can. I'll teleport us as far as I can, but it's still pretty new, and I imagine I'm going to screw it up a time or two. Or, you know, every time. It's hard enough to teleport myself."

The tiger rose onto her massive paws, and Arryn finally realized how the Chieftain must've felt when riding Zobig. Just as they were about to take off, a small voice spoke from behind Arryn.

"You made it," she said.

Arryn turned to see a woman standing there, her eyes wide. She looked disheveled—not quite dirty, but unkempt. She saw a flicker of movement in her peripheral vision and looked over to see Roger standing in the door, a bow drawn and aimed directly at the woman.

"Leave her be, Widow," Roger ordered, his voice cold and authoritative. "Arryn, leave. Now. I'll take care of this."

"No," the Widow said, her voice barely a whisper. She gave Arryn the creeps, but Arryn didn't think the woman meant her any harm. "I'm happy you made it. I was the one who changed your bandages when she brought you here. She got mad at me, hoping your wounds would fester and cause you more pain. I couldn't save the others she took from me, but I did what little I could to save you."

"Thank you," Arryn said. "You *do* realize what I plan to do."

The woman stepped forward, and Roger pulled the bowstring farther back as she did. Cautiously, the woman reached into her cloak pocket and pulled out a piece of parchment. She handed it to Arryn.

"I don't know if this will help. This is her birth record, signed by her father. It's the only copy, and I promised Adrien I'd destroyed it when he decided he didn't want anyone knowing about her."

The woman's voice was quiet and weak. She couldn't even make eye contact with Arryn. It was obvious that Talia had destroyed this woman as surely as she'd destroyed everything else.

"She won't be able to hurt you anymore," Arryn said. "I can promise you that."

Tears spilled down the woman's face. Arryn thought it might've been because she was about to lose her daughter, but then the widow smiled. "It's a terrible thing to wish for the death of your own child, but she was never mine. She was his from the moment she was born. I gave birth to her. I raised her. But she was Adrien's. May we both find peace."

After saying her piece, the Widow turned and walked back down the street in what Arryn assumed was the direction of her home. With one last goodbye to Roger, Arryn headed south for Arcadia.

After she'd traveled a few miles, she heard a familiar screech ring through the sky. Looking up, she saw Echo flying above. Without even questioning it, Arryn knew she was on the hunt for her.

"Echo!" Arryn called. "I'm heading to Arcadia. Tell Cathillian I'm on my way!"

The bird screeched again and then veered off toward the west. Arryn was confused for a moment, wondering why the bird didn't continue flying south. As Echo continued to head west, Arryn realized then that Cathillian was no longer in Arcadia. He'd gone home to the Dark Forest, more than likely to get Elysia and the others.

There was no need, Arryn thought to herself. *I'll be home soon.*

IT WAS NEARLY DAWN when Arryn finally reached Arcadia. The sun would rise soon, but it was still plenty dark enough for her to sneak into the city. She had teleported several times, stopping to kneel in the warm grass and feel the blades against her hands as she fed on the energy of the earth, allowing it to heal her. While it used some of her energy to take from the earth, it replenished much more.

It had allowed her to make several jumps, and the tiger had carried them the rest of the way. As fast as the big cat was, they completed the trip before sunrise.

They approached the northern wall, and Arryn found herself debating what to do with the cub. He was still too small to fight, so she couldn't take him with them, but he also couldn't be left alone.

Eventually, Arryn decided to hide him on the top of the wall. He would be well concealed there, and no one would be on the wall—Arryn knew that for a fact. Arryn wordlessly gave the tiger the instructions, and the big cat jumped all the way to the top of the wall. It was impressive, Arryn had to admit.

She wouldn't be able to do that, so she called vines from the ground to wrap around her and the tiger cub and lift them onto the wall. Once her feet touched, she knelt and placed the baby down.

"You have to stay here," she whispered. "We'll be back for you. If you stay here, no one will be able to find you."

She kissed the top of his head, and the mama tiger licked him before they began moving as quickly as possible toward her objective while crouching low enough to avoid being seen on the wall.

The Capitol building wasn't far from there, and Arryn wanted to get to Amelia as quickly as possible. If she could, she wanted to teleport inside. After several moments' thought, Arryn realized she'd been gone for quite a while. It was possible things weren't the way she'd left them. If Cathillian was no longer in the city, it stood to reason the worst might've happened.

Arryn nearly growled, thinking about it. And the more she thought about it, the angrier she became.

As they came to the center of the northern wall, Arryn risked a peek over the edge into the city. Everything looked quiet, but she knew better. From her position, she could see the Capitol building, and even farther away, the Academy.

Capitol building or Academy? Which one? Where would she be?

Sighing, Arryn decided the Capitol building would be her first choice. It was closer, and if she was wrong, she could head toward the Academy. She didn't know where Talia actually lived, so this would be the best option.

Arryn slid over the edge of the wall, landing on a shed behind one of the more secluded noble homes. Making her way to the edge of its roof, she jumped down to land on the ground. Though her tiger weighed several hundred pounds, the large animal was even quieter than she'd been when she landed.

They were both completely silent as they snuck through the yards, keeping to the shadows and making their way to the back of the Capitol building. As Arryn approached, she felt a familiar buzzing in her brain, alerting her that Scarlett was now very aware of her presence.

"Shit," Arryn whispered quietly.

Taking a deep breath, she led the tiger to the rear of the building. At the very bottom of the wall, just at ground level, were several small windows. They were the only source of natural light—a very pathetic excuse for it—in the dungeon.

Dropping down, Arryn peered inside to see where she would need to land. Her teleportation still wasn't as accurate as she'd like, so she wanted to make sure she had a good look at where she was going.

Her eyes turned black as she reached back and grabbed her tiger's leg. The magic surrounded her, pushing in all directions as they disappeared, Arryn landing hard on her side on the floor and the tiger managing to land on her feet.

Arryn groaned as she rolled over on her hands and knees, then stood. "Perfect," she whispered to the big cat with a wink.

As she turned, her eyes widened. Next to the door frame that led to the stairs she found her staff, her bow, and her quiver. The quiver was empty from the battle against the remnant, but there they were.

The tingling feeling in her brain returned. *Enjoy your gifts,* came Scarlett's voice. Arryn froze in surprise. *I spent the last week minus a couple days waiting for you. I expected you back a while ago, but I'm happy now.*

What is this? Where are you?

Why would I tell you that? Scarlett asked, her internal voice sounding almost offended that Arryn had asked. *I'm here, but nowhere you can find me. I thought I would give you some time alone with Talia. She's in the Chancellor's office, by the way.*

Arryn didn't understand. None of this made sense. *This is a trap. You knew I was coming. How?*

Because you're annoying. You were so weak that day that I saw straight through you. There was no way in hell you were going to give up. It's been a real treat watching Talia collapse into her own psychosis, and now I get to enjoy you taking revenge on her. The best part is that she has no idea you're even alive, let alone back in Arcadia.

Well, after I'm done with her, I'm coming for you next, bitch, Arryn sent, her internal voice flat and angry.

Oh, I'm counting on it. Have fun now! Do tell Talia I send her my best.

With that the tingle in her brain was gone and she was left to her own thoughts. Scarlett had set Talia up, or so it seemed. That was okay—Arryn didn't care if it came easy, though she *was* happy she wouldn't have to fight her way in.

Arryn slowly made her way through the door and up the stairs, hoping the wood wouldn't creak under her tiger's weight.

CHAPTER TWENTY-TWO

Arryn didn't trust Scarlett as far she could throw her, so she didn't believe for an instant that the mystic hadn't alerted Talia. While the mystic fully believed she was capable of betraying the Dean, Arryn didn't feel that luck would be on her side when it came to catching Talia off-guard.

When Arryn reached the top of the stairs, the landing's boards whined loudly. Her entire body froze as she watched the door, waiting for someone to investigate the noise. She didn't have to wait long.

The door swung open and a woman stepped through, one Arryn didn't know well but was certainly familiar with. Rebecca was her name, and she was a teacher at the Academy.

Rebecca smiled as her eyes locked on Arryn's. The tiger had ducked out of sight, lying flat on the stairs while Arryn stood on the landing above.

"Oh, Talia is going to *love* this."

Arryn smiled. "Not nearly as much as *I'm* going to—trust me."

Arryn stepped to the side, flattening herself against the wall. The landing was a slightly wider area than the stairwell—more like a foyer—but Arryn didn't want to be in the way.

Rebecca regarded her with a confused expression, and Arryn winked. She had no more than thought about the big cat before she appeared at the top of the stairs. The woman's eyes widened when she saw the oversized tiger pull her lips back over her long, sharp teeth.

There was a low growl coming from the cat's throat, and the rumble was so deep it gave the illusion that the walls themselves might rattle.

"As I said, I think I'm going to enjoy this far more." Arryn stepped forward and placed her hand on the tiger's neck. "Make it as quiet as possible. I have an office to sneak into."

With a wave of her hand, Arryn magically yanked the woman farther into the small area and slammed her against the wall across from her.

"How many people are in the building?" Arryn asked.

"Fuck you! I'm not telling you anything."

The tiger walked forward, placing her nose a couple of inches away from the woman's face. Rebecca's breathing became ragged as tears formed in her eyes. She squinted them shut as the tiger pushed forward, licking the entire side of her face.

"Did I mention she climbed all the way down a fucking mountain yesterday? Oh, and then she traveled all the way here tonight. Haven't seen her eat once. I'm starving, and I *rode* her here. I can't imagine how famished she must be."

While Arryn hadn't ever enjoyed being particularly nasty to people, after having spent a couple weeks nearly freezing to death on the mountain while torturing herself in the worst way possible with the exhaustion and training, her rage was even more satisfying than she'd imagined.

"Five, counting Talia!" Rebecca said quickly. "Five. Please. Please don't kill me."

Arryn shook her head. "You know, I couldn't remember anything from the day I was taken. A couple of flashes, that was it. Nothing made sense. But you? I remember your face. You helped take me down in the alley. You helped put me there. You helped a murderer. You helped dump me on that mountain and expected me to die, so you're a murderer, too."

Arryn turned and made her way to the door and slowly poked her head through, scanning for people. The immediate area seemed to be empty, but that could change at any moment.

Looking back at the tiger, Arryn ordered, "Make it quick and quiet."

Ducking low, Arryn stepped into the outer room, searching the area again. She heard a sound down the hallway. She closed the door to the dungeon without latching it so the tiger could walk out when she was ready.

There was a low rumble followed by a thump against the wall, and Arryn knew it was done. She took a few careful steps before stealthily running through the building, making as little noise as possible.

As she sped down the hall, she followed the sound to a room on the right. Sensing the area, she felt three people inside, and one of the life energies in the room was familiar to her.

Arryn smiled as she straightened and kicked the door in as hard as she could. It blew open, smashing into the wall and crumbling some of the plaster to the floor.

As she stepped inside, Arryn saw William, who was also a teacher, Brandi, a student, and Hugh. He had been the one with the familiar energy. When the western side of the Capitol building had been destroyed—not far from where they stood now—she had engaged three people in combat.

Two of those three, she'd managed to kill. The last person, Hugh, she'd subdued on the ground with vines, but she hadn't killed him. Those were just two more of the deaths she'd been blamed for, when in truth she'd been defending the city and trying to save lives.

"Hey, Hugh! Good to see you, buddy. How ya been?" Arryn asked, her smile exaggerated.

Hugh laughed. "Better than you're about to be. You look like shit."

"Ha! Funny story. Hilarious, even. See, I spent a couple weeks on top of a mountain. Isn't that funny?" she asked, aware that her wide smile and dishevelment made her appear slightly insane. She went with it.

"Hilarious," William agreed flatly, arcing his hands over his chest and creating a fireball in each.

Arryn waved her hands in the air and shook her head, smile never failing. "Wait, wait, wait! I haven't told you the best part. I spent all that time up there with no shower. No way to brush my hair. Or my teeth. I must look *hot*." At that moment, she reminded herself of Cathillian. He was incapable of taking anything seriously, including battle—he would make a joke in any situation. She continued, "But I also picked up a couple neat tricks."

William laughed. "I doubt that. You spent two decades with teachers. I doubt very seriously two weeks on a mountain taught you anything."

Arryn shrugged, and her eyes turned black. William launched his fireballs, but he was too late. She'd allowed the magic to swell around her and she teleported behind her enemy. She jumped forward, pulling her daggers from her belt, then wrapped her arms around his neck and pulled.

William fell to the ground before he was able to make another sound, bleeding his life out on the floor.

The other two jumped into action, but Arryn was quicker. She threw a knife, hitting Brandi in her shoulder before planting a hard kick in Hugh's stomach. She quickly sheathed the knife in her left hand before running for Brandi.

She ducked under a fireball before coming up, punching her in the face hard enough to knock her off-balance. Arryn kicked the student hard in the knee, taking her to the ground before finishing her with a hard stomp to the throat.

She heard his footsteps before she saw him. She bent forward at the waist, narrowly avoiding a punch aimed at the back of her head, then twisting her body and twirling out of the way. Hugh rounded on her, charging without really paying attention to what he was doing.

Arryn squatted as Hugh reached out with both arms to grab her, keeping her fists up by her face to guard it. She jabbed, punching him in the stomach with her right fist before quickly repeating the move with the left. As he doubled over, she stood, planting an uppercut on his jaw. She followed it up with an elbow to the nose.

He was staggering when she rushed forward to kick his feet out from under him and dump him on the floor.

He groaned as he laid there, struggling to get up. "Oh, no, big boy. That's not a mistake I'll make twice. I *won't* fight you again."

Arryn grabbed the knife from her left hip, squatted, and thrust it into the man's heart as he reached for her. She pulled the blade from his chest before cleaning it on his cloak and sheathing it again in her belt, repeating the process for the knife in Brandi's shoulder.

Rising from her crouch, she turned to the door to see her tiger standing there with blood on her face, watching her closely. "Bet ya didn't know I was a badass, huh?" The big cat made a noise that translated loosely to *"hmph."* Arryn smiled as she walked to the door. "Come on, let me have my two seconds, okay? You'll get to see some *real* badasses when we go to the forest. Until then, I'm the only one you got."

The tiger backed out of the doorframe and let Arryn into the hall, and she used her senses to search the area. Rebecca had said there were five people including Talia. Had that been five people including Rebecca? If so, Talia was alone. If not—if Rebecca had excluded herself from the count—there was one more person in the building.

As Arryn traveled through the halls to the front of the

building into the receiving area, she felt the energy of two people in the Chancellor's office.

Fuck, she thought to herself.

Arryn slowly moved forward, her breath coming hard and heavy even though she tried to calm herself before she got close to the door.

This was it.

This was the moment she'd awaited for weeks. Not just the two weeks she'd spent on the mountain, but the many she'd spent before that, knowing what this woman had done.

But before her visit to that small village, Arryn hadn't even come close to knowing *everything* Talia had done. She'd spent her entire life terrorizing her own mother and murdered the men in her mother's life, starting from the age of five.

She had been cold and heartless from the beginning, and the next few minutes wouldn't only settle the wrongs she'd committed since she had come to Arcadia, it would settle the wrongs that had been committed since her birth.

Arryn reached the door to the Chancellor's office and debated whether she should open it and walk through, or spend the energy to teleport inside. She shook her head, knowing that once all was said and done, she would have to teleport to the Dark Forest.

She couldn't risk traveling on foot with Scarlett on the loose. It was hard to say where the mystic was.

I hope you're ready for this. If it comes down to the two of us, let me die. Your baby is on the wall, and he can't live without a mama. Take him and go west to the Dark Forest. You'll be safe there.

Taking a deep breath, Arryn decided to do what she did best.

Arryn flung the door open and walked inside. Talia jumped up from her seat behind the desk, her eyes widening. On her desk sat Camdon, which Arryn found quite interesting, but she let it go

"Amelia! Oh, *Amelia,* it's so good to see you. Though, I must say..." Arryn took a step forward, giving another award-winning false smile. "I'm a little disappointed in the welcome party. And *Amelia*, you've really let yourself go. You look like *shit*."

Talia shook her head, her shock replaced by confusion and rage. "It's good to see you haven't changed a bit."

"Quite the contrary, *Amelia*, I've changed a *lot*." Arryn looked around the office before turning back to the Dean, or the Chancellor, as Talia now styled herself.

"Call me by that name one more time—"

Arryn laughed loudly, interrupting the Dean before she could finish her threat. "And you'll what? Kill me? You've already proven you fucking *suck* at that. Let me tell you a few more things I discovered you suck at. Being Amelia, for one. You're a bitch—can't quite pull it off. Actually, I've been compiling your failures into a nice list, but I didn't get a chance to put a tune to them yet. You see, I thought they were worthy of a song. I'm not the best singer, though. Maybe we can get your boyfriend there to sing it for you."

As Camdon rose from the desk, obviously ready to attack, a deep, guttural roar rolled into the room from just outside the door. The tiger had stayed out of sight, but she was more than happy to allow herself to be heard.

Talia's eyes widened. "What the fuck was that?"

Arryn smiled. "Like I said before, not only did you not kill me, you abandoned me in a place that allowed me to get stronger. That was the sound of my familiar. She announced herself because she's bored. Did I mention she's as tall as I am?"

Arryn gave Talia only a moment to react to the news before she continued, "You failed to kill me. You failed to kill Amelia. The remnant attack was a failure. You failed to pick a group of people who were worth a fuck. I should know, since I've killed almost all of them. You also failed to pick a confidant who liked anything about you."

Talia's eyes narrowed. "What are you talking about?"

Arryn smiled, tilting her head to the side as she regarded Talia with great amusement. "Wow, you really had no idea! I'm talking about Scarlett. Before I even approached this building, I felt her messing around in my head. She knew I was here, back in the city. She could have warned you, but she didn't. In fact, she sends her regards."

Talia shook her head. "You're a liar."

"She told me to pass them along when I discovered she'd placed my bow and staff in the dungeon where I could find them. She knew it was coming, Talia. She'd been waiting. Why do you think she isn't here? The city was never yours. It's not hers either, but she has taken it for the time being. So, as much as I love talking to you, I'm done playing. It's time to end this. I'll take this victory now, and come back for the rest later."

Talia slowly walked around the desk, the expression on her face enough to turn the very building they stood in to ash. "I'm going to destroy you. I'm going to rip you apart and dump the pieces in the Dark Forest just before bu—"

"Burning it to the ground, blah, blah, blah. Yeah, yeah. You've made that speech before." Arryn squinted her eyes, giving an exaggerated smile as she leaned forward. "How has that worked out for you?"

A fireball came from Camdon's direction, but Arryn had enough time to react. Thrusting her hand out, she used telekinetic force to send it directly back at him. "Not today, pretty boy."

He screamed as his fireball hit him in the shoulder. Arryn could actually hear him sobbing from across the room.

Talia's eyes turned black, and Arryn immediately recognized the energy she was pulling. She threw both hands out, creating a barrier around the Dean before she could teleport out of the room. It distracted Talia enough to halt her attempt, and Arryn dropped the barrier, shoving her magic forward and slamming Talia into the wall.

Camdon disappeared behind the desk. She had no idea what he was up to, but she would have to keep an eye on him as well. She'd meant to kill him when she sent the fireball back, but she'd missed his chest.

Talia recovered and sent two fireballs flying at Arryn. She was able to dodge them, but not the surge of telekinetic energy that came directly after. Talia had anticipated her movements and slammed *her* into the wall this time.

Arryn could hardly move, pinned by magic to the wall as Talia and Camdon both advanced on her.

Talia laughed. "Here we stand again. Little girl, I've been at this for a *very* long time. You're never going to be a strong as me."

It was true that Talia was strong. She may have even been *too* strong. The force pushing against Arryn was almost enough to keep her from breathing, but Arryn managed.

Summoning all the strength she could muster, Arryn tried to wiggle her fingers and was happy to see that she could. "I don't have to be stronger. I just have to be smarter."

Arryn's eyes turned vibrant green, the white parts turning obsidian. She could hear the rumble of the tiger outside of the room, and she silently willed her to stay there.

Talia looked terrified for a moment, but it was only a flash. She quickly recovered and took a step forward. "If you were smarter, you never would've come here."

The Dean had become overly confident, exactly as Arryn had hoped. Her force had weakened some, allowing Arryn to move her hands. She took advantage of that, causing a gust of wind to blow through the window, raining shattered glass down to the floor.

Talia laughed. "Really? That's all you've got?"

Arryn smiled. "Not even close."

Arryn twisted her hands and the shards of glass lifted from the ground. Talia's eyes widened as she stopped pushing against Arryn to create a shield around herself, but she failed to create one around Camdon before Arryn loosed the glass. Camdon was dead within seconds, and Arryn set her sights on Talia.

Arryn's eyes turned blacker as she created an ice shield around Talia that enveloped Talia's own barrier and began to push. Spikes of ice pressed harder and harder against Talia's magic, Arryn's rage and force causing the furniture and other items in the room to tremble.

Talia screamed, her face contorted with the massive amount of power she was drawing on. But Arryn had had weeks of practice, building her strength and her rage. Talia could not compete with the sheer amount of white-hot anger Arryn had saved up for this moment.

She pressed harder, and Talia's shield began to crack. "One last thing," Arryn said, enjoying the look of terror on Talia's face. "Your mother says, 'Rot in hell.'"

Arryn stepped forward, shoving her magic toward Talia with incredible strength. Talia's barrier crushed under the weight of it, and the ice shards impaled her from every direction. The last one sheared straight through her neck, fulfilling the promise Arryn had made when the Dean's severed head hit the floor.

Though it hadn't been Arryn's intention, she couldn't help but feel satisfied knowing she'd kept her word.

Exhausted, Arryn collapsed to the floor and took a moment to gather herself. The tiger walked into the room, coming over to sniff Arryn's face and check on her. "I'm okay, monster paws, but I need to get outside and touch the ground fast. I don't have much remaining in me, and everything I have left will be used to get us to the Dark Forest."

Pulling herself together, Arryn went to grab her staff, bow, and quiver. Then she and the tiger quickly made their way out of the Capitol building, careful to avoid any attention. The sun would begin to rise any time now, and she had to be out of the city before that.

They returned to the wall, Arryn having stopped on the

Capitol lawn to heal herself before climbing up and returning to the tiger cub. Just as he'd been told, the little guy had stayed put, lying down to remain out of sight.

The mama jumped down from the wall, but Arryn had to use vines to lower herself and the cub to keep from injuring themselves. Taking a deep breath, Arryn summoned all the strength she had left, her eyes turning black as she allowed magic to swell around her once again. In the blink of an eye they were gone, teleported over halfway to the Dark Forest.

When they landed Arryn collapsed to the ground, her breathing shallow. Her body was exhausted, and she could barely keep her eyes open. The tiger laid on the ground and allowed Arryn to climb onto her. It reminded her of the day she competed in the *Versuch*. Nika had worn her out physically, but she'd done it to herself magically.

Cathillian had put her on Chaos' back and she'd passed out, not unlike now. Darkness surrounded Arryn as consciousness began to fade. She used her last waking moment to tell the tiger to head west and not to stop until she reached the Dark Forest.

CHAPTER TWENTY-THREE

Cathillian awoke to the sound of repeated screeching above his hut. It took a second, but he felt Echo's familiar energy, so he threw the blankets back and rushed out of bed. When he arrived outside, he saw Echo perched on his house, and Elysia, the Chieftain, Samuel, and a fully healed Celine coming to see what the commotion was about.

"What is it, Echo?" Cathillian asked.

Echo called to him again, and Cathillian reached through the bond to see what she had observed.

His eyes widened. "It's Arryn. *She found Arryn!*" When he looked around, he saw similar looks of excitement on the faces near him. Tears filled Celine's eyes as she reached out and hugged Samuel without thinking. Cathillian continued, "She found Arryn up north, riding back here on a… Riding a *what?*"

Elysia stepped forward. "What is it?"

Cathillian's jaw was slack as he turned away from the golden eagle to face his mother. "She says Arryn was riding on a tiger. A huge white tiger. She had a tiger cub with her, too. Said she was headed toward Arcadia, and she'd come to the Dark Forest soon."

The Chieftain and Elysia looked at one another. "Surely, she wouldn't try to take Talia out by herself," Elysia said.

Nika snorted. "Have you *met* her?"

Cathillian nodded. "Nika's right. There's no doubt in my mind that Arryn went after her."

Elysia started to protest, started to get upset with the possibilities, but Samuel stepped in. "In case all of ye fergot just who we're talkin' about here, the girl was taken weeks ago. Wherever she was, she survived it. And if she has two white tigers with her, well, those're snow cats. It's too warm in the valley fer snow, so that means she was *way* up north—I'd say in the mountains. If she was dumped up there, and lasted two weeks, she ain't dyin' today."

The Chieftain smiled. "She's stubborn. Takes after me."

Elysia sighed and rolled her eyes, shaking her head. "We can argue the stupidity of that statement later. Right now, I want our warriors to fan out on the eastern and southern sides of the forest just past our border, no more than twenty feet apart, to search for her. Familiars, too. Keep the *Schatten* in the trees by the barrier."

Cathillian smiled, fighting back the emotions he been holding in since she disappeared. There would be time for those when she was with them. Right now, he just wanted to focus on searching for her.

ARRYN WAS STILL UNCONSCIOUS, but the tiger trekked on. The cub managed to keep up on foot. Arryn had gotten them close enough it had been relatively safe to make the rest of the trip at a leisurely pace. It had taken nearly all day, but they were now moving through the forest.

This was all unfamiliar territory for the tiger, but she didn't mind. A couple hours later, the tiger became aware that Arryn was losing her balance. The big cat growled loudly, trying to wake her mistress, but it did no good, so she quickly dropped to the ground to keep Arryn from falling such a long distance.

Even after she landed on the cool ground, Arryn remained unconscious. There was no way for the big cat to put her back up, so she did the only thing she could think of.

The tiger grabbed Arryn's cloak, dragging her as she headed toward the barrier. In the unfamiliar territory, the tiger felt out of place and overly cautious about which animals might attack. She knew what creatures existed in the mountains, but had no idea what to expect in the forest, and her fur could be seen a mile away in this environment.

A loud growl echoed in the forest, and the tiger stopped and looked around. She pinned her ears back and her lips curled over her teeth for a moment before determination pushed her on again.

The tiger grasped Arryn's cloak again and continued pulling her, but much faster this time. Another roar, only this time much closer. The animal was big; the tiger was sure of that. It was also approaching very quickly.

Not giving up, she continued to tow Arryn, hoping that whatever she was seeking in the Dark Forest would find them.

Sounds of heavy footfalls filled her ears, and the stink of a large animal approaching filtered through her nose. The tiger dropped Arryn's cloak and stood over her, facing the direction the animal was approaching from.

A massive black bear jumped out from behind the tall overgrowth, lurching forward and roaring. The tiger returned the greeting, pinning her ears back and leaning forward, letting loose with her own war cry. But as big as she was, the bear was still almost twice her size.

He charged and the tiger leapt forward, not wanting to let him anywhere near Arryn. The bear rose to his hind feet, towering over her for a moment before he dropped and swatted a massive front paw at her. She managed to jump back, but then charged forward again. She found an opening to go for his throat.

Just as she was about to take it, voices filled the area.

"Zobig!" a man cried out.

The bear stopped in his tracks, continuing to growl as he backed away. The tiger remained in her crouch for a moment, still roaring at the bear and all the approaching people, then quickly retreated, straddling Arryn and lying on top of her, remaining mindful of her weight so she didn't crush her.

The bear took a few steps forward, and the tiger roared again.

"Zobig!" a man shouted again as he ran into the area, followed by several more. "Easy, boy. Look, she's protecting her."

The tiger's ears stayed pinned back and her jaws parted as she growled deep in her belly. Her eyes darted from person to person, ready to pounce on anyone who got too close. The tiger cub stayed close, hiding behind his mama where he knew he belonged.

A woman with long blonde hair that hung in a braid over her shoulder stepped forward with tears falling onto her cheeks, and a man who looked quite a bit like her ran forward and dropped to his knees. The tiger didn't understand their expressions, and she refused to take any chances.

"Easy, girl," the kneeling man said. "We're her friends. The grumpy old bear is, too."

The old man who had stopped the bear from attacking stepped forward. "He thought you'd hurt her. He was protecting Arryn from *you*, but now he knows."

The kneeling man spoke again, tears in his eyes and a smile on his face. "She is yours, and you are hers."

He leaned forward, carefully and slowly crawling towards her and Arryn. The tiger was cautious, but held her ground, letting him approach.

"I'm Cathillian," he told her, slowly reaching out.

That word. The tiger recognized that word. Arryn had told the bird to "tell Cathillian she would come back to the Dark Forest soon."

The tiger relaxed some, her mouth closing and her ears rising as she leaned forward to sniff the hand of this man for a moment. Then she slowly backed away, allowing him access to Arryn, but stayed close and mindful of his every move.

CATHILLIAN HAD NEVER SEEN anything like her—the animal was beautiful. He'd seen panthers and leopards, but she was far larger than any big cat he'd ever seen. Given the way she had protected Arryn and the fact that she'd brought her back to the Dark Forest, there was no doubt in his mind.

She was Arryn's familiar.

When the tiger had backed away and he saw that Arryn was whole, his heart felt like it would stop in his chest. His friend appeared weaker than he'd ever seen her before, and she had come back with a familiar. He wanted to rush over and pull her into his arms, but he had to be careful. He didn't want to do anything the tiger would interpret as threat.

Slowly, he made his way to her side, gently putting his arms under her and continuing to judge the reaction of the big cat as he moved. His eyes turned dark green as he called upon his magic, pushing it forward to heal her of what he was certain was magical fatigue.

Within moments, her breathing sped up to normal, and her eyes began to flutter open. When she looked at him and smiled sleepily, he pulled her tightly against him in a big hug.

"You have no idea how happy I am to see you," Cathillian said.

Arryn sighed. "Trust me, I don't think anyone here is happier to see anyone than I am."

He laughed. "I can't even begin to imagine. You'll have to tell us all about it. You also have to tell us all about your new friends here."

"They're clingy. I escaped from the mountain, and they tracked me down. Stalkers," Arryn said. The tiger grumbled, lightly swatting her on the hip with her large paw. "Ouch! They have bad attitudes, too. Being hit with one of those is like being kicked by a horse with hooves twice the size of Chaos'."

Cathillian laughed and kissed the top of her head. "Welcome home, Arryn."

EPILOGUE

S carlett stood outside the Capitol building wondering what she would find inside. She sensed nothing, so she knew anyone she'd find in there wasn't going to be alive.

When she walked inside, she could smell it—the stench of death had already permeated the building. She made her way from room to room and found three people dead in one, but the corpse she found on the landing above the stairway to the dungeon made her smile.

Rebecca.

Arryn hadn't killed her herself, that was for sure. It had been an animal of some kind. The woman had been mauled to death. It had been a terrible way to go, but "terrible" was how Scarlett liked it.

Finally, she made her way to the Chancellor's office, opening the door and walking inside. Even Scarlett gasped in shock, her eyes wide as a smile spread across her lips.

Talia was dead.

Talia wasn't just *dead*, she was *dead dead*. She'd been impaled several times, and her head had been severed from her body.

"Well, she did say she'd do that," Scarlett mused.

She heard footsteps behind her and turned to see her four mystic friends entering the room.

"Wow," one of them said. "This is one hell of a mess. You weren't joking about getting her out of the way."

Scarlett shrugged. "I didn't do this, but I'd like to think I helped."

One of them, a man, stepped forward, his eyes wandering around the room before coming to rest on Scarlett. "What now?"

Scarlett smiled. "We start planning." She turned to the window and looked out at the city. "We convince the city of the truth, that Arryn killed Talia and her followers. First things first, though—we need to influence the Guard. We're going to need all of them to be absolutely loyal to their new Chancellor."

She couldn't help but feel triumphant as she gazed over what she now saw as hers. It was all she'd dreamed of since learning of Adrien's death, and with the help of the people behind her, nothing could stand in her way.

ARRYN HAD FALLEN asleep almost immediately after lying down in her hut, and she stayed asleep for hours. After Cathillian's healing, only a little rest was all she needed to feel more like herself. Not the coma-like sleep she'd needed the other times.

She was awakened by laughing and carrying on outside, so she got up and went to see what was going on. Stepping onto the cool forest ground, Arryn sighed in contentment. *Home.*

As she made her way forward, she saw friends, both new and old, sitting around the fire as they laughed and told stories. Cathillian, Samuel, Celine, Amelia—even Maddie—sat around the fire, and of course the Chieftain and Elysia were there, too. It looked like everyone she really cared about had gotten out of the city.

But there were far more than that.

It had been years since she'd seen their colors, but she recognized uniforms of the Cellan guards who were standing around drinking and carrying on. As she watched everyone, she realized that the myth of the murderous savages who were the terrifying and elusive druids was dead.

Everyone here was getting along great. Those people would take back the stories and tell them to their children, and their children's children. It would begin to build a bridge after all the years of hate.

Arryn sat down on the ground across from the warm fire. She had been there for no more than a few seconds when the cub pounced on her, curling up in her lap and purring like a kitten. She smiled and scratched his neck.

The mama made her way to Arryn as well; everyone stepped out of her way as she flopped down next to Arryn.

"What is the name of your familiar?" the chieftain asked.

Arryn looked up and smiled. "You mean to say 'familiars,' as in 'both of them.'"

The Chieftain's eyes widened and a smile grew on his face. "Look at you! I guess it was worth the wait, huh?"

She nodded. "More than worth the wait. I always thought I'd end up with a wolf or a fox. As for names, I haven't given them names yet."

"That's not a bad thing," Cathillian said. "If a familiar is bonded within the forest, it's customary to have a ceremony. You've been to a couple, mine and Echo's included, but I'm not sure if you actually knew what was going on. Well, it's not really an official ceremony—it's just a party. Family, friends. We gather and celebrate the coming together of two companions. The druid picks the name of their familiar during the gathering and announces it to everyone in the tribe."

"Am I excluded because I didn't bond with mine in the Dark Forest?" Arryn asked.

Elysia laughed. "Not at all—that's why we're all here. We

assumed you'd already named them, but since you haven't, let the ceremony begin!"

Arryn looked at her beautiful familiars, thinking hard to find good, strong names. She was great at coming up with nonsense names, but that was because she couldn't name every animal she spoke to. If she had, she would've named hundreds by now.

"I'm going to call my mama cat 'Snow.' When I met her, I was holding her cub. He was covered in blood, and she thought I'd hurt him. I passed out in the snow when she attacked me. Nothing was more beautiful or terrifying than seeing her in her natural element. I woke up in a cave, where she'd dragged me to safety after she realized I'd *saved* her cub. And this little fuzzball here, I will name 'Dante.' The name itself means 'enduring,' and he is quite the strong little guy."

The Chieftain stood and raised a cup that she had no doubt was full of wine. "To Arryn and her companions, Snow and Dante!"

Everyone cheered and shouted their names. As Cathillian had mentioned, she vaguely remembered a gathering like this for Cathillian and Echo, but it had been much smaller. She hadn't truly realized what it was for until now.

Amelia came over to sit next to Arryn, handing her a glass of the Chieftain's wine. "It's done, then?"

Arryn nodded and took a sip, sighed, and smiled as she took another. "Yes, it's done."

Amelia sighed and nodded. "Did you rip her fucking head off?"

Arryn smiled. "Funny you should ask that!"

They sat and talked for a while, and everyone quieted down as Arryn told her story. She started from the beginning, reliving every moment of it. The crowd was in awe of everything she had been through and survived.

Cathillian looked at her with pride, but also with something more. She tried to push that out of her mind as she finished the story by telling everyone her biggest accomplishment—what had happened in Arcadia when she returned.

"The mystic is still alive?" Cathillian asked.

Arryn nodded. "Had she been there, I'm not sure I would've been quite so lucky. There's still a fight ahead; I have no doubt about that. But tonight, we're all here. We're all safe. We're all alive. Let's take the night to celebrate. We can feel like shit in the morning."

Everyone cheered and raised their glasses, Samuel cheering louder than anyone. She'd meant what she said about wanting everyone to celebrate their good fortune, but it didn't stop her from worrying about what tomorrow would bring.

Mystical magic was not something she was very familiar with, and she would need its help to defeat her enemy this time around. Luckily for her, she was surrounded by the best damn army Irth had ever seen.

FINIS

Book three! I'm so excited. This is a big one—one I've been so, so crazy over since the beginning. It's quite a bit different than anything I've ever written before, and I can't wait to see what everyone thinks!

This one had a lot of emotional bits for me. I actually cried writing a couple of the parts because I was so excited. I'll give you a hint without spoiling… There is a part where Arryn meets a blacksmith named Roger. While she's there, a visitor (or two) comes to the door. That was a huge moment that really had me fighting back.

I admire Arryn a lot, and I think we as readers enjoy reading about strong characters because we want to see those qualities in ourselves. The ability to fight through anything, to never give up, to force success even when things are at their worst. I love that. That's certainly a huge motivator for writing them anyway!

I want to say thank you to everyone that has reviewed both books! Especially the last one because I actually gave a challenge to everyone! I wanted to hear everyone's goofy kid stories—mostly the hilarious things they mispronounce or just funny things they say in general. I said I'd mention my favorite one!

Theresa Barber—thanks for leaving your story! It's super cute, and you should head over to the reviews to check it out. <3 (I'll leave the link: https://tinyurl.com/yaulfsgn)

I love reading reviews, and I love seeing who reads the author notes—so as I'm writing this, I'm trying to think of your next challenge, should you choose to accept it. Ha!

I'm set to begin outlining the next one today, and I have some things that have to happen, and they need to be epic. So, I'll be paying close attention to those.

This experience has been so incredible. Through this, I've learned how to write in a much different way and with others. If I'm to be completely honest—I'm spoiled as hell. I have NO idea how I'm going to go back to the old way. Writing alone. No critique partner. Definitely gonna have to do something about that!

More than that, writing for all of you has given me a taste of what it's like to have a massive audience. Something I hope to recreate with future series of mine. Thanks to all of you for all of it!

The Age of Magic is growing all the time, and I love that. We have so many active series now, and even a couple more to come. There are loads of different powers that the main characters have, and some of them are incredibly unique—like Justin Sloan's lead. She uses shadows, and that's just badass. I wish I'd thought of that!

Having read damn near all of these books (for those of you who are huge KGU readers/fans), if you were to have a super power (even if it hasn't been mentioned in the books yet), what would you have? There is your challenge! I'm curious to know which fan favorites are out there—maybe even which ones you wish to see if they haven't been seen yet.

I love hearing from you guys! As always, remember to keep an eye out on the Facebook Fan Page for the KGU as well as the Age of Magic. Both of those pages are updated daily (sometimes multiple times a day), and we always have new and awesome stuff coming!

Thanks again for reading. <3

Hello! Thank you for not only reading this story but ALSO reading all the way to the end (my stuff!)

Today is Candy's third book. It is, in a way, a major accomplishment for any KGU author. The third book (and the fourth) represent two small milestones which fellow whale readers like myself respect.

Quantity.

I know, I know – we get this 'qty vs. quality' discussion all the time. However, the secret is if you are reading THIS note. You have already decided these sets of stories and characters are good enough for you.

Quality question solved.

Now, we see what Candy has in store as we take these characters and grow them. Book four is a tough book, and I think she now has it in her to pull it off.

I can tell you, when you fans review my books and tell me "I usually stop between books 6-8 because the story is repetitive, but I'M STILL HERE!" and I'm on book 18?

Damn, that makes me feel cool, I will admit. It means that the characters are still real, the story still puts them into situations that matter and we keep going on.

Now, I'll loose between 4-10% between books, usually. BUT, I've got enough fans asking for the next Bethany Anne or Michael book that I feel I'm blessed.

Blessed with great fans, great reads, and great comments. Now, I get to share YOU with authors (and friends) such as Candy.

If you read her author note, you know that she is experiencing the fun of her author career right now.

And I couldn't be more satisfied to share.

Ad Aeternitatem,
Michael

CONNECT WITH THE AUTHORS

To see ALL of Candy's different books check out her website below

Website:
http://www.candycrumbooks.com

Facebook
https://www.facebook.com/groups/thecandyshopgroup/

Michael Anderle Social

Website:
http://www.lmbpn.com

Email List:
http://lmbpn.com/email/

www.ingramcontent.com/pod-product-compliance
Lightning Source LLC
Chambersburg PA
CBHW050247110726

47898CB00007B/2307